A PLUME BOOK

MARGARET FROM MAINE

Dr. Ted Taigen

JOSEPH MONNINGER lives with his wife in a converted barn near the Baker River in New Hampshire.

Margaret from Maine

A Novel

Joseph Monninger

A PLUME BOOK

PLUME
Published by the Penguin Group
Penguin Group (USA) Inc., 375 Hudson Street, New York, New York 10014, U.S.A. • Penguin Group
(Canada), 90 Eglinton Avenue East, Suite 700, Toronto, Ontario, Canada M4P 2Y3 (a division of Pearson
Penguin Canada Inc.) • Penguin Books Ltd., 80 Strand, London WC2R 0RL, England • Penguin Ireland, 25
St. Stephen's Green, Dublin 2, Ireland (a division of Penguin Books Ltd.) • Penguin Group (Australia), 250
Camberwell Road, Camberwell, Victoria 3124, Australia (a division of Pearson Australia Group Pty. Ltd.)
• Penguin Books India Pvt. Ltd., 11 Community Centre, Panchsheel Park, New Delhi – 110 017, India •
Penguin Group (NZ), 67 Apollo Drive, Rosedale, Auckland 0632, New Zealand (a division of Pearson New
Zealand Ltd.) • Penguin Books (South Africa) (Pty.) Ltd., 24 Sturdee Avenue, Rosebank, Johannesburg 2196,
South Africa

Penguin Books Ltd., Registered Offices: 80 Strand, London WC2R 0RL, England

First published by Plume, a member of Penguin Group (USA) Inc.

Copyright © Joseph Monninger, 2012
All rights reserved

 REGISTERED TRADEMARK—MARCA REGISTRADA

ISBN 978-1-62090-926-3

Printed in the United States of America
Set in Horley Old Style MT Std • Designed by Eve L. Kirch

This novel is dedicated in loving memory of my mother,
Mary Deborah Brennan Monninger.

When lilacs last in the dooryard bloom'd
And the great star early droop'd in the western sky in the night,
I mourn'd—and yet shall mourn with ever-returning spring.

—Walt Whitman

Margaret from Maine

Lilacs

Chapter
One

The last sound Maine Guardsman Sgt. Thomas Kennedy heard was the whine of a mosquito. At least he thought it was the last sound, although what he thought and what actually occurred had little to do with each other. He raised his right hand to brush it away, conscious of the heat under his helmet, the dry, sweltering sweat that soaked his uniform. And now a mosquito.

As his hand lifted, he saw a glint—just a fracture of light—and he glanced down at Private First Class Edmond Johnson, who happened to be changing the back rear tire of the team's Humvee. In that instant, many things did not make sense.

What were they doing here, in Afghanistan, to begin with? How had he come all this way—from Bangor, Maine—to be standing beside a beached Humvee, beside a private named Johnson who had arrived at this point in time from Solon, Maine? And where, after all, had the flash of light come from? They were in a dry, featureless plain, and the mountains, arguably the most rugged mountains in the world, were too far away to provide a sniper with sufficient height. So how could there be a flash of light, gunfire, when all the world lay flat and even and empty?

That's when it occurred to Sgt. Thomas Kennedy that a mosquito is not always a mosquito.

Because he felt his hand shatter, the bones flying apart under his skin, his cheek exploding so that he tasted teeth and blood in the same instant. *Oh*, he thought. Just that. What they had feared, what they had all feared, had finally arrived. They were pinned down and a mosquito is not a mosquito and he turned and spread his arms—ridiculously like a crossing guard—and tried to protect Private Johnson.

The second bullet went through his shoulder and he only felt it spin him. It didn't hurt. It felt like a bird. Someone yelled at him to get down, but Johnson still kneeled behind him, completely exposed, and Sgt. Kennedy spread his arms to expand his protection, and he knew that was a bad idea. He hardly even *knew* Johnson. The kid had arrived a month and a half ago from Basic, and he was supposed to be an excellent mechanic, a diesel engine mechanic for Freightliner, but taking a bullet for him was another matter. But Sgt. Kennedy was fourth-generation Maine, and it was part of his Yankee nature to use things up, so it made no sense to him to let two people get shot when one was already plugged. It would be like punching a hole in a second bucket when the first was already punched, and so when the third bullet hit him, in the right knee, he figured he was done for anyway.

He kept standing, shielding Johnson.

Strangely, Sgt. Kennedy knew, absolutely knew, that what he was doing would be called brave. And that was simply curious. Because it didn't feel brave. It all felt stupid, and he thought of Margaret, the new baby, the dairy cows plodding quietly into their milking stations, and he wondered why the sniper couldn't see how the entire thing was absurd. Why were they shooting at each other? He had no idea what an Afghan wanted in this world, but he figured that most humans wanted to live a peaceful life, and so as he held out his arms to protect Johnson behind him, he could not imagine that the sniper would not cease. Couldn't the sniper put the situation together? They were just grunts, just stupid soldiers doing what they were told, and if the milk prices hadn't fallen through the floor, Sgt. Kennedy would still be on the sweet dairy farm in Maine, watching his herd. But the farm had debt, and the military promised to help, and now here he was with a man shooting at him.

Sgt. Kennedy held up his hand to tell the shooter to stop, but instead he felt the fourth bullet go into his shin.

And then it became a perverse game.

See if you can knock me down.

Sgt. Kennedy was a big man. He had played center for Millinocket High School, All-County selection, and he had hands as strong as any man he had ever met. His strength was always a *fact*. He knew it existed inside him, in a deep, quiet place, and he had scuff-ups with stronger-looking kids, more-muscled men, but Sgt. Kennedy had always come out on top.

Maine strength, they called it Downeast. It came, he felt, from
growing up on a farm, handling cattle, pushing and shoving
the goofy bastards every single day of his life. He had lifted
more calves than he could count, had engaged in wrestling
matches with Holsteins, their warm flanks pressing him into
the stall walls until he had pushed back, used his bulk and
strength and shoved. *Moooooooo over,* was the joke they used
on the farm.

And so that. That was his strength.

The last bullet, the one that did him, as they say, shattered
his spine at the spot where neck and backbone joined. He fell
like a Slinky. So much for seeing if they could knock him down.
He went slack, his body piling up on top of itself, and vaguely
he heard more bullets ricocheting off the Humvee. So it turned
out that the mosquito was not the last sound after all, but he
didn't make a conscious correction. In the last nervous jolt he
would ever know on this earth, he remembered a fall day right
before he enlisted. It had been a perfect autumn day, no insects, and the farm ran all the way to the pine forest. And he
had seen Margaret walking toward him, her hair blowing in
the wind, and the backs of the cattle catching the sunlight. It
was a happy memory. The white farmhouse shone in the sunlight, the red barn beside it, and Margaret raised her hand to
wave. And then, like a movie ending abruptly, the image fiz-
zled and his spine snapped in two, and Sgt. Kennedy of Bangor, Maine, fell into the puddle of himself and became a brown
box of meat stored forever, an electric hum not dead but no
longer viably alive.

Chapter
Two

Light came over the house from the east. A phoebe, nesting this year in the crook of the cowshed door, sat on the top line of a barbed wire fence and dotted its tail up and down, up and down, as if jacking the sunlight over the horizon. Light continued to spread and search, touching the muddy cow yard, the curled green hose near the water tank, climbing, at last, the 173-year-old white oak that guarded the house and shaded the front parlor. The phoebe began to call, *pheeebeee, pheeebeee, pheeebeee,* and an easterly breeze, passing from the Maine coast a hundred miles away, carried a single gull overhead toward the Androscoggin watershed.

In that moment, Margaret Kennedy's eyes rejoined the world. She was thirty-one that morning and she slept on the same side of the bed she had always occupied: the left. Her husband's side remained empty, tucked and smoothed, the pillows undented for six long years.

She did not have to consult a clock to know the time. She

read the oak's shade and from the color of the light and the fritter of the leaves, she judged it to be shy of five o'clock. She closed her eyes a moment more and heard the phoebe calling. She wondered, absently, if it was the same phoebe year after year, or whether the barn proved such an attractive nesting opportunity that any phoebe would count herself lucky to grab it. She preferred to think of the phoebe as an old friend, a true harbinger of spring, a bird that fed her babies—once, Margaret had seen this—the translucent wings of a dragonfly. For an instant as she watched—how many years ago was it?—she could almost believe the babies ate light, because the wings sparked and glittered as they slid down the chicks' gullets.

Margaret stretched. She felt old this morning, and weary, but such thinking did not help. She pushed her legs over the side of the bed, stepped into her slippers, and went to use the toilet in the master bath. When she finished, she washed her hands and face, then gazed for a second at her features, wondering if she had ever been pretty. People said she had been. She always felt she had been pretty enough for Maine, for rural life, but that if she had moved away her looks would have suffered by comparison with other women. Thomas had marveled at her looks, but he was no judge, honestly, and she stared a moment longer, noting that her hair—red as flame, her mother said years ago—had dulled to the color of certain apples after frost. Burgundy now, she thought, like a good leather chair in a British drama.

Before she dressed, she heard the milk pump switch on and its insistent sound sped her along. She pulled on jeans and a heavy sweatshirt that read *Maine Black Bears* across the chest, then fished a pair of leather work gloves out of the belly of the sweatshirt. She clumped down the center stairs and kept going right out of the kitchen and onto the farmer's porch, pushing the screen door back, then stopped and slid her feet out of her slippers and into shin-high muck boots. A glance informed her that Thomas's father, Benjamin, had already made it outside. The sound of the milking machine told her that anyway, but she liked confirmation in the world and appreciated being able to avoid surprises.

"Morning," she called as she entered the milking parlor.

Benjamin didn't hear her. He was doing something to Sally Mae, one of the thirty-three cows that stood with their heads in stocks while the milking machine sucked them dry. Margaret yelled a little louder, "Morning." She didn't call so much to say good morning as to let Benjamin know she had arrived. It was loud in the milking parlor and it was common practice to make sure you didn't startle a person by suddenly appearing. Margaret saw Benjamin raise a hand without turning, indicating hello, he had seen her, all was well, and she nodded and went to the milk sink and began cleaning. She stood a moment and let the water run to hot, then she began passing teat tubes and sponges under the stream. She did not think as she performed the work, but her hands moved like elves, like small skilled creatures that could carry out a function without guidance. When she finished, she set everything to dry in an old dish drainer, then she made a circuit of the northern wall, checking the cattle. She stopped next to Tinkerbell, her favorite, a sturdy old gal with remarkable consistency as a milk producer, and patted her flank. She bent down and breathed the cow smell, which she loved, and it came to her quickly: skin and sun, clover and hay, mud and rain. She wondered if she was crazy to like the cows so much, to like farming. A battalion of flies flickered near the windows, tapping against the glass and turning to embers in the flashing light. Now and then she saw them land on a cow, and the cow, with her gifted tail, swatted and swayed, or lifted a foot to throw shadow at them, the pendulous milking apparatus dangling like a bell's tongue beneath the cow's wide stomach. She tapped Tinkerbell's flank again and continued on her rounds.

"Morning," Benjamin said when she had bent down to remove the suck cups from the first three cows. "Gordon awake yet?"

"Not yet. I'll get him up when we finish here."

"That boy likes his sleep."

"I know," Margaret said, feeling short with her father-in-law. "But we're going to run over to the hospital. Remember, he doesn't have school today. They have an in-service day."

They had gone over this the night before. In that specific way—his slowness to store information, or recall it—he reminded her of Thomas. She had kept her head down when he spoke to her, but now she lifted it. He smiled. She smiled back.

"He's a slow boy in the morning," he said.

"It's still early. There's plenty of time to get ready. You sure you won't come along?"

Benjamin shook his head. He preferred to visit alone, she

knew, though she couldn't say why exactly. Maybe he liked a private moment with his son. Thomas was the proverbial stone in the pond, and the ripples went out in unexpected ways, caught people by surprise. She nodded and let it go.

"You make up your mind about Washington?" he asked. "That Mr. King called and left a message last night. He seems like a nice man."

She had been asked to attend a bill signing sponsoring improved veteran care for coma patients. Thomas's status as a Medal of Honor winner was attractive to the legislators and she felt it was something she could do for him. Requests occasionally arrived, sometimes surprising ones and not always with good intent, but this invitation had come directly from President Obama's staff. A weekend in Washington, D.C., a signing ceremony, a few photographs. She had put off making a decision, but it was coming right up. She needed to give the organizers an answer.

"I'm leaning toward going," she continued. "If you think you and Gordon can hold down the fort."

"Of course we can. No worries there."

"We could all go, you know? They'd be happy to have Thomas's dad. The invitation is for our family."

Benjamin shook his head. He had the dairy to watch, she knew, but it was not every day you were invited to meet the president of the United States. He claimed he had been to Washington once, when his son was awarded the Congressional Medal of Honor, and that was enough. This trip, to stand behind the president when he signed into law a bill sponsoring increased funding for veterans in a vegetative state, seemed too political and too far from life on the Maine farm. At least that's what he said. Margaret suspected that Benjamin found the social demands—the chitchat, the stuffy meals, even the mandatory coat and tie—difficult to endure. He preferred the cows' company, and in that she did not blame him. She liked the cows better than she liked most people.

"You're better at that sort of thing," he said finally.

"I'm not much good at it, but it seems to be for a good cause."

"'Course it is."

"I'm tempted to bring Gordon, but he's a little young. I'd like him to see Washington, but maybe he's not ready yet."

"He'll be fine here with me."

"I'll give Mr. King a call back then and say I'll do it. It's a little something we can do for Thomas."

Benjamin nodded and smiled. For an instant, she spotted the family resemblance. It had passed from Benjamin to Thomas and now to Gordon. They were all big men—at least Gordon seemed headed in that direction—with plain, solid features and strong chins. Margaret often thought of them as trees, as a circle of oaks growing out from a central grand oak, their lives established by acorns carried deeper into the forest by slow, gradual progress. She found nothing hurried about any of her men.

It was a short morning. By the time she finished her chores, the sunlight had already become a bright bar in the barn doorway. As she returned to the house, she passed by the phoebe nest. Her boots made a loud clumping sound against the ground. Dew flicked up from her toes. A nice breeze moved across the north pasture and it stopped her for a moment. She put her hand to her eyes, shading the morning sun from her vision while she looked slowly around the farm. Spring, she thought. Late May. She took a deep breath, then another, and she watched for a moment as the breeze pushed the large web of a barn spider into a shimmering dance. She thought of *Charlotte's Web*, the story by E. B. White that always came to mind whenever she saw a spider's web. *What a pig,* she thought, then she continued across the dooryard, climbed the back porch, and pulled one foot, then the other, out of the muck boots. The boots released her feet slowly, gasping as they did, and she closed the screen door behind her, the weight of her step setting the china in the dining room cabinet to rattling and gossiping.

The boy—Gordon, six years old—had been waking for a half hour, sleep coming and going over him like a drawer hesitantly opened and closed. He lay in his single bed, his body making a bulge only halfway down the tube formed by the blue Hudson Bay blanket his mother had tucked around him the night before. A red plaid curtain lifted and fell, lifted and fell with the breeze that pushed across the farm. It was the same breeze his mother had felt when she stepped out of the barn, but the boy couldn't know that and neither could she.

Around the boy, in the mountainous contours of his

blankets, several dozen green army men enjoyed a quiet peace in their endless war. The men—cheap plastic army men, perfectly green, stamped out in a factory near Shanghai, China—replicated poses more closely associated with World War II than Iraq or Afghanistan or even Vietnam. Near the boy's chest, fallen into a bunker near his armpit, a radioman, kneeling, held a World War II walkie-talkie to his ear and chin, listening for messages that never came, detailing their positions, which changed nightly depending on the boy's whims. On the other side of his arm, set up in an ambush, seven riflemen lay on their bellies and pointed their plastic rifles at the foot of the bed. One of the rifles had broken away, and the boy, hearing accounts of sawed-off shotguns, had decided the rifleman had one of those for a weapon, although he called it a saw-chuck shotgun without knowing better. The soldier with the saw-chuck shotgun was Gordon's favorite, although he resisted having favorites for fear it would prejudice the war games and make them hollow. Still, he often wondered if the saw-chuck soldier wasn't a little like his father, who also lay on his belly in the white bed, and whose snoring reminded him of sawing, which probably had something to do with that type of rifle.

He slept a little more, and then finally he felt a hand on his forehead, then lips. He opened his eyes. His mother sat on the edge of the bed, a white terry cloth robe wrapped around her. She wore her hair up in a towel, and Gordon saw a drop of water fall from her neck to her shoulder.

"Morning, buster," she said.

"Morning, Mom," he answered.

"You ready to wake up? Grandpa Ben said he's coming in to have coffee with you soon."

He nodded.

"Where are we going today?" she asked him.

He knew the answer, but he felt shy suddenly and wouldn't reply.

"To the hospital," she said, filling it in for him. "To see Daddy."

"Daddy," the boy repeated.

"That's right, sweetheart. Grandpa is finishing up with the cows. I've run a bath. Will you jump in and I'll be in in a second to help you wash, okay?"

He nodded.

He didn't want to get up until she left, for fear of knocking the soldiers out of their positions. The red plaid curtain lifted and fell. His mother brushed his hair back one more time, then stood and walked out of the room. He grabbed the saw-chuck shotgun guy from near his armpit and carried it with him when he went toward the bathroom.

On the back porch, Margaret stopped to smell the lilacs. They were common lilacs, purple, and smelled like wind mixed with something floral and difficult to name. She breathed deep and stretched her back. She liked what she wore—a simple cotton dress that hung smoothly around her frame—and she was glad she'd allowed her friend Blake to talk her into buying it. It was a good run-errand dress. She had a sweater to put over it if the hospital proved too cold. Blake had been right. Blake was usually right about such things.

She turned to go back inside, but then paused for a moment more beside the lilacs. Thomas loved lilacs; he cut them each spring, bringing them inside in bundles that he left in a small watering can beside their bed. There they stayed, trembling with each footstep over the bare wooden floors of the bedroom, the moisture of the can occasionally sweating a moat onto her bedside table. Even with them so near, she could not depend on smelling them. The scent rose and fell, disappeared altogether at times, then suddenly reappeared at the fluff of a blanket or the tuck of a pillow.

She cupped one of the lilac heads in her hand and brought it to her nose. Yes, the scent was there. She had already cut a half dozen and put them in the car for Thomas. She had no idea if Thomas could sense such things, but it couldn't hurt, and maybe, she liked to think, in some small, primitive part of him he still recorded sensations like these. *The doing of it would be the good of it,* she liked to quote.

Back in her kitchen, she watched Gordon row through his bowl of Cheerios. Benjamin, large and red and smelling softly of cattle, sat beside the boy, drinking coffee. Benjamin drank his coffee black, as Thomas had taken it, and she liked that in the Kennedy men. She went to the sink and rinsed out her coffee cup and set it to dry on the drainer.

"Do you have an appointment to see anyone over there?" Ben asked.

"I'm going to try to catch Dr. Medios. That's why I want to move along. He has early rounds."

"I never understood why hospitals have to start up so early in the morning."

"I don't know. That's a good question."

"Is he the Indian fellow?"

"Yep."

"I remember talking to him. He's okay. Always looks above your eyes at your forehead. That's what I noticed."

"He's been good about Thomas," she said, then she turned her attention to Gordon. "Come on, buckaroo. Let's get moving here. Finish up."

Margaret wiped down the sink with a cloth. She did it unconsciously. When she remembered what she was doing, she hung the cloth on the neck of the faucet to dry. Then she ducked quickly into the front powder room and checked her hair once more. She looked fine, she decided. Her hair, actually, hung the way she liked. She pushed at it and resettled it above her shoulders. On her way out, she ran her hand over Gordon's hair. She loved the feel of her little boy's hair. It was short and soft, like a deer's, she decided, or what an otter might feel like. Yes, an otter. She often thought of her little boy as an otter, as strange as that sometimes seemed to her. She liked thinking of him as a sleek tuck of muscle, a gamboling, happy boy at large in streams and rivers, gliding and playing all day. Her otter-boy, she sometimes called him.

She lifted his empty bowl of Cheerios away; he was finished but stayed in place gazing at a maze on the back of the cereal box. Margaret went to the sink, ran water in the cereal bowl.

"Okay, buddy boy," Margaret said to Gordon, "brush your teeth and we'll get going. Maybe if you're very, very good, we'll stop at Hot Dog Depot."

Gordon shot upstairs without any additional urging. He loved Hot Dog Depot. She heard Gordon turn on the water upstairs, then she lost track of him as she walked quickly past the screen door and shut off the television in the den. A pretty morning, she thought. Spring had definitely arrived at last.

Chapter
Three

She let Gordon carry the lilacs from the car and though it
slowed them down, she smiled at the seriousness with
which he carried out this small function. He held the flowers
out, the broad heads nearly large enough for him to hide behind, the silver handle of tin foil bright in his hand. The parking lot was familiar; she had visited the hospital ten billion
times, she felt, and she knew each crack she passed, each
patched section. She noticed that the red maple in the center
island had become green suddenly. It was a magic trick played
each spring. One saw the buds emerge, forgot to look for what
felt like a moment, and miraculously the tree adorned itself in
fresh, sweet leaves. It made her happy to see it.

It was visiting hours and she knew the way. She was glad
that Gordon had the lilacs. They obscured the inevitable hospital odor, the combination of cleaning products and still water
and decay. She could never enter the hospital without recalling
her aunt Lucy's final year in a nursing home, the halls lined

with old folks in wheelchairs, their heads like drooping dandelion puffs. But this was a veterans' hospital, and there remained in the air something fierce and proud and broken. She shook herself to get rid of that train of thinking. She asked Gordon if he needed help, and he said no.

She could not imagine what it must be like from her boy's perspective. How did he reconcile in his small world what these men meant? She worried that it frightened him to come here, and she had talked to her pediatrician about it, and they had both concluded that some visits, spaced appropriately, made sense. Without the visits, they risked turning "Daddy" into Santa Claus, a mythical figure that was always good and observing and never arriving. Only this was different, Margaret often wanted to say: no Christmas morning waited, no climax ever came due. No other side to the calendar existed, no before and after.

When they entered the ward, Margaret noted the silence. It always impressed her. It was a library, she felt, a place of stored lives, and she couldn't help lifting Gordon up into her arms—not for his benefit, but for her own. She passed the familiar beds: Mangan, Fitzgerald, James, Phillmore. The men stared up at the ceiling, their eyes closed.

"There's Daddy," she whispered to Gordon.

He nodded. She kissed his small, sweet head.

"Oh, aren't those pretty?" a nurse said, suddenly appearing. Where had she been? Margaret wondered. She must have been bending down below the sight line of the beds, because she whisked past, stopping for a second to sniff the lilacs in

Gordon's hands. Margaret didn't recognize her, which was surprising because she thought she knew all the nurses.

"Lilac season," Margaret said.

"Oh, we've got a great big stand between our yard and the next one," the nurse said, "and I go out there with my coffee whenever I can and just breathe it all in. You can hardly believe something smells so good."

Margaret smiled. She wanted the nurse to move on, especially because she was conscious of Gordon looking about, first at his father, then at all the other cocoons living in the ward.

"There's Daddy," she whispered again, and this time the nurse smiled and peeled away, promising to bring a vase when she returned.

Margaret walked to the bed and held Gordon carefully, letting him set the pace. She saw his eyes running over everything: the monitors, the small finger clip on Thomas's index finger, the bed railings, the silver bags dangling from the rolling stand.

"Want to get down?" she asked.

He didn't answer. She let go with one hand and reached down and cupped Thomas's forearm. The gesture meant, *See, here's Daddy, he will do you no harm, he wants nothing from you, he would have loved you if he could,* but what did that mean to a six-year-old boy?

"Want to give him the lilacs?" Margaret whispered.

He nodded and held them out. Margaret lowered her son enough so that he could place the flowers on Thomas's chest. Like putting flowers on a grave, she realized, and she quickly raised him up and then lowered him to his feet. When she was sure he was steady, she leaned over the bed and kissed Thomas's forehead. She removed the lilacs and made a place for them on the bedside stand. They sent up their fragrance in small, nearly imperceptible waves.

"Your daddy always loved lilacs," she said to Gordon, touching his hair. "He would cut a bunch of them and bring them into our bedroom so we could smell them all night long. Do you like lilacs?"

"Yes."

"I think they may be my favorite flower. Although I don't really know if they are a flower. Maybe they're a shrub. I don't know if there's a difference."

"What's that?" Gordon asked, his head nodding at one of the silver bags of liquid suspended over the bed.

"That's food and water."

"Oh," Gordon said.

"It's okay to ask things. You don't have to worry. He's your dad, that's all. He was injured in the war."

Gordon nodded.

"Will he get well?" he asked, though they had been over this.

"No, sweetheart. He won't."

"Why not?"

She had been over this, too, but she took an even breath and explained it again.

"The injuries are too severe," she said, "too deep inside him. It's hard to explain. He's just kind of asleep now. It's called a coma. But it's not regular sleep, so you don't have to worry. He had a bad injury and his body can't catch up to what he wants to do."

Gordon nodded. And Margaret, for just an instant, felt herself losing it. Her jaw trembled slightly and she forced herself to straighten up the bedside table, to tuck the blankets closer on Thomas's frail body. How was she supposed to explain her husband's condition to his son? If she said he was merely asleep, why wouldn't Gordon assume sleep could do this to him, too? But a coma meant nothing to a child. It was all a confusing jumble, a rat's nest of poor answers, and she finally squatted down next to Gordon and hugged him. She made a decision not to wait for the doctor. Not today. Not with her son here. There would be plenty of other days for doctor consultations.

"After the nurse comes back, we'll put the lilacs in the vase and then we can go to Hot Dog Depot. Would that be okay? You've been very good. Very, very good."

She pulled him close. Her heart turned to dust, to a bright cloud of sparkling dust pushed by a wind, pushed by spring, pushed by the tiny arms coming up around her shoulders.

In the final sunlight of the day, Margaret carried a cup of tea onto the back porch and sat down on the glider. Dinner had passed; the dishes stood stacked in the drainer. She had swept the floor and put away the meat loaf in a Tupperware container. She would make sandwiches tomorrow, maybe open-faced

ones, and the mashed potatoes could be moistened and recon-
stituted and served with chopped carrots. Not terribly origi-
nal, she decided as she sat and pulled a small afghan over her
shoulders. She considered getting up to find *The Gourmet Cook-
book*, a favorite for browsing, but then she decided she felt too
comfortable to move. The last light of the sun reflected softly
off the metal roof of the barn, and she watched to see how the
day would end.

Her body slowed and sleep made its first approach, though
she did not give in to it. She reached forward and took her tea
and sipped it. She loved this moment. The day was done but
night had not arrived, and the scent of lilacs drifted and curled
in unpredictable ways. Behind her in the house she heard the
television news. Benjamin listened and she knew Gordon
played around his feet, his trucks and soldiers a village beside
a giant's boots. Shortly, it would be his bedtime. Then night
would settle on the house, and she would hear it blend into the
darkness, the winds finding it and teasing it to come away. And
sometimes coyotes called, their chirps like eager pups, and the
cows might answer in their dull, heavy lowing, and rest would
come. Sleep would close around the house like a summer lake,
like the bright glisten of moonlight on water, and it would lin-
ger there until the next morning. That was what she thought as
she sat and watched the sunlight pull back to end the day.

A few minutes later Gordon appeared, a fistful of soldiers
clutched in his small fingers. She patted the seat beside her and
he climbed up, tucking himself against her. She spread the afghan over him and for a moment he did nothing except savor

the warmth. His little hands felt cold. She kissed the top of his head.

"It's almost bedtime," she whispered, deliberately setting her voice low so that he might calm himself.

He nodded.

"School tomorrow," she whispered.

He nodded again. Then he rolled over slightly onto his back so that he could watch his soldiers in his hand. She wondered for an instant what war he fought. It seemed perpetual and it occasionally worried her. She could not help wondering if it had something to do with Thomas. It seemed obvious that it must, but she had never been a little boy and so she couldn't say what motivated him.

"You want to watch to see if there's a star tonight?"

"Hmm-mm," he murmured, a sound meant to say yes.

"Your daddy put that star in the cupola. It's a prism."

He nodded. She watched the top of the barn. Years ago, Thomas had hung a prism in the cupola. It was a star, he said. All year the sun found it in entertaining ways, sometimes flashing a rainbow onto the side of the house or shooting a bright, combustible pin-light onto the ground or water trough. At this time of year it usually caught the late sunlight, turning to fire the instant before the light left for the day.

She pulled Gordon closer. The lilacs threw their scent into the approaching night. The tea tasted sweet and warm on her lips. Part of her now wondered why she had agreed to go to Washington. This was where she belonged, but earlier in the evening she had made the call to Charlie King, the escort provided by the administration, and the conversation had been comfortable and informative. He seemed like a good guy, as she had told Grandpa Ben, not at all a bureaucrat, and he had competently outlined the travel arrangements, the per diem, and so forth. After the call she had been glad she had agreed to go, thinking of it as something concrete she could do for Tom, but now, with her son pressed against her, the day burning out, she wondered why she had ever consented to leave the farm.

"Here it comes," she whispered.

He straightened against her and looked up. For the last three sunsets the prism had caught fire and it did not disappoint her this night. It sparkled bright white for just an instant, and she thought of Thomas, and she thought of good grace falling over the farm, and she hugged Gordon as the prism accepted light, bent it, and sent it on its way. She felt a lesson rested in its performance, that she, too, must accept what came toward her and pass it on its journey, but that seemed too grand an idea for the moment. Better, she realized, to concentrate on her boy, and the star her husband had hung for her, and to let day pass to night so that light might swiftly return.

Chapter
Four

Charlie King, thirty-three, slid across the backseat of the town car, preferring to climb out on the blind side rather than the house side of the vehicle. As much as he tried to ignore it, he was conscious of his right leg and of the prosthetic that dragged beneath the stump of his thigh. Although he walked well with the prosthetic device—he had himself filmed as part of his therapy and he was pleased with the results—the artificial leg caused a problem occasionally climbing in and out of vehicles. It caused other problems, too, of course, but none that he could not overcome. As always, as he climbed out of the car—his hands on the door opening and hoisting his weight like a man levering out of a small window—he wondered how long it would take before the subject of the leg came up. It always did eventually. Still, he took it as a small challenge, a gauge of his returning health, that people sometimes failed to discover his leg at all. He did not think he was deluded in that.

He stood to his full height, six feet, two inches, and straightened his suit jacket. It had been pleasantly cool in the car's air-conditioning, but now, in the yard before the farmhouse, he felt the day's warmth growing. He hated wearing a jacket, or a tie, for that matter, but if the occasion demanded it he did not complain. It was better, at least, than a dress uniform, something he had worn both at West Point and for five years in the army. This suit, a deep navy with a trace of a pinstripe through the fabric, fit him well. He put his two thumbs under the front of his pants and ran them to the points of his hips. He did this unconsciously, a tiny tic that he had kept since boyhood.

He bent back into the car and grabbed a small bouquet for Mrs. Kennedy, Margaret, and a stuffed meerkat for the boy, Gordon. The driver—a local man whose name Charlie hadn't fully caught but sounded like Caleb or Callum—turned slightly to see over his right shoulder.

"Be a minute," Charlie told him, his head still in the interior.

"No rush," the driver said with a Maine accent. "We have time."

Charlie closed the car door, self-conscious of the flowers and the meerkat. The flowers and stuffed animal were not strictly protocol, but they had seemed, when he left the Bangor hotel in the morning, like an appropriate ice-breaking gesture. *Why not?* he thought when he purchased the items in the hotel lobby. He particularly liked the meerkat, which seemed to take an interest in the ride out to the farm, its button eyes glowing with the lovely spring scenery as if actually alive. He tucked the meerkat under his left elbow, the same hand that held the flowers.

On the short walk up to the porch, he smelled the heavy odor of cows and manure. He also smelled lilacs and something less familiar that he could not name. He turned a little to see if he could spot its origin, but he came away with the general impression of a farm and little else. He saw sheep fencing and a faded red barn; three Barred Rock chickens pecking in the field beyond the barn; and black and white cattle—Holsteins, he thought—grazing on the spring grass.

When he turned back, an older man stood on the porch, watching him.

"This is the right place," the man said. "Did you find it okay?"

"Yes, sir," Charlie answered.

"Well, you're right on time. Margaret should be ready in a jot."

"Yes, sir."

Charlie climbed the steps, aware of his leg not behaving properly as he did so. He felt the tiniest bit unsettled that the man had appeared on his porch so soundlessly. But the man had a kind face and held out his hand.

"I'm Ben Kennedy," the man said. "The boy up at the hospital is my son."

"An honor to meet you, sir," Charlie said and meant it.

Charlie had never felt a hand with more work in it.

"I was going to come down to Washington, but we have the cattle to care for," Ben Kennedy said. "You thank the people for asking me, though."

"Yes, sir, I will."

The man turned and called softly into the doorway.

"Come on now," the man said. "Don't keep the gentleman waiting."

A boy came out first. He pushed open the door, obviously excited, but then became shy in the next heartbeat. The boy turned and held the door, waiting, though he glanced quickly at the meerkat and then looked back into the house. The boy, Charlie saw, wore clean khaki shorts and a sweatshirt. His hair was cut short and he had a child's tan even this early in the season. He looked fresh and wholesome. A country boy, Charlie thought.

The woman following the boy through the door caught him by surprise.

She was younger, for one thing, than he expected. He quickly did the math—adding together a husband in the service, a young child—and realized she was essentially his age. Call it twenty-seven or -eight, thirty at the outside. Charlie was not sure why he had assumed she would be older. Perhaps it had been in her phone voice, he thought, or maybe it was merely the idea that someone living on a farm with a child in Maine was likely to be older. That made no sense whatsoever, and perhaps betrayed a slight prejudice against rural people on his part, but his mind, always fair when it grasped the facts, rapidly made the necessary revisions. His mind was further pushed in that direction by the woman's beauty. Prepared as he was to behave in his official capacity, he could not ignore her loveliness. She did not dazzle. No one would mistake her for a runway model or a social climber down in the District of Columbia, yet he could not remember feeling so attracted to a woman in a long time. Part of the attraction, he imagined, came from the sense of the house, the open door into a fine old parlor, the sight of the boy leaning on the screen door, the benevolent father-in-law beaming his good wishes. She reminded him of a woman in a painting—was it Andrew Wyeth's pictures of Christina?—her beauty somehow matched to the landscape. She possessed a natural lightness, a grace fortified by the ease with which she moved through the open doorway. Her hand reached out and brushed her boy's hair, and then she smiled a deep, warm smile that carried upward into her eyes. The small crow's-feet at the corners of her sockets crinkled with pleasure. She wore a plain dress that did not reveal her figure, and yet it suggested simplicity and elegance in a way that many women in D.C. sought but failed to capture. He found he could not look away from her eyes once they met his.

"Mrs. Kennedy," he said in a voice he had practiced, "on behalf of President Obama and the people of the United States, it is my honor to escort you to Washington, D.C. My name is Charlie King."

"How do you do, Mr. King?" the woman asked.

She held out her hand. His eyes stayed on hers.

"If you're comfortable with it, please call me Charlie."

He shook her hand.

"If you'll call me Margaret," the woman said, her eyes still on his. "I feel as though I already know you from the phone."

"But Lord save you if you call her Peggy," Benjamin chimed in.

"And this is Gordon," the woman—Margaret, Charlie repeated in his mind—"our son."

"Hello, Gordon," Charlie said. "I've brought you something to keep you company this weekend while your mom is in Washington."

Charlie held out the meerkat. Gordon turned back and put his forehead against the screen door, effectively hiding his face. Margaret squatted next to the child, her knees pushed away and back toward the house.

"Can you say hello to Mr. King?"

The boy nodded but didn't unwind.

"And these are for you," Charlie said, not sure the flowers were the right touch after all. They seemed slightly familiar, perhaps claiming greater personal territory than was strictly required by an escort.

"Well, thank you," Margaret said, standing and accepting the flowers. "I'll put them in a vase right here and they will welcome me home when I get back."

She held the flowers to her nose. Her eyes smiled again over the buds. At the same time the boy slowly left the security of the screen door and swung over to his mother's hip, his arms up to bracket her. She lowered the flowers so that he could sniff them, too. The boy nodded and buried one eye behind his mother's hip. The other eye, Charlie noted, stayed focused on the meerkat.

He was handsome. He was very handsome, Margaret decided. Funny, because he did not strike her as handsome immediately. Certainly he was good-looking, no question, but he stopped somewhere short of handsome in her first appraisal.

She felt, glancing at him as she did now, that he possessed a sort of jigsaw handsomeness, a manner and a look that had to be assembled rather than taken on first bounce. Maybe, she thought, she was getting old: older women, she knew, broke men down and analyzed their features. They did not swoon, as young girls did, taking a man in one large gulp. Charlie King, she decided, was greater than the sum of his pieces.

She liked best of all the meerkat. Specifically, she liked the tenderness with which he offered it to Gordon. He held it forward, and bent, and she had seen the stiffness of his leg, making it difficult for him to lower himself. And he did not become annoyed or offended when her son did not respond at first. Smart man. He smiled and said he would leave it and if Gordon decided to play with it, okay. Then he let it go. Where some men might have made the child's shyness an issue, Charlie simply smiled and went off to the next thing. She respected that. So often, given her circumstances, men overcompensated around Gordon, trying to be an instant father figure, trying to be especially warm out of an odd consideration for her husband. She detested that kind of bargain, and was pleased, many times over, when Gordon routinely saw through them. But Charlie King had struck the exact right note. She awarded him points for that.

He was also polite. Part of it, she assumed, came from his duties on this trip. He was paid to be her escort, at least at some level, and naturally he would be selected for manners. But good manners, she had always felt, provided an insight to a person's character. Charlie King was not falsely polite, but he moved and acted with slow consideration, putting her comfort before his with a naturalness that she found appealing. His leg, of course, made some of his movement the tiniest bit awkward; he had insisted on carrying her bags to the car, his gallantry highlighted by the difficulty he faced going down stairs. She had caught her father-in-law's eye. Benjamin had not missed it. Charlie King had turned sideways as he went down the steps, lowering his body as a man might go cautiously down a slick loading ramp.

She glanced across the airplane aisle at Charlie King. He looked up—he had been reading the *Boston Globe*'s sports page—and met her eye. He smiled. It was a good smile, full and genuine, with a single dimple on his left cheek.

"I'm not much of a flier," he said. "I never liked it much."

"I don't mind it. It's not my favorite thing, but it's okay."

"How old is Gordon? He's six?"

"Yes, six."

"My friend's son is six. I figured they were about the same age. What grade is he in?"

"First grade. I thought about holding him back a year . . . he's a little young for his class . . . but then I figured the social-ization would be good for him. He likes it well enough."

"It must be fun for him, living on a farm."

"He likes the animals. But not the cows so much. He thinks they're too big. I like the farm for him, though. And I like cows, as odd as that sounds."

Margaret watched Charlie smile. He put the paper down on his lap.

"So are you with the Obama administration?" she asked. "I'm sorry. I don't know your official capacity."

"I suppose I am," he said. "I've just been posted to West Africa with the Foreign Service. I'm in Washington to do language and cultural training."

"How wonderful. That's the diplomatic corps, isn't it?"

"Yes."

" And you served in the military as well. Army?"

"Yes. I went to West Point, the whole nine yards. Now I've decided I'd rather push a pen than a sword. That's the little phrase I've been using for shorthand."

"How did you end up escorting me to Washington?"

"I volunteered for it, actually. I have a brother who is in a vegetative state. My family lives in Iowa, and he jumped into a quarry and landed on rocks. Summertime, swimming, you know. He broke his back."

"I'm sorry," she said.

"He was a young kid, too. He was my older brother. So I've been interested in this bill. It won't do much for my brother, but it will help other people in these circumstances. And I have to say, I respect what your husband did in Afghanistan. I read the report of his injury."

"Thank you," she said.

"It took a lot of courage."

"Did it?" she asked.

He looked at her. She wasn't sure why she made such comments, but it wasn't the first time she had done so. She did, in fact, believe her husband, Tom, had acted bravely, but she did not see it in quite the same light as others wanted to see it. Although he had had a patriotic reaction after 9/11, he had also gone into the service for a salary. It had made financial sense, and she found it unsettling to hear other people attribute patriotic reasons for his service. For his heroism. She knew her husband—saw him bracketed by his son on one side, his father on the other—and she did not believe he would have acted courageously for a concept as vague as patriotism. No, it made perfect sense that he would raise his arms and try to protect a fellow soldier, but that had nothing to do with God and Country and flag waving. It had more to do, she long ago decided, with his innate decency, his willingness to rise out of bed at four thirty in the morning on the coldest day of the year to milk his cows, to treat them tenderly, to chip ice off their drinking water while his hands and cheeks turned bright red. Thomas had always acted kindly, gently, and he could no more have ignored the man behind him, fleeing for safety himself, than he could have ignored a broken-down vehicle on his way to town or a cow floundering in a muddy rut. He did what was in front of him, and the irony was that he had no strong political impulse, but he would stand up and take a bullet for any human being in need of his protection. So was it bravery, she wondered, or simply the fate his character brought about? She was not sure the distinction mattered anymore, and she only thought of it when others commented on his actions.

"Yes, I believe it did," Charlie King answered simply. "I admire his bravery."

"Well, thank you."

"Have you been to Washington?"

"Only once, for the medal ceremony."

"I find it a little exhausting to live there. Everyone has some sort of game going. It's probably always been that way, but it seems worse these days. All these political winds."

"More polarity?"

He nodded. He turned a little to face her. She liked the way he talked, the intent way he had of holding her eyes with his own.

"So you grew up in Iowa?" she asked, partially to rid herself of political thoughts. "I saw it on your bio sheet. You must have felt right at home on our farm this morning."

"I grew up in farm country, but we weren't farmers. My mom and dad are both teachers at the high school near Carroll. That's in the center of the state. I had a pretty average upbringing."

"And you got an appointment to West Point?"

"I did. I don't want you to think I was some sort of born soldier, though. It was one of the best ways to pay for school. I would have done National Guard if I hadn't received an appointment to West Point. I'm just cheap."

"And you served . . . ?"

"In Iraq."

"I read that," Margaret said. "Three tours. And is your brother still alive?"

He nodded.

"Yes, still. He has pretty good care. Ups and downs. You know how that is, I'm sure."

He smiled. Margaret smiled back at him. For an instant, just an instant, she felt a ridiculous, nearly forgotten flirtatiousness rise up in her. How strange, she thought. How absurd and how ill timed. She would have given a great deal to have her friend Blake beside her, if for nothing except to verify that his gaze actually contained interest. Sexual interest. She felt her face flush and she became aware of her body, of his opposite maleness, of the pleasure of talking to a man. How long had it been? She could not say precisely. She did not even permit herself to think of it, to believe fully that such a thing was happening, but she could not dispute the warmth and attraction of his eyes. She nearly blurted out her feeling because it came as such a surprise she could not take it seriously. She wondered if he felt the same thing. At any moment she imagined they would both burst out laughing, except his eyes remained on hers and in a pulse, maybe two, she understood that his interest was genuine.

She moved her eyes away when the plane bounced a little on an air pocket. She felt grateful Charlie sat across the aisle and not directly beside her. It felt more comfortable that way, more casual. The plane dipped again and Margaret braced herself on the seat.

"We're supposed to have decent weather, I think," Charlie said. "Not sure where this disturbance is coming from."

"Thank goodness it's a short flight."

"No flight is too short for me."

"I would think you'd be pretty accustomed to it in the army."

"I can tolerate it, I guess. I just don't like it."

The plane dropped twice, then steadied. Margaret felt a little nervous and uneasy. She understood that part of the unease came from speaking to a man to whom she felt attraction. It had been years, more than half a decade, since she had engaged in any type of flirtation, and even that had been with Tom, her husband. And was this truly a flirtation? She couldn't even know that for certain, although she could guess Blake's answer. She felt entirely out of practice. She spoke to her friends' husbands at social functions, of course, and to Grandpa Ben and Gordon, but that was a different kettle of fish. What did men talk about? With Blake she could talk about anything, but with a man she felt out to sea. What did they care about? Sports, probably. In Maine, at least near her home, they talked about farming and milk prices and tractors, and occasionally hunting. But what topics interested a man out in the larger world, she couldn't say. She smoothed her dress a little against her legs, and when she looked back at Charlie she saw he had gone back to reading his sports page. She nodded and looked across him and out the window. The plane's wings sliced through the clouds. A red light at the wingtip turned the mist hazy and soft, and she watched the clouds fall back and away from the plane and swirl like a bad movie flashback to introduce memory or forgetting.

The city felt hot and humid, as it usually did, and Charlie felt the heat build inside his suit and rest there, as if reluctant to leave. A strange custom, he thought, for gentlemen to wear jackets in such heat. And ties. As he lifted Margaret Kennedy's bags into the trunk of the waiting town car, he was relieved to see storm clouds on the southwest horizon. A rain, he knew, sometimes cooled off the city. Sometimes, too, a storm merely nailed the heat down tighter, giving everything a swampy, malarial feel. He had not paid attention to the weather reports, so he did not know for sure what the rain might do. For Margaret's sake, he hoped for a bright, cool wind to help her through the weekend.

"Looks like weather's coming," he said to the car in general as he climbed inside.

The driver, a black man with a thin mustache across his top lip, nodded and caught his eye in the rearview mirror.

"We're going to get a break from the heat," the driver said. "Should be a good weekend."

"Well, that's fine," Charlie said, at the same time thinking that he should have sat in the front seat. On one hand, it felt friendlier to join Mrs. Kennedy in the backseat, but it also felt perhaps a shade too casual. Maybe. He did not want Margaret to think he presumed a certain familiarity, that he had forgotten his official function on this trip. But he admitted to himself that he had felt . . . what? What was it, exactly? He could not name it to his satisfaction. Warmth, perhaps. Or interest. Sitting across the aisle from her on the plane, he had felt sensations he had not indulged in for a year or longer. She was undoubtedly a beautiful woman, and a kind one, and he confessed to himself that he felt comfortable in her presence. He had felt it on the phone. It felt like calling home somehow, as if they had already met. Maybe it was all tied up with the cows and the Maine farm and her valorous husband, but he felt a deep tidal attraction growing in him. He liked her, simply put. And if he felt a few tiny sparks, a little acknowledgment of the man-woman thing, what of it? More than anything, he wanted her experience in Washington to be fun and meaningful, a break in what he knew from his brother's life could be a long, unending wait. A futile wait. To his way of thinking, even the rain counted. If it cooled the city, if it made her weekend more enjoyable, then he wanted it to rain. It was that simple. And if he could serve a little as the rain—that was stretching it, but it had a basis in truth—then he didn't mind. He would pay attention. That was all. He had not counted on liking her so much.

"What time is the signing tomorrow?" Margaret asked. "I know I know it, but I just need someone else to tell me."

"Ten o'clock."

"And is it close to the hotel?"

"A three-minute walk. We should allow for a little time to pass through security. It's at the hospital, so the security attachment won't be quite as smooth as it would be at the White House."

"It was very smooth when we went for the Medal of Honor ceremony. That was all my father-in-law talked about for months afterward."

"And he lives with you?"

"For the time being. We're a little in limbo. There's a second house on the property that we're renovating, but there isn't much time or money. We'll stay on the farm no matter what. It was to be Tom's farm, but things don't always turn out the way you expect. Of course, you know that. But I like farming. It sounds odd, probably, but I do."

"And I take it the farm in Maine is a lot like the farms in Iowa. Tough making a go of it."

"We could sell the land and do a lot better."

"Are you tempted?"

"Oh, sure. Tempted. But we've had the farm through four generations. I think it's four. I lose count sometimes. It's never been flush. We've never made a lot of money at it, but you know how it is. It's your way of life, everything. I'd hate for Gordon to grow up without experiencing it."

The car moved through traffic.

"Did you grow up on a farm?" Charlie asked. "I hope I'm not asking too many questions. You don't meet many farmers in Washington."

"No, it's fine. My dad leased a farm one town over. It's been sold out for condos for, oh, I don't know. A couple years, anyway. Maybe longer. My dad and mom moved to Tennessee. They couldn't take the Maine winters any longer. Dad works at Home Depot and Mom does party cleaning. You know, if a woman is hosting a big party, then she calls my mom to come in and do a top-to-bottom cleaning. Before and after. She isn't afraid to charge."

"Good for her," Charlie said.

"They miss farming, though. They don't say as much, but

I can tell. If we can get the second house renovated, maybe they can come up and give a hand in the summers. I must be boring you to death with all this. I didn't mean to go on about myself."

"Not at all."

She smiled. There it was again, Charlie told himself. He liked that smile a great deal and he felt it pull him in, draw him closer. He wondered if she had any idea how fetching her smile could be. Meanwhile, the driver managed to hit the highway and Charlie felt the car accelerate. The driver's window, down a crack, made a high, noisy hum as they sped along. But the air felt good and Charlie smelled the rain. It was beginning somewhere. The leaves on the trees beside the highway turned their white sides over.

"Now you know my life story," Margaret said. "Not exactly an exciting life."

"It sounds like a good life," Charlie said.

"Well, it has its moments. After Tom's accident, his situation, I needed to stay busy and there's no place on earth that will take more work from you than a farm. The schools are good and it's safe. No crime at all, really, except a domestic blowup now and then. No one locks the door and people park and leave their keys in the ignition. That's worth something, I figure."

"Sure it is."

"But you're going to be a diplomat," she said. "That sounds more exciting."

"Well, we'll see. I like the sound of your Maine farm. It reminded me of home when I saw it this morning."

He felt his eyes go into hers again. He didn't mean it to happen, but it did anyway. Lust, probably. People called it love, but maybe it was simple lust. Charlie couldn't say. But he felt their eyes teetering, holding on to each other's gaze longer than any required need. He only managed to pull his eyes away when the car veered sharply to the right and the driver tapped his horn. Charlie looked forward. The driver, for the barest instant, met Charlie's eyes in the rearview mirror and nodded.

Margaret loved a late afternoon rain. Stretched out on the bed, she listened to the rain slash and move against the window. She felt good in her body; her limbs felt warm and solid. Her face, washed and scrubbed, glowed with the polish of soap and Noxzema. She felt a deep, wonderful, guilty luxury. She had nowhere to go, nothing to do, except, perhaps, to get herself something to eat. But even that was a simple matter. She merely had to lift the phone and it would be brought on a silver platter. She could eat what she liked, then pack it all up and stick it outside her door, and then the hotel elves would come and take it away and that would be that. Wouldn't it be wonderful, she thought, if life always came complete with room service?

She had nearly fallen into a doze when her cell phone rang. She grabbed it and glanced at the number, but she didn't recognize it. It was a Washington, D.C., number.

"Yes?" she whispered when she opened the phone.

"Margaret, I'm sorry. Did I wake you? This is Charlie King."

"I dozed off," she admitted. "Or almost did. Hi, Charlie. Is everything okay?"

She reached over and turned on the bedside lamp. She felt fuzzy and slightly hungry. She tried to clear her head.

"I wanted to invite you to a ball," he said. "It's a spur-of-the-moment thing, and I apologize, but a friend of mine has tickets. They throw these things from time to time and this should be a pretty good one. I thought it might be fun for you."

"A ball?" she asked, not quite getting her mind around it. But her stomach had started to flutter noticeably. "I have nothing to wear, Charlie. I didn't come planning to attend a ball."

"I have a friend . . . she lives here and has helped me with a few things. Anyway, she has a couple ball gowns she can lend you. She has three. She's looking at me right now and nodding. You can pick, she says. If you want, I could put her on and you two could talk."

"Oh, Charlie, I don't know."

Margaret swung her legs over the side of the bed. Where had this come from? She admitted, deep down, that it felt good to be asked. Very good. At the same time, it made her nervous and a tad distrustful. What was the game here? He knew that she was married. Obviously. Then again, she wondered if she wasn't overthinking it. Maybe he simply meant to be polite, to give her something to do on a Friday night in D.C. She pushed back her hair at the hairline and switched the phone to her other ear. She closed her eyes and tried to concentrate.

"Here, just talk to her for a second," Charlie said. "Her name is Terry. I'd really like to escort you to a ball tonight,

Margaret. If you'd like to go. It should be very pretty. It's at the French Embassy. It's sponsored by the London School of Economics."

Before she could answer, she heard a woman's voice on the other end of the phone. Terry, obviously. Terry giggled and the phone rattled as she came on.

"Now, don't worry about a thing," Terry said, her voice deep with a southern accent along its edge. "Margaret, I have three dresses and you're welcome to any of them that suit. What's your dress size, darling?"

"I want to say six, but probably an eight."

"I'm an eight, too. Maybe a six in my good stretches. Trust me, you'll have a wonderful time. It's a beautiful building and they have a rotunda or whatever you call it. Everyone will be dressed up, but that's not to scare you. These tickets just fell into my hands and I can't use them and you two can. What do you say? Let us do this for you."

"You're very kind," Margaret said. "But I was just getting relaxed. . . ."

"I understand. I do. It can feel awfully good to be quiet for a while, especially for a woman with a child. But you're not in Washington very often, Charlie tells me, and we just happened to come into these tickets. Charlie can come over, bring the dresses. . . . I'll send over some wraps and a few pairs of shoes . . . size eight if that works. There's not a thing in the world to worry about, and if you end up having a terrible time, well, what's the worry there? You just go back to the hotel, right?"

Margaret felt her stomach churning. She had never expected this, not in a million years. She wished, somehow, that she could pause the whole procedure, hit stop, like you did on a DVD, and then call Blake and get her thoughts. But she was on her own and she had difficulty reading the weather inside her head.

"This is just out of left field," Margaret said, mostly to give herself time to think.

"Well, of course it is. But it's a ball in one of the prettiest embassies we have in D.C. They serve French food and a symphony orchestra plays. I mean, it's right out of *Cinderella*. I went two years ago and we had a marvelous time. Do you like to dance?"

"It's been so long, I don't really know."

"There's lots of dancing, naturally. And the food and drinks are excellent. I mean, it's French, so you can expect a certain amount of skill. It's a pretty big affair, and you can be relatively anonymous. It will just be you and Charlie, and he's a great guy. Then you can go back to the hotel, and it won't be a great night's sleep . . . but you're not leaving tomorrow, are you?"

"No, Sunday night."

"There you go, then. Sunday can be your sleep-in day. And tomorrow after the signing ceremony, you're free then, right?"

"Yes."

"Am I making a good case to go?" Terry asked.

"Yes. You are. Yes, then, I'd love to go. If it's not too much trouble with the gowns and everything, yes, it would be wonderful."

Margaret felt herself blush. She waited while Terry said good-bye, said something to Charlie, then heard Charlie clear his throat.

"I'm so happy you agreed to go," he said. "It starts at eight, so would it be all right if I swing by at seven? Or six thirty? Will that give you enough time to dress?"

"Yes, that would be fine. Maybe six thirty. I'll need a little time."

"I'll bring the gowns and we can leave the two you don't want in your hotel room."

"I'm a little overwhelmed," Margaret said.

"It's just like going to prom," Charlie said, "only you can have a drink and not get into trouble with the chaperones."

"Six thirty then?"

"I'll be there."

Margaret listened to him hang up. She closed her own phone and set it on the bedside stand. She felt a giddy, happy rush in the pit of her stomach that mixed with an equal flood of reservation and hesitation. If it hadn't happened so quickly, she probably would have fended the invitation off. But it had arrived out of the blue, and she had accepted, and now, one way or the other, she was going to spend the evening with a man. At a ball. At the French Embassy. She looked at the window, where the rain still drizzled down the panes. *I have a date,* she realized. She shook her head at the thought. It felt incomprehensible. But the notion came again to her and it felt good and strange and undeniably exciting. She hated that it made her feel good to be asked. She hated that her true heart knew what her conscious mind did not: that loneliness was her companion, and she did not dare risk asking it to leave.

―☊

"Of *course* it's a date!" Blake said, her voice leaping with pleasure. "You're going to a ball? That's amazing. Tell me how it happened."

"He's going to be here in a few minutes."

"You have to remember everything. I want to hear every detail. Tell me again, what's he like?"

"He's tall and handsome. I mean, he's not a movie star, not that kind of handsome. But he's very sweet. He brought Gordon a stuffed meerkat."

"A what?"

"A meerkat. It's like a prairie dog, I guess. From Africa."

"And Gordon is home safe. I just called over there. They're eating lasagna."

"Good, I'm glad to hear that. I called earlier and shamed Grandpa Ben into reheating it."

"You go and you have fun, Margaret Kennedy. Don't put anything in the way. You deserve a night out. Do you hear me loud and clear? Don't try to decide what it is or isn't. Just enjoy it. You've got to have a little fun, too."

"It's been so long since I've done anything like this. And I can't help wondering what Charlie is thinking here. What's his game?"

"He must have liked what he saw to ask you to a ball. Don't complicate it."

"I think he's just being kind," Margaret said. "He's taking pity on an old farm woman. And the tickets were available."

"That's crazy talk. You're gorgeous. You will be stunning. Do you know anything about the gowns?"

"No idea. A woman named Terry is lending me one."

"In some ways it's easier," Blake said. "I mean, having only three gowns to choose from and you have to do it on the spot. You could kill yourself with shopping for something like this."

"I know. And I'm not really responsible for how I look. The pressure is off."

Margaret heard Blake change hands with her phone. Blake always weeded when she talked. Margaret pictured her walking around her deck, the phone crunched into her neck, her hands biting and nipping houseplants.

"So," Blake said, dragging the word out a little like a kid on a playground, "how much do you like him?"

"That's ridiculous, Blake. You're such a cornball."

"Is it ridiculous?"

"I'm still married, you know."

"I know that, Margaret. But Tom is Tom, and you know I have a whole lot of love for him. It's been six years since you so much as looked at anyone. Don't judge yourself so severely."

"I'm trying to stay in the moment. Okay, to answer your question, I told you, he's very sweet. Charlie is."

"And you like him?"

"I like him very much. From what I know, I like him."

"That's all that counts then," Blake said. "I'm happy for you, Margaret."

"I'm married, Blake. Don't go crazy here. I don't even know why I said I'd go. It caught me by surprise, and I admit it was nice to be asked."

"That's human, Margaret."

"I have half a heart for anything. You know that."

"I do, sweetie. I know that. But you don't get to go to a ball at the French Embassy too many times in your life, so just enjoy it. Stay in the present, like you were saying."

"Okay, I should get off. He could be here any minute."

"Call me first thing tomorrow. And remember everything. God, I am so going to enjoy this vicariously. Take pictures, because I want to see how you look and what Charlie King looks like. And remember what they serve for dinner and how things look. You're like Cinderella."

"I'll do my best. No glass slipper."

"I love you, sweetheart," Blake said, her voice warm.

"Love you, too."

"Don't put up obstacles," Blake said. "Don't limit anything. Be open, Margaret."

"I'll try to be."

Margaret hung up. She bent to the bathroom mirror and traced a thin line of eyeliner under her eyes. She flecked mascara on her lashes, combing them up and away. She couldn't deny she felt excited. The conversation with Blake reinforced everything. A man, a nice man, would arrive any minute to take her to a ball. How had that happened? It felt as though a minute ago she had been clumping around in muck boots and listening to the phoebe sing a welcome to spring. Now she had a fluttery stomach and a teenage girl's anxiety about how she would look, how she would act, what the night would bring. Then, almost in the next breath, she warned herself not to get carried away. It was likely that Charlie's innate decency had provoked him to ask her. Maybe, she thought, it might even be part of his official function. In any case, it didn't bear thinking about. She was going to a ball, and she had never been to a ball, and she decided simply to enjoy herself and observe everything she could. She let out a long, slow breath and let herself relax for a moment. *Meet life openly,* she reminded herself of one of her mother's dictums. *Do not climb a mountain before you arrive at its foothills.*

As she bent back to the mirror to inspect her eyeliner she heard steps outside her door and the crinkle of plastic dress bags. Then a knock came sharp and hard, and Margaret felt her breath shorten, felt like a girl again, her hand to the top of her robe to keep it closed.

Chapter
Five

Gordon placed the saw-chuck soldier on the side of the sink and then brushed his teeth with the Colgate bubble-gum-flavored toothpaste his mother had set on the bathroom counter. He brushed a little up and down, flicking the bristles along his upper teeth, but he found it difficult to concentrate with the saw-chuck guy standing so close. He heard Grandpa Ben coming up the stairs. The stairs sounded like shells crack-ing the way they squeaked and he could tell how far his grand-father had come by the rising noise each step released.

"You about finished there, Gordon?" his grandpa asked.

Gordon nodded, even though he didn't hear all the words clearly because of the toothbrush, but he understood the gen-eral idea. He reached over and made the saw-chuck guy crawl forward on his belly. He made a shooting sound in the side of his cheek and a dot of toothpaste spattered out onto the sink.

"Okay, hip-hop into bed," he heard Grandpa Ben say from down the hall.

He nodded. He swirled water in his mouth and spit it into the sink. He turned on the water and rinsed off his toothbrush. He grabbed the saw-chuck guy and made him slide fast on his belly until he reached the end of the sink. Then the saw-chuck guy flew through the air like Superman.

Grandpa Ben had the covers pulled back and the chair set beside the bed. Gordon jumped into the bed and shoved down under the covers. He kept the saw-chuck guy in his right hand and kept him down, out of the way, so that he could make him move and fight if Grandpa Ben's story got boring.

"What will it be tonight, buckaroo?" Grandpa Ben asked, reaching to a pile of books beside the bed.

"Is Mom coming home tonight?"

"No," Grandpa Ben said, sitting on the chair. "You know that. She told you she would be home Sunday night and you would see her Monday morning, bright and early."

"Monday morning," Gordon whispered.

"How about the rabbit story?"

Gordon nodded. He stretched his legs out and made the saw-chuck guy climb his thigh. He smelled straw and hay and wondered if his grandpa had cleaned off the cuffs of his pants. His mom always made Grandpa Ben clean the cuffs of his pants because he tracked. People tracked a lot, he knew, although he wasn't entirely sure of the concept.

He fell asleep before his grandpa had read one full chapter of the rabbit story. The saw-chuck man rested cradled in Gordon's fingers, suspended above the bottom sheet and still a minute weight that the boy perceived. His breath grew gradually deeper, and slower, and his grandfather closed the book and slid it back in its place. He brushed the boy's hair back and tucked the blankets up a little higher. The movement of the blanket spun the saw-chuck soldier out of Gordon's fingers, but the grandfather did not notice. He stood and turned off the lamp, and in the last instant of light saw the resemblance between the boy and his son, Thomas. The passing of time made the only difference, and he felt a momentary dislocation between the present and past as he tiptoed out to the hallway, his cuffs carrying two wands of straw that he had forgotten to brush away.

She wore the black gown. Black always worked, Terry said when she fished the dress out of her closet, and Charlie could not say what the other colors might have looked like—a pale peach-colored gown with a wider skirt and tight bodice and a cream-colored gown that was longer and more fitted through the hips—but he thought the black absolutely suited Margaret. It more than suited her; it surprised him by how easily it had transformed her. She had disappeared into the bathroom a mother and had stepped out—well, how exactly? He couldn't say. The peach, he realized, might not have flattered her coloring; and the cream would have made her pale and mothlike. The black looked beautiful on her and as he stood he could not help but smile.

"You look lovely," he said.

"I had no idea these gowns . . . they're really quite extravagant. Are you sure Terry won't mind me wearing one?"

"Believe me," Charlie said, "these are hand-me-downs from her friend Trish. Trish has plenty of gowns, I promise you."

"It's a Vera Wang," Margaret said in a nervous whisper, and Charlie saw her eyes go a little wide. She looked down at the dress and combed it against her thighs. She looked charming. She *was* charming in her modesty and lack of pretension. She had been excited about the gowns and had made the entire outfitting attempt fun.

"That's what Terry said," Charlie said from his position near the bank of windows, "and the other two . . . one's a DK and I forget . . . the peach one is a Gucci knockoff, I think. Trish goes to a dozen balls a year and she can't wear the same gown every time. Honestly, you really don't need to worry about a thing."

Charlie felt grateful for the fuss about the gowns. They had been a convenient icebreaker all the way around, preventing the first moments together from becoming too conspicuously datelike. And now the dress—a black ballerina-style gown, halter top, with simple lines that Charlie admired—felt to be the culmination of a satisfying project.

"I feel like I'm driving a Mercedes after being in an old pickup," Margaret said. "We don't wear many gowns in Bangor, Maine."

"Well, you look very natural in it," Charlie said.

"You look very handsome, too," Margaret said. "In all the fuss about the gowns, I didn't properly compliment you."

"Thank you," Charlie said.

He wore a tuxedo; it was a good-quality tuxedo he had bought in a secondhand store on Avenue B. Terry, in fact, had pointed him to it nearly a year before, when he had come for his first interviews with the Foreign Service office. He had attended two formal affairs—a dinner at the vice president's mansion and an opera premiere—and had been glad to have the tuxedo in his closet. Besides, he actually enjoyed dressing up a little. Why live in Washington if you didn't become involved in the social life at least to some degree? He cut a decent figure, he knew, and it felt like make-believe to wear a tux. As long as he didn't take it seriously, he enjoyed the experience.

"We should get going," Charlie said. "Did any of the wraps work?"

"I picked this one," Margaret said and stepped back into the bathroom quickly and returned with a beige wrap.

Charlie took the wrap from Margaret and held it while she slipped under it.

"Ta-da," he said. "That worked out, didn't it? And the shoes are okay?"

"They're fine. I told my friend in Maine that borrowing a gown took a lot of pressure off. I can simply blame the gown if it doesn't look right."

"You look wonderful, Margaret."

He saw her blush. It was natural and complete.

"This is really a treat. Even dressing up. . . . It's been so long," Margaret said.

"Well, you haven't danced with me yet. That may not be much of a treat."

"I bet you're a fine dancer."

He stepped past her and opened the door. She grabbed a small clutch—another thoughtful detail from Terry—and dropped her key into it. She nodded that she was ready. She stepped through the door and he closed it after her. She smelled of soap, he realized, and faint perfume. The movement of her dress sounded like groceries being bagged far away and in a bright kitchen, and Charlie followed.

Margaret heard music as soon as she stepped out from the taxi and she felt a delicious wave of joy and happiness fill her. She loved music. To hear it now, carried out from the embassy on the warm spring breeze, made her eyes moisten. How long had it been since she had felt so free? she wondered. The idea that she had no responsibilities, no Gordon, no house to clean, no cows to look after, felt nearly incomprehensible. She wished for time to slow. She worried, as she watched Charlie pay the driver, then turn to face her, that the evening might pass too quickly. Dear Charlie. He looked handsome and happy. He smiled easily and she liked his smile. On the taxi ride he had told an amusing story about a basset hound wandering into the last ball he had attended. The dog, he said, had begun to bay at the music, its hangdog look comical and piteous, and when someone on the waitstaff went forward to grab the dog's collar the basset hound had trotted off, staying just out of reach. The dog had received an enormous round of applause, and the rest of the night people had remarked about it, wondering where it had come from, to whom it belonged, and so on. Honestly, Margaret had not been able to concentrate on the story, because she had been too keenly aware of Charlie: his size, his maleness, the warmth she experienced sitting close to him. She had felt his shoulder against hers; the satin stripe running down his trouser leg had brushed her knee. For a moment in the midst of his story, she had stared at his hands—large, strong hands, so entirely masculine and different from her own—and she had resisted the ludicrous impulse to reach over and grab one. What would he have said? she wondered. And why was she even tempted by such a thing?

But the music chased such thoughts from her head. She reached behind her and straightened the fall of her dress. She felt, she admitted, prettier than she had in years. She liked the dress, a feminine sheath that clung to her back and breasts. Black had been the correct choice after all. The peach had been tempting, but in the end it had made her feel like a pastry, something soft and comestible and not quite stout enough to stand up to the evening air.

"They've started—do you hear them?" Charlie asked, finishing with the driver and stepping over beside her. "There's something wonderful about these buildings being all lit up at night, isn't there?"

"Oh, it's beautiful," she said.

"Well, shall we?"

He held out his elbow and she took it, grateful for the relative darkness so that he would not see her blush. A curse of redheaded women everywhere, such flushing. But she took his arm and held it, and became aware again of his size. How nice to walk beside a man, to have his arm, to feel as though they presented to the world a pairing. And when he moved slightly right to go around a cement planter, she felt his arm clamp her hand a little to guide her, and unconsciously she tucked her arm more completely under his and an undeniable warmth spread through her. She felt impossibly aware of these minute accommodations and she wondered if he did as well. Rather than dwelling on it, though, she gazed around her, remembering her promise to Blake to record what she saw. Everywhere she looked she was rewarded: a hundred women in gowns, all flowing toward the entrance, their escorts beside them. Men in uniforms; Indian women in saris and Arabs in head cloths. The music acted as a magnet, drawing them closer, and she heard French spoken somewhere behind her, though it was a different French from what she heard in Maine, the French-Canadian variety she sometimes caught during the summer tourist season. She resisted turning her head left and right, gawking like a rube, but little passed her notice.

At the door Charlie produced the tickets from his breast pocket. He did so, she noticed, without releasing her hand from his elbow. They stood in a small line while security guards went over them with wands, then exchanged the tickets and stepped inside.

"Ready?" he whispered, dipping a little to gain her ear.

"As I'll ever be."

He smiled. Then they entered.

The music overwhelmed her instantly, its bright, fluid

sound sweeping her along the floor. It felt extraordinary to be in an enormous room, with the orchestra arranged on the right as she entered, the dance floor directly in front of them. Large pillars divided the left-hand side of the room, so that people could gather and converse without obstructing the dancers. Margaret tried to name the music—she recognized its rhythm, but it drifted away from her in the excitement of entering the room—and she let it pass over her, her hand nervously gripping Charlie's forearm. Ahead of them, all the way across the ballroom floor, massive French doors opened onto some kind of terrace. She saw lighted lanterns holding back the spring night, and to the right of the doors, a buffet table glimmered white and silver.

"Oh, my, how pretty," Margaret said, when they paused beside one of the pillars, her eyes gathering details. "This really is a treat, Charlie. Thank you for inviting me."

"Do you like it?"

"It's just how I pictured a ball would look. Just exactly. I've been picturing it this way since I was a little girl."

"Did you get anything to eat at all at the hotel? Are you hungry?"

"I don't think I could eat right now."

"Well, maybe we can share a plate later. I think we should dance. That's the fun of these things."

"I'd love to dance."

"Let's find someplace to put your wrap, then have a drink, and then we'll dance. How does that sound?"

"A glass of wine, please."

And did he squeeze her arm again against his side? She thought so. She held on to his arm as they navigated the crowd. He stopped her near a statue-vase and took her wrap and gave it to a coat check girl. She used the moment to pull the front of her dress up. It did feel wonderful to wear a halter-top gown, to feel the warm air on her shoulders, to know, to be certain, that she looked good. And the music! She turned and saw the orchestra, all of the musicians dressed in burgundy jackets, their instruments gleaming. The sound was powerful. Then Charlie put his hand on her back and began steering her toward the terrace where people lined up for the bar. She observed people as they pooled around her, but she also felt his hand on her back, the strength of it as it flexed slightly to guide her. Once, when they moved around another couple, she felt his hand fall to her waist, his fingers brushing slightly above her hips, and blood rushed to her face and arms. It was the music, she tried to pretend, that caused the tiny riot in her stomach.

A small moment followed. She felt, remarkably, as though she could hover above herself, watching their progress across the floor. Here was a woman with a man, she thought, the most natural thing in the world. With each step, she felt herself casting away her caution. She did it deliberately, bravely, like a child consciously approaching the edge of a diving board. It felt, for an instant, as though a thousand tangled roots drifted behind her, each of them snapping and pulling her back to the earth, but she resisted. She took several deep breaths, glad to feel the warm spring air fill her lungs, glad to feel Charlie beside her. For once in her life, she decided, she would not try so desperately to manage things. For once she would let the world take her where it liked, and she felt something nervous and empty in her stomach, but joy, too. She understood what Cinderella knew: that the splendor of the ball was made sweeter by the approach of midnight, that the pumpkin carriage and the ratty chargers waited patiently to collect their passenger at the end of the night.

In dreams, Gordon turned and tossed, and he heard the cows mooing in their evening movement to the barn for milking. He heard a crow calling and the dishwasher running and the sound of his mother opening a window. It was spring, but he had no name for the season. Time meant little to him, especially in the dream, and he watched the saw-chuck guy creep forward and fire at a pair of robins perched on the white oak outside the parlor window. Then the saw-chuck guy became his father and he saw his father hanging upside down in a special bed, a bed like a hamster wheel, and someone promised him it was his father although it didn't look like anyone he knew. Then he listened to the wind slither down the chimney. He hadn't told his grandfather or mother, but he believed someone spoke through the chimney, someone lived inside it, because he had heard it calling his name. It was a secret, not a bad secret, a secret that lived in the house. Maybe, he thought in the tangled logic of his dream, his father's voice had left the hospital and had come to live in the bricks and mortar of the fire flue. Gordon turned again in sleep and drew his knees up closer to his chest, and the saw-chuck man rolled once again and landed on his back, his stunned reaction prompting him to shower a spray of bullets at the ceiling.

—☙

The floor felt wonderfully slippery. That was a detail she needed to remember to tell Blake. It was a ball, of course, and naturally they would wax the floors properly, but Margaret loved the way the surface felt beneath her feet. And the flowers! She made a point of slowly surveying the room to take in the flowers. The planners had selected spring blossoms, understandably, and she easily identified irises and oxeye daisies, salvia and candy tuft, but someone had forced peonies and they gave off their strange, compelling fragrance in bursts of perfume as people passed. In the end, she decided, that was what most impressed her: the tender, exquisite details; the floor, the flowers, and the lighting. Someone had given great thought to the lighting and managed to work small ponds of illumination into an otherwise overly large banquet room, and the resulting effect was intimate and appealing. One could imagine stopping anywhere beside a light and having a conversation, even a romantic exchange, but the larger flow of the room made such potential moments only part of the evening. The music controlled much of the atmosphere in the ballroom, and Margaret delighted to see the burgundy jackets, the gleaming instruments, and the serious indifference with which many of the band members played. They were pros, obviously, and they had doubtless played these standards countless times before, but now and then a moment of genuine pleasure and virtuosity jumped out and took possession of the musicians, and then the band played with more enthusiasm and relish, and the dancers responded. Margaret particularly liked that the ball had no spokesperson, no planned agenda. No one tapped a glass or demanded the group's attention. It was very French, she felt, to give over the night to music and dance and drink and require nothing of the attendees. It should be a rule, she decided, to require nothing of guests except their own pleasure. That was something she would definitely tell Blake.

"So," Charlie said, arriving with two glasses of white wine and a small plate of appetizers, "are you taking it all in? You're not planning to run off at midnight, are you?"

"Oh, Charlie, it's wonderful. It's a beautiful event. I'm glad you persuaded me to come."

"Can you grab one of these wines, please? I ran into a fellow I knew and he insisted we try this food. He called it *amuse-bouche*. He's a Frenchie."

"What is it?" Margaret asked, taking one of the wines. "Did he say?"

"Pâté of some sort. I didn't listen very closely. I wanted to get back here to you."

"Well, when in Rome . . ."

"Or Paris. But first a toast to your husband. To Thomas Kennedy."

"To Thomas," Margaret said and touched her glass to his.

"Here's how," Charlie said as she sipped. "How's the wine?"

"French, I'm guessing. It's good. It tastes sweet, but not too much."

"Try one of these appetizers. You need to lead the way."

She tasted what looked like a spring roll. It crumbled a little as she bit into it. The pastry gave way and underneath it Margaret tasted a dark, tangy meat with an odd consistency. She didn't much care for it, but she held it while Charlie sampled a different one.

"What do you think?" she asked.

"Not a fan."

"I'm a complete peasant when it comes to food, I'm sorry to say. Pot roast is exotic for me."

"I bet you're a good cook. Here, put that back on the plate and we'll just drink wine. Is that okay? Maybe we can grab something a little later. The buffet table was jammed."

She put her half-eaten appetizer back on the plate, and Charlie managed to hand the plate to a passing busboy. It was a relief to be without something to juggle, Margaret decided. She took another sip of wine and found it excellent. It tasted of dry barrels and something bright and sharp that stung the tip of her tongue a little.

"How do you like the band?" Charlie asked.

"Very much. I like seeing the musicians playing. I realized it's been a while since I was around live music. It's not like going to a rock show when you're a kid . . . all those strobe lights and stage theatrics. You can actually see the musicians and watch their faces turn red when they blow hard on their trumpets. That fellow over there . . . the one with the mustache . . . he's quite dedicated to his instrument."

"And the clarinetist. Do you think people end up resembling their instruments?"

"They must. And their dogs."

"You look very beautiful tonight," Charlie said, changing the subject and catching her off guard. "You should know that. The gown is perfect for you."

"Well, thank you, Charlie. And you're very handsome."

"I mean it sincerely. My friend, the one who recommended those horrible appetizers, he said you have stolen the night. That was his phrase, not mine, though I concur."

"You'll make me blush."

"And he's French, so you have to believe him."

"But he doesn't know food."

"I'd give my arm for a pig-in-a-blanket," Charlie said with a warmth that made her smile.

"Those little cocktail wieners? Everyone loves those. They're ridiculously good."

"We probably shouldn't confess to liking them in the French Embassy. They could kick us out of here," Charlie said. "But at least I like the wine. It has a strange aftertaste, but I like it."

"So do I."

"I've been trying to understand why the London School of Economics throws a ball at the French Embassy."

"To raise their profile?" Margaret asked. "I don't know. It's a good question. They need excuses to have balls, I suppose. We have a venison ball up in Maine to commemorate a successful deer season."

"See?" Charlie said. "It's not very different."

"It's held in the VFW, and it's big on camouflage gear. There's a door prize of one hundred pounds of venison. Sometimes if it's been a tough season, they'll substitute moose meat."

"And I bet they serve pigs-in-a-blanket."

"They sure do."

Charlie sipped his wine, then extended his hand to her. She met his eyes and handed him her glass. He stepped away and put the glasses beside a small vase that stood near one of the columns.

"Could I have this dance, Margaret?" he asked.

"Of course, Charlie. I'd love to."

Yes, she realized as she followed him a few steps toward the dancing people, the floor was wonderfully slippery. She walked on the balls of her feet, careful not to slip. *Here goes nothing*, she thought. It was an absurd line to come into her head, but she couldn't chase it out. *Here goes nothing*. It meant, Here goes a dance with a man at the French Embassy. Here goes a dance with a man who is not my husband. She did not let her mind dwell on the thought. Not now. Maybe later, but not now. She concentrated on the fall of her dress, the pleasure she felt in the warm air. When she reached the halfway point on the dance floor, she turned and faced Charlie. She raised her arms. *Here goes nothing*.

———⌒〇⌒———

Charlie was conscious of his leg in the moment before he took Margaret in his arms. He had been kidding himself, he realized. People always noticed his leg. It was impossible not to, and it struck him as perverse that he insisted on dancing on it as if to wave it aloft in public for the world to see. He was not ashamed of the leg, precisely, but he felt it had to be treated with respect. He had to *know* his leg, and dancing with a beautiful woman, a woman he hoped to impress or at least not injure, struck him as an odd choice. After all, they could have spent the evening in a hundred ways, ways more suitable for a man with one leg than dancing, but, then again, he loved the excitement in Margaret's eyes, the obvious pleasure she experienced coming into the ball. He loved the way she looked; it was more than the dress, although that worked out far better than he could have hoped. No, it was her innate goodness and openness that he found so appealing. She reminded him of his neighbors he had known in Iowa as a boy. They were not puffed up, as so many easterners tended to be. Margaret seemed grateful for things, for any small joy that came her way, and he found that remarkable in a woman whose husband had been shot into a vegetative state in the first year of their marriage.

"I'll do my best," he said to her and watched her smile.

Then he took her in his arms. She fit perfectly; it was strange how well she fit. Nearly everything about their meeting had been easy and comfortable. Her body felt slender and long, and yet her softness pressed against him and made him aware of her breasts, the line of her thighs. He began by doing a sort of slow two-step, following the music, his hand spread wide on her back, her hand in his. His right leg trailed slightly.

He could not get it to move as adroitly as he might have liked, but there was nothing for it. He hoped he did not strike her as a comic Igor, Dr. Frankenstein's misshapen assistant. But the music covered many things. It rose and fell, and he believed he recognized the song—Ella Fitzgerald did it, was it "April in Paris"?—and it moved gently through its measures, while Margaret stayed in his arms, her body blended into his. It was not natural, he decided, that they should fit so well. Under her charm and openness, he sensed her sexuality, and that surprised him. He hadn't guessed it, but he felt her warmth, felt her body move against his, and he could not determine if she deliberately made him aware of her femaleness, or whether she simply danced naturally and abandoned a portion of herself to the music. Either way, he turned her slightly in his arms and danced her backward, moving as well as he could while her hand, perhaps for steadiness, tightened on his shoulder.

"I'm afraid I'm not much of a dancer," he said.

"Funny, I was just thinking you're a wonderful dancer."

"I like to dance," he said, "but my feet don't share my enthusiasm."

"The main thing is to like the person you're dancing with; then it doesn't matter what anyone does."

"I like dancing with you, Margaret."

She glanced at him. A flittering glance. Then, like water rising, she filled his arms completely. They danced for a little longer. The music moved and closed over itself, and, yes, it was "April in Paris," he recognized it fully now. It was a riff, he imagined, on the idea of the ball taking place at the French Embassy. A little fun note.

"I like dancing with you," she whispered after he thought she had forgotten his remark.

He could not prevent his arm from gathering her closer. He wondered, as he did so, how this had happened. He could recount the steps they had taken, could remember his first glimpse of her when she passed through the screen door on her porch in Maine, but that did not explain how she felt now in his arms. He wondered, frankly, if he had ever felt so comfortable with a woman. He waited after pulling her closer to see if she would return his movement, and she did, gradually, shyly, until her body fitted against him more perfectly than ever. He marked how sweetly she acknowledged his increased pressure; he felt the dress under his hands, the slickness of the material as she moved to match his awkward steps.

"Would you like some air?" he asked when the music ended.

"Yes, please."

He took her hand. He could not walk through the entire night with her hand perched on his forearm like a pirate's parrot. She closed her fingers over his and he walked her onto the terrace, the evening air sweet and warm and fresher than the inside air. The band broke into something a little more lively, something vaguely familiar, and he watched as a number of couples headed back inside to the dance floor. He was glad to see them go. He brought her to a marble railing where they

could look down onto a fountain. He smelled the mist from the
fountain, and something fragrant and sweet.

"Are those lilacs?" she asked.

Instead of answering, he turned and kissed her.

Chapter
Six

O*h,* she heard herself say when he lifted his lips away from hers.

She moved her forehead against his shoulder. *Oh, my,* she thought. The oddest memory came to her at that moment. She recalled the game they played as kids, something about cracking the egg over your head, then feeling the yolk running down your back and shoulders and then cracking the egg again, and feeling the yolk running down and down. . . .

That was how the kiss had made her feel. She felt the kiss run like yolk down through her body and she had to concentrate not to shiver. How strange. She could not sort the many thoughts that rushed at her, especially because they became tangled in the warmth that suffused her body. She felt her hand on his arm, her head against the material of his dinner jacket. She liked his size. She liked the warmth of his skin on the cool spring night.

"I'm sorry, Margaret," he said. "I shouldn't have done that. I'm so sorry."

She shook her head against his shoulder.

"That was inexcusable," he said. "I just . . . you're very beautiful tonight and I got carried away, I'm afraid. Please forgive me."

She rose onto her toes and kissed him.

She felt a momentary shame at the hunger her kiss revealed. What must he think? she wondered, but she was powerless to stop. She had intended, if she had intended anything at all, to kiss him lightly, to show goodwill, to let him know she was not a prude, she did not take offense at his kiss, and then, in the instant before her lips met his she felt herself turn to water. It seemed an entire sea had pushed her harder into his arms, and she kissed him with everything she had, her body pressing into him, and tears came to her eyes.

"I'll be right back," she said when she released him. She turned and walked away.

"Are you . . ."

She didn't hear what else he had to say. She walked quickly back into the ballroom, her eyes scanning for signs of the ladies' room. She spotted it off to her left, partially behind the orchestra, and she went along the wall, dodging people when necessary. His kiss, Charlie's kiss, still moved through her body. A giddy, girlish feeling inside her warred with bright tears that came from no place she understood. What in the world was she crying about? she wondered as she pushed into the ladies' room and stepped behind a line of women at the vanity. She understood the tears' source, of course, and she ducked into an empty stall and pushed the toilet lid down and sat for a moment, her breathing rough in her chest. She felt as if she might be sick; she felt also, she confessed, a sexual stirring that she had believed had been paralyzed when Thomas had been paralyzed. How could this be happening? she mused as she pulled toilet tissue from the roll and pressed it to her eyes. Was she really so desperately lonely that she would collapse at the first male attention she had received in a half decade? She decided she was a weak, horrible person. All her cheerfulness, and her laughter about farm life, it had all been a bluff. She felt herself a phony. She pressed the toilet tissue into her eyes for a second more, then sat straight and pulled her shoulders back. Poor Charlie, she thought and nearly laughed. He had chosen to kiss a nutcase.

She stepped out to the vanity and found a faucet unoccupied and ran water on her wrists for a few moments. Then she bent carefully to the sink and dabbed at her face. The little makeup she had applied hadn't been washed away. After she had examined her face one last time—not bad, none the worse for wear, really—she reached around a woman and grabbed a paper towel and dried herself. Then she pushed back through the door, dodging past two women as she went, and followed her trail back to Charlie. He stood where she had left him, two glasses of wine in his hands.

"Just what the doctor ordered," she said, taking the wine. "Thank you, Charlie."

"Are we still friends? I apologize."

She kissed him. Softly and simply. She held her lips against his, her glass out to one side.

"I'm flattered, actually, Charlie," she said, moving away from him and turning to watch the dancers. "And very moved. It's been . . ."

He nodded. He understood.

He bent to her ear and whispered.

"The thing is, we work too well together. Do you feel that, too?"

She nodded.

"You were the last thing I expected," he said. "I didn't mean to cross any boundaries."

"You didn't, Charlie. You read me exactly right. You read me more accurately than I read myself, actually."

"It's not some sort of seduction scheme," he said. "You know that, right?"

"I know that."

"I need a drink," he said and took some of his wine.

She had a drink, too.

"Now what do we do?" she asked.

"I want to dance with you some more."

"I want that, too."

"Everything a little at a time."

"Yes."

He put his hand against her back. Crack the egg, she thought. She leaned back into his arm a little. She listened to the music. *The lilacs, the damn lilacs*, she thought. Her heart beat hard under her ribs. The impression of his lips on hers remained scalding. She tried to remember her last kiss, Thomas's last kiss, and she could not. Probably at the airport, she decided. Probably when he was leaving. A kiss of parting. He had stood in the airport with his uniform on, his chest broad, his shoulders draped with duffel bag straps, and he had kissed her good-bye. He had never kissed her hello again, and she had not felt a man's lips until this moment, this evening, and it flustered her. Each thought that came into her head chased its tail. She could not say what would happen next. She could not say what she hoped happened next.

"Terry invited us for Sunday brunch," Charlie said.

He held Margaret in his arms. The music had shifted to something slow and hypnotic, a song he didn't recognize. The sax player ran a low line of notes that suggested cities and alleyways and street cats. Charlie couldn't decide if it was too much, given the venue. Still, he liked having Margaret in his arms no matter what. He felt no space between them any longer; when he moved, she was there, receiving him, anticipating him.

"Who is Terry exactly? She's been awfully kind. I can't thank her enough for the gowns."

"I am going to be working for her husband in Burkina Faso. In West Africa. She runs in a pretty rarified circle, but she's down-to-earth. She has two kids. She arranged for some congresspeople to sponsor a bill on hand surgery for veterans . . . it's a long story. Her husband was the deputy ambassador to Ghana under Bush. She stayed back in Washington to raise the kids. If Washington were a big high school, she'd be student council president."

"How old is she?"

"Late forties, maybe. Maybe early fifties. She has a beautiful home overlooking the Potomac. She throws Sunday
brunches once a month. They're informal and friendly, unlike
a lot of get-togethers in this city. She'll make you feel welcome.
You *will* be welcome."

The music began to curl back and close on itself. Charlie
pulled Margaret a little closer. Her body fit his. You could never
tell when you took a woman in your arms how she would fit, he
decided. He had known runway model types who had felt like
coatracks to dance with; Margaret fit him exactly. It had something to do with the way she moved, with her body's willingness
to meet his. It took fortitude not to pull her absurdly in to him,
and the tension of not doing so proved more pleasurable than
he would have guessed.

"I need a little air," Margaret said when the music stopped.
"Could we step outside again?"

"Of course."

He led her out. In the same spot they had occupied before,
she took her phone out of the small clutch bag she carried and
checked for messages.

"Sorry," she said as she folded it closed, "I know that's
rude to do, but with a little boy I have to do it."

"Everything quiet on the western front?"

"No messages, so that's clear."

"Well, that's good news."

"Gordon's a good boy. He doesn't make many waves."

"He struck me as a nice boy."

"He'll play with the meerkat, you know? He's just a little shy. I don't know if it's a phase or just his disposition. It was kind of you to bring it."

"I thought it might make taking his mom away easier on him."

"I'm sure it did."

"Do you need more wine?"

She shook her head.

"More dancing?" he asked.

Instead of answering, she leaned into him and kissed him. He kissed her in return. The kiss grew and tightened and advanced.

"Would you like to leave here?" he asked when they broke apart.

"I don't know. I honestly don't. My brain feels like a bee's nest."

"We can stay or go."

"Where would we go?"

"We could go eat something. There are plenty of restaurants open around here. Or you could come back to my place. It's not far. It could be anything you want it to be. No pressure. I like you, Margaret. I think you understand that. I've liked you from the minute we started talking."

"I'm so out of practice for all this, Charlie. It's complicated."

"I'm sure it is. On the other hand, it's just us being together. We can stay right here, too. I'd like that. That would be fine, too. We can dance until they kick us out of here."

"I think I want to be alone with you," she said. "If that's what you want, too."

"That's what I want."

"I might change my mind. I can't promise what I'll feel like."

"I understand."

"We've just met."

"I know, but it doesn't feel like that."

"No, it doesn't. I'm still a Catholic girl at heart. I can hear the priests and nuns whispering in my ear."

He laughed. She looked at him for a moment, surprised, then she laughed, too. He wanted her to realize it didn't have to be so serious.

"It can be whatever we want it to be," he said. "No expectations. I like spending time with you."

She nodded.

"Another dance," she whispered, leaning into him.

"Okay."

"Then let's see."

"Okay."

"I didn't expect any of this. This is out of left field."

"For me, too."

"Is this now officially a date, Charlie?"

"I think it qualifies."

"My friend Blake said it was a date, but I didn't believe her. I thought you had to keep me busy for the weekend. That it was your responsibility and you were simply being kind."

"To tell the truth, I was looking for a way to ask you out without it being awkward. Then Terry suggested the tickets."

"You're a tricky devil."

"No, interested in a woman. A beautiful woman from Maine."

He led her back to the dance floor midway through the next number. The crowd had thinned, or people had moved closer to the bar, but now they had more room to dance. Charlie held her close. She put her cheek against his shoulder and kept her eyes closed.

Chapter
Seven

His apartment was charming. From just inside the door, Margaret looked around the small living room, the tiny kitchen, and felt herself at home. It reminded her—at least at first glance as he went about turning on lamps and moving a set of dishes off the kitchen island—of a well-provisioned ship. She had been on a sailboat once with Thomas, up in Bar Harbor, as a passenger on a lighthouse tour. She had loved that boat and especially its size, the efficiency of its features and cupboards. She felt the same affection now as she examined Charlie's apartment. Tidy, she thought. Shipshape.

"This reminds me of a boat I was on once," she said, scanning the room, her eyes falling on knickknacks, picture frames. "I've always liked small spaces."

"It *is* small," Charlie said, still moving through the kitchen. "But I like it. The State Department provides it for people in transit. So a lot of this stuff doesn't belong to me."

"I meant it as a compliment," she said, seeing how he

could have taken it the wrong way. "Our farmhouse is a second job all in itself. There's so much cleaning and so much clutter, and on a farm . . ."

She trailed off.

"I'm going to open a nice bottle of wine," he said. "A small glass?"

"Yes, please."

"Please make yourself at home. Have a seat, or you can come in here and sit at the island while I get the wine."

"Yes," she said, "I'd like that."

She moved into the kitchen, feeling slightly absurd in the ball gown. How silly ball gowns were, really, when you came down to it. She had to tuck the skirt of the gown behind her legs as she climbed up onto the stool next to the island. She felt a tender wave of emotion seeing a bouquet of faded wildflowers in a vase at the center of the table. The flowers had been kept too long—daisies and a purple flower like a bearded iris, but not quite—and their petals had fallen on the smooth, black top of the island. She fought the urge to grab a sponge and rid the table of the petals. Too many hours cleaning up after Gordon, she decided. She took a breath and tried to remember what it meant to be alone with a man.

He moved around the kitchen well, his trailing leg not an obstacle, apparently. The situation could have been awkward, she imagined, but she did not feel that it was. Perhaps it was for him, she couldn't say, but he didn't seem bashful or nervous. He kept his attention on the wine bottle and smiled when he stuck the bottle between his thighs, yanked, and then held up the cork as though he had removed someone's appendix. He smiled.

"Success," he said.

"How long have you lived here, Charlie?"

"Oh, a little over a month and I'll be here another month before my posting. I just finished grad school. People who are injured, military folks, I mean, they generally have to decide to go on with a military career or refocus somehow. A lot of us go to grad school. It's free, essentially, and it gives us a little time to acclimate back to civilian life. In my case I went and now I'm training."

"Where did you go to grad school?" she asked as he poured her a glass of wine. Red, and a dot spilled out onto the countertop. She caught that he mentioned his injury but didn't explain it.

"The Kennedy School at Harvard."

He looked at her, the bottle cocked before he poured his own glass.

"Okay," he said, his eyebrow arching slightly, "that sounds more impressive than it is. A ton of these grad schools are very happy to get ex-military folks, especially from the academy schools. We're good bets and we bring our own funding, so, yes, I did fine there, but it isn't really as laudable as it could be. There were plenty of people a lot brighter than I am who didn't get a place."

"You should be proud of it. It's an accomplishment."

"I had a lot of questions after my service. A lot of opinions. The Kennedy School was a terrific place to ask those questions and to air those opinions. I didn't always like the answers, or agree with them, but the discourse was sincere. They have an amazing faculty."

"It sounds like time well spent."

"It was," he said and raised his glass, which he had finished off filling by giving the bottle a twist. "To you, Margaret. I admire you."

"Me?" she asked and took a small sip. Her stomach felt empty and she cautioned herself not to drink too much.

"It can't be easy being a single parent. And the circumstances, with Thomas, well, you know what I'm saying. Have you always wanted to be a farmer?"

She smiled. It was often humorous to see people stumble over the whole farm business. People valued farmers, at least in conversation, at least in a theoretical sense, but they knew little about them.

"I'm not sure anyone ever decides to be a farmer," she said. "For Thomas it was simply a family occupation. He had always done it, and when he returned from the University of Maine, he fell back into it. The land tempts you and you forget about the work sometimes. But I like it. A good part of the year, I love it. The winters get rough."

"And that's where you met? At UMaine?"

"After, actually," she said. "My plan was to teach. I had just started in a second-grade classroom one town over when I met Thomas. He was local and so was I and we were of a similar age. It's funny how that happens, isn't it? It's almost like it was when you were a kid on the playground. You made up teams from whoever was around. A lot of my girlfriends found they weren't so choosy about guys once a little time went by. But I liked Thomas immediately and I could see he was a good man. We courted for a year and a half or so, then we got married. I was twenty-four, almost twenty-five. He was two years older. We lived on the farm for a while, planning to fix up the other house, and then he decided to join the reserves."

"Did he know he might go over?"

"As an abstract possibility, maybe. It's hard to stand on a farm in Bangor, Maine, and imagine you have some future responsibility in Baghdad or Kabul. But he went with his eyes open. I can't say he didn't. He wasn't there very long when he was injured. It all seemed sort of make-believe. That sounds strange, probably, but that's how it struck me. He had a group of young kids with him and they were gung ho, but Thomas just wanted to come home."

She looked at Charlie. He listened with a soft smile on his face. He took another sip of wine.

"After he was injured, the bottom dropped out of things for a while. And we had been living on the farm, well, I told you about the extra house on the property . . . and it seemed natural to remain there. It was good for Gordon. At least Thomas knew he was a father. I'm glad about that."

"Do you think about going back to teaching?"

"Think about it, but I've gotten so lazy I don't know. The idea of putting on school clothes and driving in a little car to a job and then hurrying to get Gordon from school, then dinner, and so on, it feels overwhelming. It felt like too much at the time, anyway. It still does, I suppose. I can be useful around the farm and I like the cows. How's that for a job qualification? Liking cows?"

Sitting with the wine warming her belly, she wondered if she was dithering. In a second chamber of her mind, she tried to calculate how long it had been since she had been alone with a man. A man of interest, so to speak. It felt—except for Thomas—as if she hadn't flirted with a man since her college days. She wondered if that could be true. And while she enjoyed talking with Charlie, and liked his gentleness more and more, she wondered how this evening would go. Had she misread the signs? And what exactly did she hope might happen? They were alone and that felt thrilling, and yet they seemed intent on vetting each other's resumes. Was that how it had always been? She supposed things had to begin somewhere, and she took another sip of wine to embolden her, curious what it would require for him to cross his petal-strewn countertop and kiss her. How difficult it must be for a man, she thought, to feel you needed to always make the first move, initiate any physical contact. Of course women could do that nowadays, and they did, but the social contract still put it chiefly in a man's hands. She wondered how she had never appreciated the treacherous waters a man had to navigate. Unless he had the nature of an ape, a man had to read a thousand signs and intrepidly move forward. She made a mental note to discuss her observation with Blake. How strange she had never considered it before.

As if reading her mind, though, he stood and moved closer

and turned her chin up slightly so he could kiss her. She luckily put her wineglass down in time to feel him step into contact with her thigh, his lips warm and pleasant on hers, his hand reaching around her back and resting on the bare skin above her bra line. It felt good to kiss him, but not as wild and as exciting as it had at the ball, and she started to pull back, falling into the idea of more conversation, when he suddenly surged forward and kissed her with everything.

Her body burned back. Again, a second part of her brain registered with wonder the powerful surge she felt spring up from her loins, her gut, her throat. She made a small animal sound, an absurd noise that she hardly knew came from her, and then slid off the stool and pressed every inch of her body into his. He was strong; he was incredibly strong and he kissed her over and over, his mouth on hers, his tongue somewhere, his maleness abrupt and emphatic and entirely present. He kissed her over and over and he began walking her backward, lifting her and kissing her, and she turned to paste. Her groin felt urgent, it felt impossibly full and in tune with his, and she let him lead her to his bedroom. She stopped to unzip her dress, and because it wasn't hers, because she did not want to ruin it, she put a hand on his chest and made space so that she could step out of it and hang it on the back of a chair. That gave him a moment to take off his jacket and then he covered her again with his arms, his body, and she moved onto the bed and he kept kissing her, his body bent absurdly forward as he stripped out of his pants. She saw his artificial leg in quick glances, but she kept her eyes on his. Then he moved on top of her, and something sharp poked at her from the bedspread, and he reached beneath her and grabbed a book and chucked it into the darkness. She sensed they both listened for it to land, but it didn't, it made no noise, and she couldn't help it, she laughed, and so did he, and he broke from their kiss long enough to say, "It must have fallen on something soft."

"Or maybe it went out a window."

She felt him laugh, she laughed, too, and then suddenly every need of his came into the room with them, and she met his needs, and she kissed him over and over and gave her body, took his, then gave her body again and again, each part, one after the other, for as long and as fully as he would have it. She kept her mind in check, not letting it go to Thomas, or to Maine, or to anything except this man beside her. Her body felt like a clatter of dice rolling across a green felt, and she did not know what number would turn up, or what the wager might be, but she gave in to the chance and her heart felt thrilled.

Chapter
Eight

Gordon dreamed of the basement stairs. The stairs led from the kitchen directly to a dark place in the base-ment. He did not like the stairs, nor the basement, for that matter. The basement smelled of dirt and water and raspberry preserves. A jar had broken there long ago, but the odor never left; the sticky juice clung to the wooden shelf and the cement floor like a bloodstain.

His eyes fluttered under their lids. His breathing became short and uneven. His bladder pressed to be released, but it was not painful, not overly full. His right leg kicked a little—at spiders, probably, at rats—and his foot happened to touch the side of a toy truck. In his sleep, in his childish obliviousness, he mistook the side of the truck for his mother's foot. Instantly his heart settled. He rolled a half turn onto his belly and spread his arms out like a man falling. Only he was not falling. He was in bed, and his mother was near, and in his universe nothing else mattered.

The basement dream disappeared. All dreaming disappeared and he slept down deep in his body, his breathing measured and quiet, his long lashes touched with the slightest moisture, his skin warm and quiet on this soft spring night. The saw-chuck guy, fallen to the floor in Gordon's newest turning, kept his rifle aimed at the dark space under the bed, his vision sharp and ready for the appearance of any monsters, any creatures of bed dust and rug scatter that dared to threaten his boy.

—cɔ

Charlie felt he could kiss her forever. He had never experienced anything quite like it. How did such a thing happen? He had been with women before, a reasonable amount anyway, but he had never felt this tremendous urge to kiss. It reminded him of high school kids groping each other in the local library, but Margaret was not a kid and neither was he, and yet here they were. It did not matter how he kissed her. He could begin softly, delicately, and little by little the kisses would build until the entire world seemed contained in them, until her body pressed into his and he had to run his hands everywhere, over every inch, and then, like the tide, like water pulling back through marsh grass, they would subside and become gentle again.

"Where did you come from? Where did you come from?" she whispered.

"Shhhh."

Then more kisses. He felt his body respond and he entered her and continued to kiss her, the kiss an anchor, and in some way he could not define, the sex, the bodies joined, meant nothing. The kiss meant everything, it obscured and conquered everything, and the movement of their bodies together was a secondary gift. To be able to kiss and to have that, too, that second thing, was nearly more than he could bear. He whispered her name, realizing that they could find this in each other whenever they wanted. He drove into her and felt his body grow urgent and heavy, but then her kisses brought him back, and they glided together in perfect rhythm. Outside a wind pushed a branch beside the streetlight and the shadows fell through the window and covered them, and sometimes he kissed her mouth, and sometimes he kissed the wavering motion of a branch, and spring air leaked quietly into the room and lifted the edge of a piece of paper somewhere on the floor.

After, after it all, he kept kissing her. She continued kissing him, rising into him, and he held her and felt his body tremble and she kissed his neck, his shoulder, and he wondered if love could begin like this, as simply as this, and if it could stay by its own power.

"You're lovely," he said a little later. "So lovely."

"I can't believe how it feels to be with you."

"I've never . . ."

She shook her head against his shoulder. The tree shadows danced on her ribs and across her breasts. She raised herself up and kissed him. For an instant everything began again, but she broke away and slid to his ear.

"Do you have any eggs?" she whispered. "I am so hungry. . . ."

"Oh, you just get better and better."

"Because I'm hungry?"

"Yes. Exactly. Exactly because of that. I've got eggs and bacon, both fresh from a farm nearby. I can make you breakfast. It's the only thing I have to eat."

"I'm famished."

"When we kiss . . ."

She shushed him. She put her fingers over his lips.

"I'm going to wear your shirt. I'm not eating eggs in a ball gown. Get up and rattle those pots and pans. It's the least you can do for a girl."

But he couldn't gather the necessary determination. He rolled on top of her and kissed her and the marsh began to fill again with water. He kissed her over and over, and what he wanted to say was something about love, about what she meant in his arms, but he remained silent and full, his eyes on hers.

❧

He cooked well. He wore a pair of jeans and a hooded sweatshirt that said *Army* on its front, and she wore a large white shirt of his, its length at midthigh. She drank an enormous glass of orange juice. She could not begin to describe how good the juice tasted. She passed it over to him and he sipped it on the run, his attention on the stove. The bacon smelled remarkable. At some point he had turned on a swing station, something low and pretty, and now and then she caught a riff of familiar mu-

sic. The music made it seem that a party took place down the
hall, in another building, and their pleasure, she felt, was en-
hanced knowing they did not have to go there. Twice while he
cooked he stopped and kissed her.

"Do you have any idea how long it's been since I was awake
past midnight?" she said.

"What time is it, anyway?" he asked and slid a plate toward
her. He put his own plate in front of his spot, but he waited for
the toaster to ring. When it did he pulled out the slices—thick
rye—and shook his hand at the heat. Then he sat down in front
of his plate and smiled at her. He took her hand and held it.

"Twelve twenty," she answered. "The witching hour."

"I'm starving. I was too nervous to eat in front of you at the
ball."

"You were nervous? About going to a ball with me?"

He nodded. She squeezed his hand. He poked his chin a
little to tell her to eat.

"I liked you, Margaret. I wanted to impress you, I guess."

"You did."

"Please, eat while it's warm. Don't insult the chef."

She held his hand with her left hand and ate with her right.
He had scrambled eggs, adding pepper and paprika, and they
tasted delicious. She bit a piece of bacon in half. She had always
been a sucker for bacon, but she rarely tasted bacon as good as
the pig they raised on the farm. Someone had matched that
bacon here in Washington, D.C., and she ate the remainder of
the piece in greedy bites.

"So," she said, "I could protest and tell you that I am not

this sort of girl, but I guess it's too late for that. Do you think I'm a shameless hussy?"

"Yes," he said, "I definitely do."

He wiggled her hand and looked at her. Then he moved off his chair and kissed her on the neck. She felt her body respond—it amazed her how her body responded to him—and then he moved back to his chair.

"I think you're wonderful," he said. "Your reputation is safe with me. It's just one of those things."

"I haven't had one of those things, but I believe you. I can't even tell you what you did to me."

"It was amazing, wasn't it? I'm not fishing for compliments. I'm just surprised at how natural it all felt. It's never been quite like that for me."

"I mean everything," she said. "You've been kind and thoughtful. You *are* thoughtful."

"It's all a pose. I'm really very shallow. How's your breakfast?"

"You even cook well."

"Just breakfast. That's my entire repertoire. Oh, and I'm not too bad on a grill. Do you like to cook?"

"I do. It's a little wasted on Ben and Gordon, but I do. I'm always trying something new. I like looking at new recipes. I make soups. On the farm we have a lot of fresh food."

"It sounds like a good life."

"It is most of the time. I have my bad days, like anyone, but for the most part it suits me. I'm a dairy farmer and proud of it! Support your local dairy!"

She smiled and he smiled back. He ate. She bit into a piece of rye bread and liked it. She wanted more juice. She stood and went to the fridge and when she passed by him he put one arm around her waist and drew her toward him. He pushed back the hair along her neck and kissed her there, just beneath the ear, and it sent a jolt through her body that made her flinch and move to one side. She nearly spilled the juice.

"Should we talk about tomorrow?" he asked, returning to his food. "Today, actually."

"Please."

She poured juice into the glass they shared. Then she climbed into her seat again.

"I'll pick you up at eight. We need to be early for security checks and so on. It will probably take us an hour to clear security, then they have a buffet for you. You can have a second breakfast there."

He smiled. He reached over and took her hand again.

"Anyway," he continued, "some of the bill sponsors will be buzzing around. Congresswoman Gilden will be there. She's one of the main sponsors and she carried it through the House. She's from Illinois. The nice thing about the bill is that it cuts across party lines, so there won't be the usual muttering from one side or another not liking it. Politically it's very safe. Then President Obama will come in shortly before ten. He's usually prompt, from what I've heard."

"Have you met him before?"

"Once," Charlie said. "He's very relaxed, very low-key, but he has astonishing charisma. Maybe all presidents do, but

he's good at working a room. That was my impression, anyway."

"How long will the actual signing take?"

"Not long. It's ceremonial. He'll want you behind him for
photo ops. And a few press people will probably ask for your
name, but that will all be handled by the PR folks. Then by ten
thirty, eleven, you're done. The president will leave and then
people will wander off."

"Have you done a lot of these?"

"No. One or two. This is the biggest bill yet."

"We can handle it."

"Then we should go somewhere fun. Do a little sightseeing. Unless you have other plans. We can go see the monuments if you like."

"I would love to see the monuments, but I don't want to
take up your whole weekend."

He looked at her. He wiggled her hand again.

"You are my weekend," he said. "I thought that was pretty
obvious."

"I was hoping so."

"I'm crazy about you, Margaret. Too crazy, maybe."

"I feel the same way."

And she did. That was the remarkable thing. She knew it
suddenly and also knew it to be true. It was that easy. She rose
and slid into his arms and she kissed him. She felt as though
she could kiss him every minute of the day and never grow
tired of it. When she lifted her lips off his she whispered that
she had to go, that she needed to get back to the hotel, that she

needed to be where Gordon could reach her. Besides, she said, it felt like she should be alone on the night before the signing. He nodded. And it did not surprise her when he pulled on his coat and made movements to go as she dressed back in the ball gown. He was the kind of man who would see her home, who would make sure the babysitter got back safely, and who would never think of putting a woman in a cab and sending her off. She wondered as she followed him out the door if someday, some distant day, Gordon would be the gentleman she knew Charlie to be. She hoped so. She could think of nothing better than to meet the world with the kindness and consideration that Charlie demonstrated in the smallest action. It was enough, almost, to wish to write a letter to his mother. *How you raised your son,* she would say, *did not go unnoticed.* One day, she hoped, a woman might think that same kind thing about her.

Chapter
Nine

It was very early when Margaret entered St. Patrick's Church. The sun had not quite cleared the city buildings and the short walk from the hotel had felt quiet and lonely and peaceful. The clerk at the hotel had outlined the directions, sketching a primitive map on the back of a receipt pad. She wondered in passing what he had thought of this woman, awake in the first hours of the day, asking for a church. A sinner, probably, she concluded. That's what he must have thought. But she had taken the map and found the church without error, her only companion a newspaper truck that stopped while the driver jammed copies of the day's edition into news boxes. The truck had leapfrogged with her as she went down the three blocks from the hotel, the driver hopping out and nodding at her the last time their paths crossed. When the truck finally pulled away, grinding its gears and letting the noise climb the building walls, Margaret watched a scatter of pigeons fly up and then sheer down and circle around a discarded pretzel.

But now the church opened before her, quiet and empty, the red votive candles guttering at the wind the door created as it swung shut behind her. Instantly she felt herself transported to Our Lady of Lourdes, the church of her childhood. The smells—candle wax and flame, polish and shoe dirt—might have been borrowed from the little church in Maine and brought without a molecule lost to this church in Washington, D.C. She wondered if the Vatican did not have a recipe for air, a mixture it promoted so that Catholics, however old, could not escape the compelling atmosphere of their first church.

To the right of the center nave she saw someone move, a person kneeling and praying, so she went to the left, walking slowly in the comparative darkness, her steps loud on the floor. It was a magnificent church, far grander than she had anticipated. Someone coughed back and to the right, and she turned and spotted a man stretched out on one of the pews. Homeless, probably. She kept walking, her eyes up at the vaulted ceiling. The hotel clerk had told her the church had been erected for the European stonemasons who built the White House. Whatever the origin of the building, it felt calm and beautiful. She walked slowly, observing the details of the building, letting her mind adjust to the stillness.

Twenty rows from the altar, she paused and took her bearings. She felt herself compelled to genuflect, to cross herself as she had been taught, but she resisted. Instead she slid into the pew and sat for a moment, concentrating on her breath moving in and out of her lungs. It felt good to be in the church, she admitted, but she could not say for certain what had brought her there. Was it guilt? Was it her hope to remember Thomas clearly and perfectly for one instant before the ceremony? She couldn't say with any certainty. Her mind felt jumbled and confused and it wanted to rush toward a contemplation of Charlie, of the night they had spent together, of his kisses and his body and his gentleness, and yet she felt herself betraying Thomas by doing so. She was here, after all, for her husband. It pained her to think that she had been so ready to be with another man on this of all weekends. It demonstrated a lack of character, she felt, and she placed her face in her hands and leaned forward to kneel.

"Forgive me," she whispered, but whether she prayed to Thomas or to God, or simply to the universe, she couldn't say. She could not even say for certain if she *did* feel guilt. A merciful God, she believed, would understand that she was not made of wood or stone. A knowing God would comprehend the scalding loneliness she had experienced these past six years.

"I'm sorry," she whispered into her hands.

Her breathing caught and she began to cry. She cried a long time, her face trapped in her hands, her knees braced on the edge of the kneeler. Twice she heard the homeless man cough a long, spastic series of explosions, and she kept her face in her hands.

Was it wrong what she had done? she asked herself. Had she betrayed Thomas in any real sense, or was it only the vestige of old, worn-out thinking? Thomas could not know and therefore could never be hurt by her actions, but she had sworn a vow to him and now she had forsaken it. Truthfully, she had never been tempted before, had never even seriously considered the possibility. Where would she have gone to indulge such feelings? To the Ramada Inn bar over in Bangor? Would she have parked herself on a bar stool and waited for a local man to make an overture? Followed him upstairs to a motel room? The thought was hideous. But had she simply jumped at the first viable occasion, letting herself yield to Charlie because she could console herself that distance and the specialness of the occasion had given her license? It made her sick to think so. No, she wouldn't believe that.

After a time she looked up and took a tissue out of her coat pocket. *Oh, my goodness,* she thought. It was almost comical, she understood, to end up in a Catholic church the morning after she had slept with a new man. How true to type she was, she realized. More light came into the church through the stained glass windows, and a single barb fell on a statue close to the altar. It took her a moment to recognize St. Sebastian, his body pierced by arrows. Like Thomas, she thought. Like my dear husband whom I love, and always will love, but who is now gone except for his flesh. Except for his spirit, which resides in my son's body and mind, and I will be true to that, to that portion of Thomas, on pain of death, on pain of torture, on pain of my immortal soul.

She sat a while longer, waiting to see if she had any new impulse, any new understanding of her behavior. She still felt mixed up inside. Charlie had not been a fling. She would not believe that. But what was he? And why had he been so interested in a woman with a child from Maine? Had she misjudged him? She didn't think she had, but women often believed what they wanted to believe when it came to men. Women wanted a connection to exist, and she realized she needed to rationalize the night in her head. It could not have been simply about sex. She avoided that possibility. But in the course of a night she had ended up with a man, and what kind of woman did that?

She put her head on her hands for a moment, took a deep breath, then crossed herself and slid slowly out of the pew. The homeless man coughed again and the church echoed and let in the morning light. *Let it go,* she thought, though she knew it would haunt her. She pushed out the door and saw the sun had found the church and washed the steps in light.

Blake Welsh watched her son, Phillip, run after the soccer ball on a bright Saturday morning in Maine. A medium-size Dunkin' Donuts coffee steamed in her hand. She felt a little guilty about the Dunkin' Donuts coffee, because the West Bangor Little League mothers ran a refreshment booth out near the parking lot—hot dogs, bottled waters, orange soda, and coffee—but she could not abide bad coffee and the mothers' huge coffee urn notoriously produced rancid dreck. *Oh, well,* she thought, *let them hate me.* She had never felt particularly at home with the West Bangor Little League mothers, and she supposed the coffee would drive another nail in her coffin of ex-urban ostracism. So be it, she figured. At least she had good coffee.

She held the coffee flat and smooth as she raised her voice

when she saw Phillip gallop close to the opponent's goal. The children ran like iron filings after a magnet, she'd often thought, chasing the ball wherever it went, abandoning any sense of scheme or strategy that Barney Rudd, the coach, tried to instill in them. Or like fish, she amended now, her eyes still fixed on Phillip. Like tiny reef fish darting in synchronicity to escape a predator. Instead of swimming away, these little fish swam to the compelling object, but in every other way the metaphor suited the situation. She pictured them as a school of bright, shimmering fish, skittering back and forth, back and forth, in unison with the rocking ocean.

She took a sip of coffee and before she removed the cup from her lips, her cell phone rang. It was Donny, her husband, and she answered it on the second ring and turned a little away from the game for privacy. He was already at work, cutting the grass on the twelve-acre cemetery in Millinocket. Mowing the dead, Donny called it, but only to her. He thought it was funny, and she was never quite sure.

"How's he doing?" Donny asked.

Blake heard mowers running behind his voice. She pictured him taking a break in his truck, the phone pinned to his ear.

"Oh," she said, "he's chasing the ball around the field with about twenty other kids."

"Any score?"

"Not yet."

"Well, tell him to give me a call when he finishes. Tell him I'm sorry I can't be there."

"You *can* be here," she said, then felt both annoyed with him and disappointed in herself for having revisited his perpetual absence from family events so quickly in the conversation. She had meant not to do that.

"Whatever, Blake. It's called making a living."

"It's called raising a son."

He hung up. Just like that. She sipped her coffee, slid her phone back into her pocket, and watched the children chasing after the ball. She spotted Phillip for a second before he disappeared in a swarm of green jerseys and bare legs. She felt her eyes glaze over, and for a moment or two she thought of Margaret. Margaret had called early—mother early, she had named those early hours—and she had recounted the night with Charlie, the ball, the kissing. How strange, Blake thought now, that Margaret, the one woman in their circle with an infirm husband, with what many might have said was a lonely life, had been swept away by passion and romance and a charming man. How out of the blue. And because Blake was a decent person and a devoted friend, she smiled and nodded slightly in honor of her friend's good fortune. It could not have happened to anyone more deserving, more kind, more human. Yet—and it horrified Blake to understand it, to grasp it fully—she felt a tiny bit jealous, a tiny bit envious that Margaret had experienced this marvelous night. *I am a bad person,* Blake told herself, *a horrible, miserable human being.* To rectify it, she closed her eyes and sent out a beam of good thoughts to her friend Margaret, sent her hope and love and joy. *Any simple joy, for my friend Margaret. Give her gladness in her heart,* she prayed, the coffee like a warm handshake sealing the deal.

—ॐ

Standing behind the president, Margaret thought about Thomas. She felt light-headed and empty. Charlie stood beside her, his dress uniform sharp and surprisingly vivid among so many civilians, but she would not let her mind go to him. Now was Thomas's time, and she focused her thoughts on him. Thomas, her husband. Thomas who'd stood and opened his arms to protect his fellow soldier. Thomas whose simple goodness was the most remarkable thing about him.

I see you, Thomas, she whispered to herself. *I remember you.*

She felt, just for an instant, his warm presence. She pictured him walking toward the barn, his body upright, his neck brown from the sun, his large boots clotted with mustaches of hay and manure. She pictured him sitting at the kitchen table, a yellow foolscap pad of paper in front of him, a calculator, a beaver lodge of pencils, a coffee cup whose rings scattered across the evening sports page. Doing the books, he called it, and she sat with him, helping to calculate the numbers that did not calculate, the sound of the Red Sox in the television room, the baby, Gordon, at rest in her womb.

"And so, today . . . in honor of those who serve . . . ," she heard President Obama say, but she could not follow his speech. Lights flashed. A person stood beside President Obama with a cluster of pens. She kept her arms at her sides.

Slowly, her eyes filled. They filled for Thomas, whose life

had been spent before it had started. Whose empty form rested in a Bangor hospital, whose son would grow up without a father. What had it been about, after all? Surely Thomas had no enmity toward the Afghans. He hardly listened to political talk and never engaged in it. It had been a job, nothing more, and as she'd known he would, he did it without question, without thought of his own safety. For an instant she nearly made a sound, called to President Obama to stop, to hold on, because she wanted to tell the world who her husband had been. She wanted her son to know how proud he should be of his father, this kind man who brought her lilacs in the spring and asters in the fall, who did not raise his voice, did not scold or argue, who met people with gentle directness, whose happiest moments revolved around his house, his family, his livestock.

Thomas Eugene Kennedy, she whispered each time the president's voice paused. *Thomas Eugene Kennedy.* When people clapped she whispered his name louder.

"Your daddy," she whispered to Gordon, though her son was not there. "Your daddy is a good, good man."

"Did you see it?" Margaret asked.

She sat on her bed in the hotel room. Her body and eyes felt dry and cried out. She wore no shoes. Her feet hurt from the morning in heels. Her hand trembled a little as it held her cell phone. A headache had begun in her forehead, pressing and pulling at her. She had swallowed two aspirins before calling and the taste of the pills felt like sand in her throat.

"Yes," Grandpa Ben said, "and a reporter from the Bangor paper called for a quote. I told him we were proud of Thomas, that's all. I didn't really know what else there was to say. But yes, it showed up bright and center . . . and we could see you behind President Obama. Blake said it's on YouTube so you can watch it yourself when you get home."

"I'm glad you saw it, Ben. I was very proud of Thomas at the signing. Did Gordon understand what was going on?"

"Not so much. He didn't understand what the signing meant. He thought President Obama was signing autographs."

"Well, in a way he was. Is he nearby? I'd like to say hello if he is."

"He's right here. Gordon? It's your mommy."

Margaret listened to the sounds of the house and knew each one. She heard Gordon's quick steps scurrying. It was late morning and he would be hungry again. She felt a momentary pang at the sound of his little steps. But then he came onto the phone, all breath and hurry, and she asked him if he had seen the signing.

"President Obama is tall," he said.

"Yes, he is, sweetheart. You should be very proud of your daddy."

"I am."

"President Obama told me that he was grateful for the sacrifice your daddy made. Do you understand what 'sacrifice' means?"

"Medal of Honor," Gordon said, falling back on the biggest concept he knew, Margaret understood. It was a phrase he used imperfectly to cover himself when adults pinned him down.

"This is a little different, but it's kind of that. All those people you saw today, they are trying to help your dad and other men and women like him. Do you understand?"

"Yes," he said, although he sounded a little distracted.

"Okay, we can talk about it when I get home. Are you having a good time with Grandpa Ben?"

"Yes."

"Are you helping with the cows? Doing your chores?"

"Yes."

Margaret understood she was now talking mostly for her own sake. Whatever interest he had had earlier had drifted away. She wondered what he was playing. She wondered if Grandpa Ben had let him watch television earlier than the house rule. She decided not to bring it up. She rubbed her forehead. She turned her foot over to see the back of her left heel. It was red and raw, probably ready to blister.

"Okay, buddy, I love you to the moon. Can I talk to Grandpa Ben again?"

" 'Bye, Mommy," he said.

She heard the phone clatter down. Then Ben picked it up.

"He's in a whirl," she said.

"That kind of day around here. Noel Grummond came over from the county and wanted to talk about using biosolids out on the two north apple meadows. We walked it and Gordon came along. I thought he was tired out, but I guess I thought wrong."

"What did Grummond say?"

"Oh, a lot of state talk. They're looking for sites where they can spread the biosolids and get them out of the landfills. Has to be at least twenty acres and we have about that up there. Some activists are worried about heavy metals, mercury, mostly, and selenium, but I don't know. We don't graze the livestock up there. It's all apples."

"Do they pay something?"

"Yes. Not much, but they do. We more or less leave the field empty for one summer. There will be some smell. But it's supposed to be safe and it's good for the soil if we ever want to use it."

"Well, Noel's a trustworthy sort."

"I've always thought so."

"Are you eating enough?"

"Now, Margaret, I've been able to feed myself quite a long time. Gordon's doing fine, so there's nothing for you to worry about. Just take a little break down there. Are they treating you okay?"

"Everything's fine here."

"Well, if you see that fellow Charlie, tell him Gordon slept with the animal he gave him. What was it called? Looks a little like a squirrel or rabbit."

"A meerkat."

"That's right. It's quite a hit right now. He has it attacking his soldiers. Looks like Godzilla marching through Tokyo."

"Glad he's enjoying it."

She felt a lump tighten in her throat, and she thought of

her father-in-law's simple goodness. It was the goodness he had given to Thomas, the same goodness she hoped he would pass along to Gordon.

"I miss Thomas," she said. "I missed him today at the ceremony."

"I did, too."

"He's helping people, Ben. Even as he is, people are better for him."

"I understand."

"I hope you're proud of him," she said.

"And of you, Margaret."

And that was all he said.

Chapter
Ten

Charlie lifted the cone of blue cotton candy away from the concessionaire and passed it to Margaret.

"Oh, good grief, I can't believe I'm eating more," she said as she bit a little off the top. "Thank you."

"You only have so many zoo days in your life," Charlie said. He paid the concessionaire and smiled. "It's a beautiful spring day and we're at the zoo. It's better than the French pâté last night, isn't it?"

"Much better. Here, take a bite."

She held it out to him. He broke off a hunk and tasted it.

"Are you sure this is covered?" Margaret asked. "There's no reason for you to pay. . . ."

Charlie put his hand briefly on her back to move her away from the concession stand.

"Ready to find the lions?" he asked. "We're fine, Margaret. Everything is good."

Margaret nodded, then glanced down at the park map.

Charlie liked Margaret's approach to the zoo. She was systematic without being dictatorial, but it was clear she wanted to make sure they saw everything. It amused him to watch her. She was a true Yankee who insisted on value for payment, her thoroughness a personality trait she hardly recognized in herself. It charmed him to see it, and it charmed him, also, to see her relax after a difficult morning. She wore flip-flops below a khaki skirt and carried a blue sweater knotted around her purse strap.

It took fifteen minutes to find the lion enclosure, and Charlie helped himself to three more bites of cotton candy as they walked. He couldn't remember a better afternoon. The temperature stood at seventy and the usual Washington humidity had drifted away. He felt relaxed and happy. He wanted to put his arm around Margaret, but he had difficulty reading her after the morning's ceremony. Had a trace of formality entered their exchanges? Charlie couldn't be certain. It might simply have been the strain of the morning, of dealing with the security checkpoints and meeting the bill sponsors. The press, naturally, snapped a thousand photos of President Obama, and for someone unaccustomed to so much activity it might have felt overwhelming. Perhaps, too, Charlie thought, the morning signing ceremony had highlighted her husband's condition, called him clearly to mind, and the events of the night before stood in contrast. Maybe she regretted having an affair with him, and so he watched her for signs, trying to read her, taking pains not to presume too much familiarity. It was difficult because he felt tremendously attracted to her, both physically and mentally, and he had to guard against his feelings propelling him forward too fast.

"Aren't they amazing?" Margaret said when they finally reached the lion enclosure. A small family group lay in the sun, clearly enjoying the fine afternoon. The male lion had a particularly impressive mane. "Gordon would love to see this. I'm kicking myself right now that I didn't bring him."

"Did you consider bringing him?"

"He's so young, I didn't know if it made much sense. He doesn't fully understand his father's condition. I think he believes Thomas will wake up someday and walk back through the door. Anyway, he loves animals. He'd love this."

They watched the lions for a minute or two and then Margaret asked if he wanted any more cotton candy. When he said no, she walked to a trash can and tossed it out. She used a napkin to wipe off her hands.

"Can we sit for a minute?" Margaret asked as she sat on a bench in the shade. "I'm not used to all this walking. And the heat! I'm afraid I'm a Maine girl through and through."

"It's pretty perfect weather. For Washington, this is about as good as it gets."

"It's a wonderful, perfect day."

"And a nice zoo. It's the national zoo."

"I love this zoo," she said, "but I meant you. You've been wonderful, Charlie. In every way."

"Are we okay, Margaret? Do you regret anything about last night?"

She leaned across the bench and kissed him. It was a light, friendly kiss, with just a touch more beneath it.

"I've wanted to do that all day," she said when she pulled back. "I didn't want you to think . . . I don't know . . . that last night was one thing and today is another. I mean, it is another thing today, but I remember last night. I'll always remember it."

"Me, too. I know what you mean. I wanted to kiss you all day, too."

"I had such a funny day, Charlie. Meeting the president, and all those political operatives. Is that what they're called? Well, anyway, the bill sponsors. I liked the woman from Illinois. What was her name again?"

"Gilden."

"Yes, I liked her. She was very kind. And I liked the president. He took time with people. That's what I noticed. But I couldn't help thinking of Thomas. Naturally, I suppose. I thought about him and it felt like he was right there for a moment. He was a good man, Charlie. You would have liked him. This bill is necessary, of course, and I don't want to sound ungrateful, but the fact of him, of Thomas's life, well, nothing can help that."

Charlie took her hand.

"And you're mixed up in my head, too. I have such strong feelings about you. It's silly, I know, and maybe it's just that I haven't been with anyone in so long . . . maybe I'm overreacting and if I am, if I'm being silly, you've been very understanding about it. I appreciate that. I talked to Blake this morning and she said I should simply enjoy my time with you and not question it and that's what I'm trying to do. So I wanted you to know that I don't have anything . . . I'm being inarticulate now, but I don't hold you to anything, if you know what I mean. I just like you, Charlie. I haven't any expectations at all. Not one. So that's my little speech and I feel better for making it."

"I'm so relieved. I thought you had decided it had all been a mistake. It wasn't a mistake for me."

"Oh, I'm sorry you had to wonder about that," she said and kissed the back of his hand. "I should have made myself clearer, but everything was jumbled up this morning. I'm sorry, Charlie. No, if anything I like you too much. That's a bigger worry for me than if I didn't really like you. You know what I mean. I don't do *this*. I haven't been with a man in over six years. I'm more surprised by it than anyone else could be. The worst part is, it feels incredibly natural. I feel as though I've known you for years. It's strange. Do you feel that, too?"

He nodded.

"Am I talking too much?" she asked.

"No," he said and kissed her. He kissed her fully on the lips and pulled her body closer.

Margaret tasted of candy. He smiled and told her and then felt her lips smile back at him. Then he kissed her deeper and far away he smelled the lions, the wild scent of them caught on the wind and scattered on a spring day as fine as any he could remember.

"He took me to the zoo, Blake. He is the sweetest man I've ever met."

Margaret studied herself in the bathroom mirror of her hotel room, the phone pressed to her right ear. She looked at her outfit, the one she had worn on Friday, and wished that she had packed something else. But the dress still looked good and she turned to look at it from behind. Not bad, really, she thought.

"And tonight?" Blake asked.

"We're going to a little Italian restaurant he knows."

"Wow, this is pretty intense."

"I want to be with him as much as I can."

"Careful, sweetie."

"I know. I know I should be. I feel like I'm fifteen years old again. Do you think it's terrible? Tell the truth."

"That you feel like you're fifteen? Or that you're spending so much time with him?"

"Oh, I don't know."

"Look, Donny isn't even home. He missed Phillip's game and now he's out having beers with his buddies. So right now I'm actually jealous of you. I'd enjoy it if I were you."

"Boy, he gets to me, though. Charlie, I mean. I'm going to be with him and I don't care what it all means in the great scheme of things. For once, I'm going to let go of the steering wheel a little."

"That's a good thing, isn't it?"

Margaret saw herself nod in the mirror before she answered. It was a good thing.

"I went to church this morning."

"You did not! Margaret . . ."

"I just needed to try to sort things out. I didn't go to confession or anything. I'm not that crazy."

"There's nothing for you to feel guilty about. Don't let those thoughts in your mind."

"They come on their own. But okay, switching subjects. I like this outfit," Margaret said. "But I wish I had something to put over it. I want to jazz it up a little."

"What are you wearing?"

"That dress I wore to the airport. In my defense, I wasn't expecting anything like this. The shoes are wrong. I wore flip-flops all afternoon. My feet are killing me from heels."

"He likes you no matter what. How did he look in his uniform?"

"Unbelievably handsome. What is it about guys in uniforms?"

"Not all guys. I hate that camo stuff they wear with the big boots and the ugly desert colors. Ick."

"They took plenty of pictures, so I can show you when I get back."

"I'm picking you up at ten tomorrow night? That's still the plan, right?"

"I can get a ride, Blake. Or take a cab."

"It's going to be late and you're going to be tired and I'm happy to do it. Have you called Ben?"

"I did after the ceremony. They watched it on television. And he told me you said it's already on YouTube. He's a sweet man, but he doesn't get very excited about things. I talked to Gordon, too, but I'm not sure how much he understands."

"Probably better in the long run."

"I'm sorry you have to be up so late to get me."

"Tomorrow night? Ten isn't so late, except for us fossils. And you can tell me everything. I want every detail."

"Connections to Bangor are just ridiculous."

"It's okay. Don't worry about it. Donny's going to watch Phillip and that's that."

Margaret left the mirror and walked into the bedroom. Beyond the sitting area the window had turned gray and quiet with evening.

"Blake?" Margaret whispered as she sat on the edge of the bed, tears coming into her eyes.

"What, sweetie? Are you okay? What is it?"

"It's all just . . . ," Margaret said, then realized she couldn't fit her mind around it. "I don't know, I feel unfair to Thomas, I mean, I'm here in Washington for Thomas and I know he doesn't know a thing about it. . . . He's in a vegetative state, for goodness' sakes, and that's the fact, that's what I've learned to accept, but I have such strong feelings for Charlie. It's been years and years and years since I felt anything like this. It scares me. And I wonder if I would feel something like this no matter what, you know, if any man showed interest in this way. . . . And it's been romantic, the ball and zoo, and his kindness with Gordon and the meerkat. . . . I feel like I'm cheating on Thomas, and in a technical way I am, but even he wouldn't begrudge me a little happiness, just a little bit. When I'm with Charlie I feel lighthearted and it's been so long since I felt that. Lighthearted. It's a funny expression, but it describes it perfectly. I have hope when I'm with him. So I'm all bundled up inside. When we kiss, Blake, I can't believe how it feels to kiss him. Tell me I'm not being a bad person. A bad wife."

Margaret felt a deep, choking sob force its way up through her throat. She cried and sat on the edge of the bed, and she tried to listen to Blake. Dear Blake, who said everything a friend would say, who reassured her, who promised her that she, Margaret, was a good person, that these were special circumstances, that life was not all one thing or another. With part of her mind she listened, and the other part, the deep, quiet center of her consciousness, suddenly remembered the farm, the back porch, the purple lilacs thrusting their heads up into the spring air. She pictured the fire pond and the phoebe fluttering on its nest, the sun finding the old oak outside her bedroom. She lifted that memory like a string and followed it to Blake's voice, and she leaned back and put her head on the bed and listened to her friend's good advice, her heart paused as if cracked open.

Chapter
Eleven

"Tell me about your leg," Margaret said.

Charlie felt himself flush. It was a beautiful evening and they had walked from the restaurant toward his apartment, and he had kissed her a dozen times—against trees, against walls, against the curled stone banisters of Georgetown. He could not get enough of kissing her. But as soon as she spoke, he wondered if he hadn't been foolish in not mentioning it earlier. It had to come up, and now it did, and he wasn't sure what to say. No, that wasn't true: he wasn't sure what had prompted her question now and the notion that she had found him flawed made him insecure.

"If you don't want to tell me, I understand. I didn't know if I should ask, or if I should ignore it . . . and then it started to feel silly to ignore it. I'm sorry. Let's let it go."

"No, it's just not much of a story. I stepped on a bomb, that's all. Nothing very heroic or wonderful. Just a stupid step and that's that."

"That's a lousy break."

He felt his stomach roll a little. It wasn't the first time he had felt awkwardness about his leg, but somehow he hoped to be spared the conversation with Margaret. But that made no sense; she was in an impossible situation, and it was rude at some level on his part not to put it in plain sight. He slipped his arm around her waist. He loved her waist.

"I should have said something," he said, holding her against him. "I'm in the same boat. I never know when or if I should mention it. Usually I beat the other person to the punch, but with you, I don't know, I wanted to prolong the illusion in my head, I guess."

"I'm sorry for what it must have been like, Charlie. For what it still is."

"Thank you. Coming from you, I appreciate that."

She stopped and turned in his arms. He smelled her perfume, the soap in her hair. He felt her touch his cheek, his chest.

"I won't ever bring it up again unless you do. It's your wound, it's your injury. I want you to know, though, that there's so much to love and admire about you that you should never, ever give it a thought. Not in the way you might. Do you know what I'm saying?"

"I do."

"You're a remarkable man, Charlie. Your leg . . . it means nothing, believe me. In that way, nothing."

He nodded. She put her arms around him and squeezed. That contact built and started urges in him and he kissed her, kissed her until it felt as though he fell into her ribs, into her heart, and that she met him there.

———⟲

"Have you ever heard of a dawn-stone?" Charlie asked.

She shook her head. She felt wonderfully lazy and fulfilled and quiet. She lay naked next to Charlie, her head on his chest, and listened to his heart. Sometimes, with certain breezes, she smelled lilacs. Or maybe cherry blossoms. She reminded herself that Washington was famous for cherry blossoms, but she could not recall if they were in the correct season. Maybe so, although she imagined they bloomed earlier. Certainly in spring.

"A dawn-stone is a hammer. A primitive hammer," he said, the air in his lungs making her head move slightly, his voice deep and lovely in his chest. "Early cave people used them to pound on objects, like a hammer. . . . Anthropologists and paleontologists, they concluded that individuals searched for stones that fit their hands. Fit them perfectly. Once the people found them, they kept them for years. The stone grew to fit the hand more perfectly as time went by. Anthropologists find them abandoned near camping spots or in caves . . . the usual locations. They were useful for lots of reasons and they also fit one person's hand . . . so, anyway, you're my dawn-stone. That's what I'm thinking right now. Long story. Sorry."

She kissed his chest.

"I guess it's not very flattering to be compared to a stone," he said.

"Yes, it is," she said and climbed onto him.

She kissed him for a while, sampling his mouth, moving her lips back and forth on his.

"You fit me perfectly," he said when she stopped and rested on his chest again.

"Where in the world did you come from, Charlie? You need to go back there. You're spoiling me."

"I don't know a million things about you. I don't know anything about the rest of your family, your brothers and sisters, your parents. The only things I know came from the little introductory bio they provided escorts for the bill signing. I know Thomas's case history, but not yours. Where were you born?"

"In Baltimore, actually. Then we moved to Maine. My dad worked for the railroad for a while. The B&M, but that ended and he went to work for a truck dealership. Big equipment, farm tractors. He was a salesman. My mom worked at an insurance company. I have a sister who lives in Oregon. Her husband is a forest ranger. And they farmed later on. My parents, I mean, not Annie."

"So your parents aren't retired?"

"Dad's closing in on retirement. Mom works part-time. They seem pretty happy. My sister, Annie, she's the rebel in our family. She was always a bit of a wild child. She and her husband have one of those rocky relationships. They break up and get back together, then break up again. That's really all of it. It sounds so simple and tidy when you say it aloud like that, but it really was an okay childhood. We weren't rich, but we didn't want for anything."

"Did you go to the prom?"

"Yes . . . ," she said and felt herself blush. "And it was horrible. My date stole a bunch of nips—you know those airplane booze bottles?—well, he had a shoe box full he stole from his parents and I had two gins. I still can't stand the taste of gin. We got in all kinds of trouble because kids drank them and a couple threw up. Small potatoes, but it felt like a big deal at the time."

"Maybe you're the rebel in the family."

"Aren't I just scary? And what about you? Did you go to the prom? No, I bet you were a football hero. Did you play football?"

"No, basketball."

"You don't seem like a basketball type. Too solid."

"Iowa basketball is more about taking up space under the basket. I did that pretty well."

"And the prom?"

"Dora. I went with a girl named Dora. How good a prom could it be with a girl named Dora?"

"There's Dora the Explorer now."

"But not then. She was nice, actually. We had a dull time, that's all. We didn't click. Our parents kind of wanted us to go together. A lot of the kids went out to the quarry afterward, but I never liked going there because of my brother's accident. I suppose I disappointed her. We were home by midnight."

"Poor Dora."

A cool, moist wind blew in through the window and Margaret tasted rain coming. She wrapped a blanket around her from the bottom of the bed and went to the window and pushed it wider. She loved rain. She always had. She leaned out of the window a little and took a few deep breaths. Yes, some sort of flower, she thought. She tried to catch its scent again, but before she could Charlie was behind her, kissing her neck.

He spun her toward him and she had to brace herself against the windowsill. She felt rain begin to patter against the sash and drops flicked up onto her shoulders and backbone. He pulled the blanket away from her body and she let him do what he liked, let him do anything, let him use the wall and floor and window frame. The room remained dark behind them and Margaret felt herself release and abandon something, a control she had lived behind for a half decade, and she kissed Charlie over and over, his lips finding hers the instant she left his lips, and his hands moved and encouraged her everywhere. In time it felt too much; she could hardly bear it any longer. She kept kissing him and the rest of her body stayed rooted to the kiss and it went on and on, moving and climbing, receding and starting again, and with each movement the rain came harder and ran down her back, across her chest. She leaned back beyond the plane of the window and she looked up along the line of the outside wall and saw the drops of rain coming like so many small meteors, like flecks of light shed by the stars, and Charlie held her, consumed her, and stole her breath and refused to give it back.

"We could delay your flight back," Charlie said, his finger slowly tracing her backbone. "I have time and you're here already. It would be easy enough to make an excuse. We could just tell your father-in-law that you were asked to give additional testimony. Monday, Tuesday. We can put you on a flight for Wednesday. You can be home Wednesday night at the latest."

"Oh, you tempt me."

"Honestly, I'm not trying to push you. But I am, I guess. We could take a ride out to the Blue Ridge Parkway. It's not so far from here . . . just down in the Carolinas, and the rhododendrons would be in bloom. They say it's one of the prettiest things to see in the South. Not-to-be-missed kind of thing."

"You haven't been?"

"No, never. And I've wanted to go. We could find a little place to stay . . . if you like that kind of thing."

"I love that kind of thing."

"I could bring a fly rod. I like to fish. We could do a little fishing and sightseeing. We could see the flowers and the mountains . . . supposed to be beautiful. I know you're probably eager to get back to Gordon, but in the scheme of things two days isn't much. It really isn't."

"It feels longer than that to a little boy."

"Of course. I'm not trying to minimize it. I'm just saying I want you here with me."

"I want to be here, too, Charlie, but maybe that's a good reason not to extend things. I'm married, Charlie."

He nodded.

"You know," she said, "I used to wonder if I would ever meet someone new. A man. Blake thinks I should start to date if I want to, but it's never felt right. I don't know. There are no rules for this. But now suddenly you appear, on this of all weekends, and I like you so much, Charlie. Any woman would be lucky to have you. To go away to see rhododendron blossoms . . . are you kidding? With a man she wants to be with? It's really not a question of making up excuses. I could extend my stay, but I'm worried I'll fall for you too deeply. It might make everything else harder in the end."

"Will you at least think about it?"

"Of course I will."

Charlie pulled the edge of the blanket over them both. He felt tired and calm and he felt Margaret edge back into him, spooning, her body tight against his. It was past midnight. It was Sunday already, and Margaret would leave this evening if she decided not to extend her stay, and Charlie held her close and tried not to think about that. How strange it all was. He had accepted the assignment to escort her to the bill signing out of loyalty to his brother, and because he had time, and because it was a good cause, and now he slept with the woman in his arms. It unnerved him a little to like this woman on so many levels. She was beautiful and passionate and kind. She was levelheaded, but not in the least dull. He thought of her at the ball, at the pleasure she took in the evening, and he remembered her against the window, the rain splashing and getting them both damp.

"I want more of you," he whispered into her ear.

She turned and faced him.

"Charlie, more sex?"

The look on her face—she looked appalled at the notion—

made him laugh. He couldn't help it. Her initial expression was so shocked, so alarmed, that it made him laugh harder each time he thought of it. It took her a moment and then she understood, and he felt her begin to laugh, too, both of them silent, holding their breath. The laughter went on a long time. It stopped and started once or twice, and eventually she pushed into his body and didn't say anything for a little while.

"I know what you mean," she said eventually.

"This is too short."

She nodded.

"They tell me airplanes even fly to Bangor these days," he said.

"But I don't think you're ready to retire to a farm in Maine, Charlie. And you could break my heart. I'm careful with my heart these days."

"It wouldn't have to be all one thing or another. We could see where it goes."

"Maybe," she said. "Maybe we could. It's pretty to think about."

"You'll come to the brunch with me tomorrow?"

"Yes, I'd love to. I'm looking forward to it."

"And then I'll take you to see the blossoms."

"I'm not sure."

"Are you sleepy?"

"Yes. I am. I like being here. I like having you beside me."

Then for a while he thought she slept. He heard the rain subside outside and somewhere down the hall someone yelled something—a party, from the sound of it. Sleep closed over him slowly. He jumped once as his body shut down, and he felt pain in his phantom leg. He often felt pain, but he had grown accustomed to it and it didn't bother him much except at night.

"I want you to know that I love you, Charlie," Margaret whispered close to his chest. "It's a kind of love I feel for you and I don't want to pretend I don't. I know, I know, it's all too quick and fast and so I don't want you to think anything of it. But I admire you, Charlie, and I think you're a wonderful man, and so I love that in you. You've made me feel like a woman again and I didn't imagine that would happen to me. Not after Thomas's injury. I'm being silly, I know, but I didn't want you to think I saw this as a passing fancy, a little sex and I don't know. Whatever name you want to call it. I like you too much, Charlie. Girls have to say this stuff, we just do, so I'm saying it now. I'm sorry if it embarrasses you. I don't mean it to. It's just love for another person. Now I'll shut up and I'm going to sleep and when we wake up it will be our last day and that's okay."

She turned again in his arms, pressing her back into him, and he held her and kissed her neck below the ear, and he took her hand and held it.

"I love you, too," he said quietly.

Chapter
Twelve

It had never occurred to Charlie how strange the Lincoln Memorial must appear to children, but to see a school group like the one that walked before them approach, their eyes up, their faces confused, forced Charlie to see the statue in a different light. How odd it was, really, to have this enormous man seated in a gigantic chair, his face pointed down in understanding and amusement at human folly, greeting strangers and inviting them nearly onto his marble lap. Without context, without knowing who Lincoln was or why he merited a statue, it might simply be frightening.

"I hadn't realized how formidable it is," Margaret said, seeing the children, too, Charlie thought. "Just the size is impressive."

"It's a lot of stone."

"Much more than I realized," Margaret said.

A man with a small rat terrier walked down the stairs in the opposite direction. The dog went to the end of its leash to smell a wedge of pizza. The man yanked the dog gently away. Finally Charlie climbed the last few steps and stood in the shade almost directly under Lincoln's shins, Margaret beside him.

"The Lincoln Memorial," Margaret said. "I have to say, it looks just like I pictured it."

"It's more impressive at night, I think."

A male docent wearing a maroon jacket with a National Park Service emblem on it patrolled at the northeast corner, keeping an eye on the school group. It wasn't very crowded for a Sunday morning.

"Did you believe in the war, Charlie?" Margaret asked softly, her eyes studying the statue.

"Which one?"

"Is there a difference, really? I suppose there is. I'm cynical. After Thomas, I don't have much faith in any of it. I imagine I did at one point. We were told so many lies and I believed them. But now . . . Anyway, it's not my business, but I was curious. I'm sorry if it's the wrong question."

"I think a lot of my friends still believe in the cause," Charlie said, not sure himself where he was heading with it, "because to go back on it now makes us . . . what? Murderers? Professional assassins? I've had trouble with it. Plenty of trouble. That's part of the reason I went to grad school. I studied the background and sources and whatever else I came across. I don't know, honestly. We can't be forever at war. That's certain. Everything you can say about the war, about either war, sounds like a bumper sticker. It's sad."

"Was it worth it? Your leg?"

"No," he said, giving voice to a thought he had shared

with only a few people, "I don't think it was. Deep down, I don't think so."

"I don't think it was worth Thomas's life, either. I'm probably wicked for thinking that. That's a horrible thing to have in your mind . . . that your husband's condition was preventable and unnecessary. I don't dwell on it and I never talk politics, but with you, standing here . . . I don't know. They always say there's a victim on each side of a bullet."

"I guess once I got there I concentrated on being a good soldier and protecting my friends. That's the irony, isn't it? You travel halfway around the globe and put yourself in danger and all you can worry about is watching out for your friends. That becomes the mission and you don't ask the bigger questions because they don't have much meaning at the time. It's only when you come back that they start to stack up in your head. Did Thomas talk much about what he was doing there?"

"He was on an escort team . . . ," she said and stopped.

Then she shook her head.

"I don't think he had a clue about the bigger picture," she said. "Do you know, when it became clear he was going to be sent neither one of us could find Iraq or Afghanistan on a map? Not easily, anyway. Isn't that horrible? To go give your life to a place that has so little weight or meaning in your existence that you don't even know where it is? I'm ashamed of that. I bet a lot of people who celebrated Bin Laden's death in the street couldn't find either country on a map."

Charlie took her hand. She turned and looked at him. He imagined she was talking to herself as much as to him.

"I'm sorry to bring this up," she said, shaking her head as

if to clear it of cobwebs. "It's been on my mind and I can't really talk about it with anyone at home."

"They're fair questions, Margaret."

"If Thomas had had an opinion about it all, it would have been easier somehow. If he had believed in some sort of cause, I guess I could rationalize that even if I didn't agree with it. He was patriotic, I don't mean to say he wasn't. But he joined to help with the mortgage and I hate him for that. I hate that our society makes war an attractive job for young men and women. I hate that we can't think of a better way to employ them than to put them in uniforms and send them off to a foreign country that wants nothing to do with them. I hate that when they come back we look for ways to cut costs on their medical benefits. And now I'll be quiet. I've said my piece. I'm sorry if it's out of line."

"No, not at all. I like your passion in saying it. If you don't have the right to speak, who does? But we should get going," he said gently and put his arms around her. "Terry will wonder where we've gotten to."

"I'm sorry to get on a bandwagon. I had to ask, though."

"I don't mind. And I honor your husband's act. War reveals character, they say. If that's true, Thomas is a brave man."

"He was a good man," she said, and Charlie noticed the change in tenses.

The docent passed by on a perpetual lap.

—☙

"So you're Margaret! No wonder Charlie has been in a tizzy! You're beautiful!"

Margaret felt herself blush, and at the same time Terry—it had to be Terry, didn't it?—leaned in and kissed her on the cheek. Margaret kissed her back, and it felt like kissing a bird. Yes, a bird, Margaret thought, watching Terry pull back, her face somewhat angled, her hair in a bun, her black silk trousers and white blouse elegant and chic. Terry smiled and glanced over at Charlie—who carried a rack full of gowns on his index finger—and went up on her toes to peck his cheek.

"Well, she put you to good use," Terry said, her hand draping a length of one of the gowns that had tangled in its cleaner bag. "You can hang those in the hall closet. We'll look after them later."

"Thank you so much for letting me wear one. They're all beautiful."

"Oh, glad to do it. You wore the black, right? That's my favorite, too. I also like the cream-colored one, but I've worn it out. They're all hand-me-downs from Trish."

Charlie had the closet door open and he pushed back clothes while Terry gently scolded him and told him what to do. Margaret used the moment of confusion to glance quickly around the foyer and the expansive living room that stretched out behind Terry. It was exquisite. Had she ever wondered if the magazine spreads in *Country Living* or *Better Homes and Gardens* existed in genuine homes, she now had proof that they did. In the quickest perusal, she saw a grand piano positioned near a long set of French doors, air moving the shimmery white drapes in and out; on the other side of the piano, she saw a brick fireplace, expansive and wide, and above the mantel a portrait of a man staring out at them. The man wore a black frock coat and a prominent white collar and he did not smile. Light and air moved through the room, and the deep blue of an enormous Oriental carpet lent the room a liquid feeling. No, Margaret corrected herself, it was not a water feeling, but a sense of the sky brought lower. She remembered a tiny snatch of poetry, nearly the only thing she recollected from all her years of schooling: *When weeds, in wheels, shoot long and lovely and lush / Thrush's eggs look little low heavens . . .* but she could not bring the poet's name to mind. Yes, that was what the blue carpet gave to the room. The light turned into a little low heaven, and Margaret turned her attention back to Terry, the woman who had designed such beauty.

"There, all stowed away," Terry said, closing the closet door after Charlie had vacated it. "You're learning, Charlie."

"Your house is beautiful," Margaret said. "Just wonderful."

"I wish I could take credit for it, but it's been in our family for ages. I'm merely the latest tenant."

"I'm sure it takes more than that."

"Well, sure, it's demanding at times, but thank you. Now, come through. We're eating out back. I don't know what terrible lies Charlie might have told you about us, but we're simple folks. Our Sundays are casual and we have a moratorium on political talk. Any other subject in the world is welcome, but no wrangling over politics. I won't stand it. We even pull out the editorial pages from the newspapers. We read the

sports pages and the arts section and maybe real estate, although real estate can be thorny, too."

Margaret followed Terry through the living room and out
onto the back veranda. The beauty of the house continued into
a gracious garden, expansive and lined with gravel walkways,
that spread and led the eye to the river beyond it. It comple-
mented the house perfectly, and it gave way in time to a spacious
lawn that rolled down to the water. Lovely, Margaret thought.
She liked, too, that children seemed at home running and darting around the yard. Someone had constructed a tree fort in an
old, hollowed oak, and Margaret spotted three boys looking out
the window. Then she received a surprise: one of the boys leaped
onto a zip-line and rode a hand trolley down to the earth, his
legs spinning as they took to the ground. Somehow the sight of
the children and the free way they explored the garden and
grounds made her feel at home.

The adults—Margaret counted eight in her initial
assessment—sat at a wide white table overlooking the water
and the lawn. The table rested beneath an enormous catalpa
tree; the leaves on the tree shimmered like small bells in a soft
breeze. The table had not been set up in a fussy manner. People seemed to sit every which way, some reading the paper,
others simply taking the spring sunlight on their skin. A small
buffet arrangement waited on a second table ten paces away
from the first. Margaret smelled food and counted five heating
trays stationed over chafing dish burners.

"Now, please, help yourself to something to eat," Terry
said, guiding them toward the food. "I never do introductions

on Sunday morning. It's up to you to mingle and to eat and to have a mimosa if you care to. I'm holding you responsible for her welfare, Charlie. Everyone, say hello."

People looked up and said hello while Margaret smiled and made a small, embarrassed wave that she immediately regretted. She wasn't sure how to navigate from a standing position to a place at the table. For an instant she felt vulnerable and nervous, but then she felt Charlie's hand touch the center of her back, leading her to the buffet table.

"I'm starving," Charlie said, "I'm always hungry around you. Why is that?"

"I'm hungry, too," Margaret said.

She selected scrambled eggs, home fries, a bowl of fruit, and a cup of tea. Charlie followed her in line and helped himself to a generous plate of bacon and eggs. She realized, as she watched him close the top on the serving tray containing rye toast and pots of oatmeal, that she did not know what he liked to eat. It struck her as strange that she wouldn't know more, but how could she?

"Here, you two," a tall, thin man said, clearing papers away from a spot near him. He reminded Margaret of a heron, a bird with patience and stature, but one that looked at the world somewhat sideways. "I'm hogging three spaces. You can sit if you know the answer to 'Cleveland third basement who stopped Joe DiMaggio's hit streak.' Starts with a *K*, probably."

"No idea," Charlie said, putting his plate down and leaving a spot next to him for Margaret. "I was always a Reds fan."

"John is obsessed with the *Times* Sunday crossword," a

woman on the other side of him said. She was the man's opposite, broad where the man was thin, and she had an open, honest
face, perhaps rounded by hope. "Don't sit near him unless
you're ready to be plagued by questions and clues. He will not
give up until he finishes the puzzle, and he's certain the whole
world shares his passion."

"How about," the man asked, ignoring the woman, his
heron face pecking at the folded puzzle in front of him, " 'Film
about Japanese mortuary arts'? Second letter, *E*."

"His name is John Philbrick, and I'm Alicia, his wife," the
woman said, leaning across him. "We haven't met, have we?"

Charlie made the introductions.

"She exaggerates," John Philbrick said about his wife, finally looking up and pulling away from the puzzle, "but I do
like the puzzle. I only do puzzles edited or created by Will
Shortz. He's my dope pusher."

"Do you do the whole week?" someone—a short, dark
man with tremendously thick glasses—across the table asked.
"I refuse to even try Saturday's puzzle. It used to take the entire day and I just couldn't stand it. I'm Lenny, by the way. My
wife's around here somewhere."

Margaret smiled and ate, happy to sit in the shade on a
sunny day and look out at the river. She listened to the conversation around her, feeling not shy, but content to observe and
take things in. She watched Charlie—how easily he mixed with
people, unlike Thomas who had never been at his best in social
situations—and she saw immediately that people liked him.
The admirable traits she found in him, his humility, his innate

kindness, his gentleness, became clear to each person who in-
teracted with him. In a different kind of man, his ability to put
people at ease, while, at the same time, making them interested
in his views, might have led to power or a seedy corruption.
But he did not have that bone, as her mother would have put
it. He answered the heron-man's crossword questions as best
he could and took a genuine interest in Lenny's job—Margaret
had difficulty following the table talk, filled as it was with government acronyms, initials for agencies that meant nothing to
her—but she enjoyed watching Charlie navigate it; and she
concentrated on her food.

It was a little later, during a lull in the conversation, that
Charlie reached under the table and took her hand. He did not
hold it a long time, perhaps out of deference to her position as
a married woman, but he squeezed her fingers gently to let her
know that she was not out of his thoughts. She squeezed his
hand in return, and she wondered for a moment how people
viewed them. She felt that they had become a couple, and she
wondered if others saw them that way. She could not deny that
she welcomed his hand, welcomed whatever construction people wanted to put on them, because she felt proud and honored
to be in his life.

After breakfast they went to stand in the sun and look out
at the water. Margaret crossed her arms and felt mildly chilled
with the breeze off the river. The tree fort squirmed with children. One boy on the ground shouted something indecipher-
able to the boys who stood guard near the top. Two girls
popped out and ran away squealing. A bigger boy—Henry,

Margaret thought she had heard, one of Terry's children—swung down the zip-line after them.

"How do you know Terry again?" Margaret asked. "You'll work for her husband in Africa?"

"Kind of in a tangential way, but yes. We'll be on the same diplomatic mission. Meeting Terry was a big coincidence. She knew the sponsors for the bill you saw signed this weekend. She also volunteers one morning a week in the hospital. We met when I was doing physical therapy at Walter Reed because of the whole diplomatic connection. One of my buddies knew us both and put two and two together. You wouldn't know it from the house and the setting here, but she's completely down-to-earth. Her family has had money for so long that it's just a fact of life. And she is a first-class fund-raiser. You can pretty much guarantee success if you get her involved in a function or a charity campaign. She's connected to everyone. That's why I admire the volunteer work. She says it keeps her grounded."

"It's a beautiful home. And I like her."

"She kind of took a shine to me," Charlie said, "probably because of my Midwest background. Her favorite uncle was from Iowa and was the Iowa Hawkeye mascot when he went to school there. I guess the rest of her family is all East Coast, so her uncle was an exotic. She said I reminded her of her uncle. The way I talk, I suppose."

"Do you come out often?"

"Sundays like this. There's a little secret you don't know about me," he said, and he bumped her shoulder with his, flirting. "It's nothing nefarious. It's simply that I'm a bit of a birder. Not a big birder, but my dad has a life list and he taught me to pay attention and to look up. Around here, the river is just terrific, especially for waterfowl. So she indulges me. I sometimes come out with another guy, an old fellow named Fritz, and we sit and use binoculars and smoke cigars. That's my confession."

"I bet she loves having you both."

"She scarcely notices us. We just sneak out to the edge of the river and set up our seats."

"It's funny you mention birds, because just before you showed up at the farm I was listening to a phoebe. We have a phoebe every spring, and I was wondering if it's the same phoebe or different one each year."

"Probably an ancestral nest, but I'll ask my dad. *Sayornis phoebe*. It's one of the few names I know in Latin."

Almost on cue, a W formation of mergansers flew down the core of the river, their wings audible as they swatted air underneath them. Margaret recognized them; in Maine they landed on the fire pond beyond the barn now and then and she had looked them up in the old Norton bird book so that she would have their name for Gordon. They flew rapidly, their wings casting forward and back, rowing, and she found their passage somehow emotional. She smiled to see them, and yet felt close to crying. They reminded her of Thomas, of his northern life, and she put a hand on Charlie's shoulder to steady herself.

"I'm a sap in the spring and fall," she said, feeling silly and oddly moved by their swift passage over the river. "That's my confession. I get all stirred up and I hardly know why. I'd like to know more about birds. Maybe you've inspired me. Maybe I'll join a bird group when I get back."

"I aim to serve, ma'am," he said and smiled.

She couldn't help it. She leaned into him and kissed him. She kissed him a long time. The mergansers, she thought, and she felt her chest flutter and she held him tighter, fearing that some part of her, some part she could never recapture, would take leave of her now and fly after the birds. After their kiss, she put her head against his chest and stood for a long time that way.

"Oh, Charlie," she said, "what have you done to me?"

Chapter
Thirteen

A little later Charlie looked back at the house and raised his hand to wave. He spotted Terry and Margaret sitting together in the catalpa's shade, cups of tea in front of them. The women waved back. At the same moment Henry slammed a shot at his sister, Jordan, and yelped when it kissed her yellow ball.

"She's out!" Henry shouted.

The game had devolved from croquet to Poison, a bastardization of the standard game wherein every ball was poison and could eliminate any other ball if it so much as touched it. If the ball touched a wicket or passed through one, or if it touched a post, it also died. As a result, the game established a wary dance of cat-and-mouse that forced players to lag shots into defensive positions before they could take a final leap at an exposed adversary. That was what had just occurred with Henry's attack on Jordan.

"It didn't touch!" Jordan countered. "Now I've got you."

"It did, too, touch! Charlie, didn't it touch?"

"I didn't see it. I was looking up at the house."

"Believe me," Jordan said emphatically. She was a cute blonde, eleven, a year older than Henry, and she wore a pink sundress and bare feet today. She also wore a pink ribbon that had come undone and now trailed behind her head like a streak of color. She ignored everyone and began aiming her shot at Henry. Henry put his foot on his ball and his mallet in front of his foot.

"Don't," he said to Jordan. "I hit you; you're out."

"Why don't we do a do-over?" Charlie asked.

"Because I hit her fair and square," Henry lamented. "Charlie, she's cheating."

"So says you," Jordan said.

"Compromise," Charlie said. "Let's just go back one turn. I'll promise to pay attention this time."

"Cheater," Henry said, but he picked up his ball and walked it back into position. He took a long time lining up his next shot, but when he finally went his ball rolled to within a foot of Jordan's. An easy kill shot for her.

"This is unfair," Henry said and threw down his mallet. "She's a cheater."

Charlie had to fight back a laugh when Jordan stuck out her tongue at Henry. Then she lined up her shot and put Henry out of his misery. It was a quick turnaround from death to conqueror. Henry, deciding finally to be a good sport, enacted a brutal death, spinning and choking, grabbing his chest and falling slowly to his eternal rest, as the rules dictated.

"Showdown," Jordan said, turning like a gun turret toward Charlie. "Prepare to die, Charlie."

"Come and get me, Jordy," Charlie answered.

Henry, from his death scene on the ground, pointed up at the sky.

"That cloud looks like an alligator," he said.

———

"I've adopted Charlie, you know? He has that wonderful vulnerability that's catnip to any woman. He is a little too good for the world, isn't he? That's always been my impression of him. This wonderful Midwestern boy who grew up going to sock hops and proms and heading out in his roadster to the Saturday football game. I suppose I romanticize him, but not by much. I keep waiting to see him do something small or mean, but he never does."

"He's a wonderful man," Margaret said. "At least he seems to be. I haven't known him for very long."

"Yes, he is a wonderful man. But he hardly knows it himself, and that's his charm. He gives everyone around him more credit than they're due. He believes people are good fundamentally, and most of the people in Washington believe people are venal. It's refreshing to be around him. He's a tonic."

It felt good to sit, Margaret realized. She watched Charlie playing with the kids. Beyond them, the river ran like a black sock. She sipped her tea.

"You helped him with his leg?" Margaret asked.

"I didn't help him, but I made sure someone did. These

damn wars. We have so many young people coming back with injuries, and of course Congress doesn't like to spend the money to fix them. And they can't really be fixed. Not deep down. But Charlie has handled his leg well. He was an athlete, so he knows how to keep his body fit and he knew how to commit himself to rehab. He's bright as a penny now, but it took time."

"He's very grateful to you. I know that."

"To be honest, I get so sick of the Washington crowd that I look forward to these young men and women who come through the hospital. I don't mean that I want them to be injured, obviously. They just come at the world from a different place than the politicians I bump into. Charlie's sweeter than most, but there are plenty of good young people coming through the hospitals. Has Charlie told you about Fritz?"

"The fellow bird-watcher?"

"Is that what he said?"

"Yes. Isn't that accurate?"

Terry sipped her tea. Margaret watched as Charlie grabbed his heart and pretended to die. Someone had won something in the croquet match, but Margaret couldn't tell who or what or why. She watched the two kids pretend to put their feet on Charlie in conquest. The boy, Henry, drummed his chest like Tarzan.

"Fritz is a quad," Terry said. "He's been institutionalized since Vietnam. He stopped talking some years back, and when Charlie was in the hospital for treatment he happened to bump into him at an X-ray station or something. Somehow it happened that Charlie learned his story from the nurses, so he decided that he would sit with Fritz for a little while each day. No big deal to Charlie, but to anyone else . . . Fritz was never a very nice guy even when he did talk. So Charlie sat with him and read to him and eventually Fritz began talking again. Nothing big, no major philosophical discussions . . . just simple companionship. So Charlie found out that Fritz was from Nebraska, and that Fritz had been a bit of an amateur birder. Something about the sandhill cranes. I don't know. I'm not much of a birder myself. Long story short, Charlie figured out a way to get Fritz a van and a driver and get him out of the hospital. He brings him here mostly, but they've gone to some other places . . . bird sanctuaries and parks. It's been a transforming thing for Fritz. He's not much less grumpy, but he communicates now and has gotten a couple other long-timers involved with birding. It's something they can do from the windows of the hospital. So, that's Charlie. And it's also like Charlie to dismiss Fritz as a guy he goes birding with."

"That's a wonderful story."

Terry reached forward and broke off a piece of croissant that she had saved on her plate earlier. Margaret watched as Charlie rose off the ground, pretending to growl at the kids. A bright yellow kayak passed by on the river.

"And your husband?" Terry asked. "Vegetative? That's such a horrible word."

"Yes, he is. He was shot in Afghanistan."

"I'm sorry. I knew the basics from Charlie. What a shame."

"He was a very good man," Margaret said and she felt

tears suddenly fill the spaces behind her eyes. "Is a good man, I mean."

"And you're a good woman."

"Oh, I don't know about that. I've felt like a traitor all weekend. Or not like a traitor, but something else."

"It can't always be about him, Margaret. I don't know your situation, so forgive me, but I know many men and women who have found themselves in situations they never dreamed of before these wars. They're good people, believe me. One of the sordid side notes to these wars is the notion that people can simply go along without it affecting their lives. I've been thinking about this lately, and of course I run into it all the time at the hospital. Because we see so little of the war on television, and we debate so little about it in any meaningful way, we've relegated it as a nation to a small parlor in the back of our minds. People aren't drafted, you see? So the war is simply a thing that certain people are hired to carry out. It's a job we contract out, like a kitchen renovation. That sounds horrible, but it's true. And if some people are injured on that job, well, we say we care and we have Veterans Day, but we've cut benefits to wounded soldiers. Sorry to unload all of this on you, but I can't always speak my mind to folks around here. The point I'm trying to make is that we have people enduring tremendous pain and suffering, all against a backdrop of normalcy for everyone else. So if you have indulged yourself to some degree this weekend, don't sit in judgment. Your husband was caught up in these terrible wars, but so were you. I guess that's what I'm trying to say in my long-winded way."

"Well, thank you for saying it."

"I knew a woman in your circumstances who divorced her husband and then adopted him. Crazy sounding, I know, but these are crazy times."

"I couldn't do that," Margaret said.

"No, I didn't think you could. And listen to me making all of these pronouncements and I hardly know you. But I feel as though I do, so forgive me. Now we should change the subject. Tell me about farm life in Maine."

Margaret smiled.

"It's not very glamorous, I'm afraid," she said. "The wardrobe consists mostly of old jeans, a down vest, and muck boots."

"Sounds good to me."

"Come visit someday," Margaret said and she meant it because she felt a warm, genuine connection to Terry. "We live in a beautiful area. We have an old farmhouse that is the devil to heat in the winter, but through three seasons it's very pretty. And the farm is set on rolling hills, so it looks like a farm should look. It's a simple life, but a good one. I love it. It's down deep in my blood."

"You know, I go up to Maine every now and then so I might surprise you. Is it near the seacoast?"

"Inland. Old logging country."

Terry moved her chin slightly to indicate that Charlie was returning. She sipped her tea and when she put down her cup she smiled at Charlie. Margaret watched as Charlie sat down.

"What kind of horrible things have you two been discussing?" Charlie asked.

"Why is it that whenever a man sees two women together he assumes they've been talking about him?"

"Because we're paranoid and it's a matter of survival."

"Who won the game?" Margaret asked.

"Just a battle in an ongoing war," Charlie said. "Each side claims victory, but I think a careful study of the replay might give the nod to Jordan."

"What time is it?" Margaret asked.

Charlie glanced at his watch.

"It's getting close to noon."

"I'm such a bad flier," Margaret explained to Terry. "And I never trust connections will go off as they should."

"You're more than welcome to hang out here," Terry said. "Airports are such horrible places."

Charlie poured himself a glass of water. He drank it down in a couple of swigs. Then he poured himself more.

"I'll be right back," Margaret said, rising.

"Good," Charlie said, "now we can gossip about you."

"Or start a fan club," Terry said and reached across the table and took Margaret's hand.

"I'm going to come visit you someday on your farm," Terry said. "I'd like that very much."

"I hope you will," Margaret said. She squeezed Terry's hand. Then she left the table and went toward the house to use the bathroom and to call the airport.

Chapter
Fourteen

M argaret used the half bath off the kitchen. She washed her face and hands and then took a moment to brush back her hair with her fingers. She felt tired and her face, she decided, appeared washed out. She wanted to pinch her cheeks, as Scarlett O'Hara had done in *Gone with the Wind*, but that seemed silly. She wished, absently, that she possessed more skill with makeup. She did not care for makeup as a rule, but there were times, times like now, when a touch of makeup would have been a welcome friend. She wanted to look her best with Charlie, and if that made her vain, so be it. She leaned close to the mirror, checked her skin, checked both sides of her mouth, then stared for a moment into her own eyes.

It was all very simple. She had fallen for Charlie, and Terry had confirmed what she already knew—that Charlie was a fine man—and then Terry had put into her head the idea that one could go around things a little in a time of war. Margaret was not sure Terry had meant it that way, but there it was: she

could divorce Thomas and adopt him so that her responsibility
to him changed from wife to mother. And, really, wasn't that a
more honest arrangement? She *was* a mother to him; her visits
had long ago changed from a wife's visits to her husband's bedside, to the practical, maternal visits she experienced now. Was
he being turned enough? Had they tried a new regimen against
staph infections? Procedural questions and discussions. How
many years had it been, she wondered, since she had climbed
into bed with Thomas and held him, used the weight of his
body for comfort? She had done that often in the first months
after his return. Wife and husband. It had not been a case of
playing the dramatic near-widow, the yearning, devoted wife,
but rather, a case of longing and desire, a case of a wife wanting
her husband to return to her. *Come back to me,* she had whispered like a prayer, saying it in their private moments, whispering it in his ear, and she had said it so much that she had
believed, in a small, delicate tissue of hope, that he would hear
her and follow her voice back to consciousness. It was ludicrous; she knew better. But it had been a wife calling for her
husband, and she wondered now, staring into the mirror, when
that impulse had changed. When had she become the mother
visiting the child with measles?

It was important, she decided, not to obscure things. Not
to pretend one thing and do another. No hypocrisy. If she
wanted to be with Charlie—and she did, down deep inside
her—then she needed to be clear and forthright about it. In
some curious way, Thomas deserved that. He deserved hon-
esty. She was going to go with Charlie to the Blue Ridge Park-

way, and she accepted that as a married woman, as a woman with a husband in a bed in Bangor, Maine, as a person whose wedding vows still remained intact. Eyes open, she told herself. No pretending or giving the choice a fancy coloring.

She examined her face one more time, brushed down her clothes, shaped the dress around her hips and breasts, then stepped back into the kitchen. For a moment she misremembered the direction of the backyard. It took her a second to get her bearings. By the time she sat on the lovely living room couch, her phone open to her ear, she heard a clock ringing noon.

"Will you go for a little walk with me?" Charlie asked and held out his hand. "Terry's turned on a movie for the kids and she's going to sit inside and watch it with them. Everyone else has cleared out. I want to show you something."

"I'd love to."

"There's a pretty spot up here and a tree you should see," he said. "We'll leave whenever you say."

"I made a call to the airport," she said, and she remembered her vow to be open and honest about her desire. "I've moved my flight to Wednesday. I want to be with you, Charlie, and that's that. I want more of you."

"Did you really? You're not joking, are you? That's perfect."

She nodded. Her color rose.

"I've called everyone and made my excuses. Blake is going to look in on Gordon. He'll be fine. I've decided I want to spend more time with you. And I'm determined to be direct about it. I'm not going to pretend anything about it."

Charlie took her hand and kissed the back of it.

"Yes, to everything."

"Are you sure? I can still change it back. I realized as I made the call that I was being presumptuous. We hadn't actually confirmed things."

"Positive."

"I want to get away with you."

"We can leave this afternoon. Let's just get out of town. I'm completely free. I know someone who will lend us a car. He's offered it before and I never took him up on it."

"I have nothing to wear. I know women say that, but I really don't. I packed for the bill signing and that was about it."

"We can shop. Pick up a few things."

She nodded and put her hand in his. Charlie waited until they were closer to the river, then he kissed her.

"Yes, I want to go away with you. I've had a wonderful weekend," he said. "The best I can remember in a long time."

"So have I. I don't know whether you've made it easier or harder to go back home."

"We're not going to talk about going home. Not for a while. We're hunting for rhododendron blossoms. It might be a little early, but we can chance it."

He kissed her hand again. The air felt cooler nearer the river. He heard frogs starting, bullfrogs and green frogs, the twangy rubber of their voices. Clouds had begun to cluster in the west. It would rain later, he imagined. It pleased him that she had experienced good weather. He clamped her arm under his elbow.

"Do you see it yet?" he asked when they had gone a little farther.

"Is that a tree?" she asked, her voice delighted. "I thought it was a tent. I didn't think a tree could be that color."

"Apple blossoms. Terry claims it's an antique variety because it blossoms so much later than the other trees."

"Do you mean to tell me I've been smelling apple blossoms all this time? I thought it was cherry blossoms in Washington."

"They're earlier. April usually."

He led her to the tree. Usually, he thought, people planted apple trees together so that their spring foliage would have greater impact, but this tree seemed wild and unruly. Clearly it had escaped the landscapers, or had volunteered on its own, springing up and growing close enough to the river so that no one bothered it. It was larger than most apple trees he had seen in Washington. Its branches spread out over the river and the reflection of its boughs created a second tree, a wavering twin that moved and shimmered in the passing water.

"Listen to the bees," Margaret said, stopping for a moment when she came to the drip line. "They're crazy for it."

"Somehow this tree feels more honest than the others around this town. It's earned its way. No special treatment."

"Oh, it's absolutely perfect. Just perfect. In another day it would begin to fade. Or a day earlier . . . . it wouldn't be the same. It's lovely."

"The tree's great hour," Charlie said. "Someone wrote that about a cherry tree."

He watched her bend a bough down and put her nose into the blooms. She looked beautiful standing beneath the ripe blossoms, like a painting of some sort, although he couldn't call one to mind. An Impressionist probably. Bees hummed and bumped into the red-white flowers, their leg sleeves stuffed with propolis, their flight drunken and contented. He walked up behind her and held her in his arms. She crossed his arms over her waist. The scent of the blossoms touched everything.

He kissed her. He kissed her until he felt their heat begin to build and carry them. He smelled the apple blossoms and heard the bees.

"We should get back," she said after a little while. "You've got me stirred up and we're a perfect scandal out here."

"You're passionate. No one would know it to look at you. Not right away. But you are."

"You bring it out in me."

"We bring it out in each other."

He took her hand and began walking with her. He felt good and calm, though he still had the impression of her kisses on him. *Rhododendrons,* he thought. He would have her for two more days. Three, counting tonight. He glanced at her from time to time as they walked. How beautiful she was; it made her more beautiful that she did not have a sense of her own fine looks. If it was possible, he wanted a mental snapshot of her standing beneath the apple blossoms. It had all been mixed together: water, light, apple flowers, bee hum. The blossoms had turned her skin softly pink and the water behind her had made her appear to be in motion or flight. He felt heat rising in him again, but he also felt the desire to have her beside him.

"I want to be in a bubble with you," she said. "Just for these next days. I don't care about anything else. I apologize to the world, but I'm going to be selfish and that's that. Or maybe not a bubble exactly. Maybe the basket of a hot air balloon so that we can see everything and feel everything, but no one can touch us."

"That's a deal."

"Let's leave as soon as we can."

She turned and kissed him. Charlie held her and kept her arm when they walked back toward the house.

———⁂———

Gordon watched the movie. It was an old movie about a dog and a boy somewhere far away and he decided he wanted a dog himself. A dog made sense. This dog, for example, could alert people to problems, or run with you when you rode a bike, and at night it slept on the foot of your bed and kept bad guys away. He wondered, as he watched, his body slumped against a rack of cushions on the couch, why he had never understood about dogs before. He hadn't understood that they could be friends, guards, a bunch of things that helped a person to live. Grandpa Ben had owned a dog years ago, he knew, but that dog had always been the butt of jokes, or stories about how stupid it had been, and so it lived in his memory in an entirely different form from the dog on the screen. This kind of dog, a collie, even Grandpa Ben would like.

Gordon turned when the door to the room opened and he saw his grandfather move in the kitchen. Grandpa Ben let him watch television more than his mother did.

"We're going to get going pretty soon," Grandpa Ben said a few minutes later. "Can you go to the bathroom and get ready?"

He nodded, but he didn't move.

He wanted to tell Grandpa Ben about dogs, about his new understanding, but he didn't know how to phrase it. He moved a little forward on the couch seat. He did that whenever he wanted to prolong his television watching. It made his mom or Grandpa Ben think he was getting up, when in fact he had merely moved a few inches.

"Come on, sport, turn off the TV and get ready," Grandpa Ben called.

They were going to the hardware store. That was Grandpa Ben's favorite place to go.

Gordon slid off the couch and took a step toward the television. He held the remote control in one hand. That was another trick. You could wait and have the remote control ready to shoot the TV dead, but you could stall and pretend it wasn't working right. He pointed the remote at the television and stood for a moment to watch the collie run across a grassy field. Yes, he thought, a dog like that. A dog exactly like that.

Rhododendrons

Chapter
Fifteen

Charlie held her hand as he drove them out of the city in a borrowed Jeep Wrangler, the top down, the wind chilly and fresh. His holding her hand was one of the small, endearing differences from Thomas, Margaret thought. Thomas had been sweet as a suitor and a husband, but he had behaved as though a rule book existed somewhere and one didn't willingly violate it. Looking back, they were not silly rules, but they took some of the fun out of life: don't call before or after nine o'clock; always clean the dishes before going to bed; two-drink maximum; thank-you note the day after receiving a gift; dinner early, usually around five thirty, consisting principally of meat and potatoes. She valued his practical nature, his three-thousand-mile oil changes, his careful monitoring of the furnace, his chimney brushes that he ran up and through each flue on a bright day every September, his handiness with the tractor; but it could at times be more weighted than she liked. In contrast, Charlie's hand holding, his impetuous kisses under the apple blossoms, his tenderness when he turned over her hand and kissed it, his overt desire for her, thrilled her and made her eager to discover what came next. Thomas suffered by comparison, and she did not like to let her mind wander to those considerations, because Thomas was in Maine and he was now locked inside his body and he had no chance to respond or to develop or to grow as he might have as a husband.

They came to a patch of traffic. Margaret didn't bother to try to see what was wrong or why things had slowed. Washington struck her as a confusing city; she had not understood where she was for most of the weekend and she didn't particularly care.

Charlie slipped the Jeep into neutral and leaned across and kissed her so hard it flattened her. She felt her blood ripen and she broke away and glanced around her, but no one noticed. She climbed across the seat, her hand scrambling at the seat belt, and she kissed him as passionately as she had ever kissed a human being. She adored each inch of him—his lips, the shape of his forehead, his proud, heavy hands that gripped and pulled her closer. She felt slightly mad, slightly out of control, and she imagined him kidnapping her, stealing away with her, taking her up through the forests of Maine and Canada, not stopping but traveling north, always north, until they found the end of the road.

She pulled back when he nudged the Jeep forward.

"Maybe," he whispered, "best lifetime kiss. Right here, right now. In a traffic jam in Washington, D.C."

"I feel as though we could do that whenever we want. You melt me."

"A gift from the gods on Mount Olympus."

"I'm serious," she said.

"We have it," he said, moving the Jeep close to the car in front of it and taking her hand again. "We have great potential, Margaret. That's all I've wanted to say. We've just spent one weekend together, but it feels longer, it feels more substantial. It's good fortune to meet someone that you like well enough to spend time with, and then to think about the whole big picture. . . ."

He had to switch lanes and they gained speed. Then he had to stop a little abruptly.

"Whatever happens," he said, "I'll remember you."

"Don't project forward," she said. "Please. That's a rule for the next couple days. I don't want to think about anything. I'm sealing my mind up. We're on an adventure, that's all. Nothing else matters right now."

He nodded. Then a lane in the traffic cleared and he accelerated into the opening, his hand returning to hers after each time he shifted.

"Larry said he has a few maps under your seat. Can you try to fish one out?"

She reached under and pulled out two atlases. They appeared the same to her. She checked the dates and slid the older one back under the seat. She loved maps. She spread the atlas on her lap.

"You're navigator," he said. "I think we want Route 66 and then it changes a bunch of times to different numbers."

"We're going to North Carolina?" she asked and started turning the pages.

"Virginia first. I guess the Blue Ridge Parkway is about eight hours away. Not that far. We'll figure it out."

It took Margaret a few minutes to familiarize herself with the maps. Wind came over the top of the Jeep, but the heater kept her feet and legs warm. The sun had already begun to slide into the earth. She squinted to see the connections on the map. The area around Washington was so congested it took her a moment to spot their destination in Asheville, North Carolina. At least it looked to be the proper destination. She ran her finger back and forth and finally found the Blue Ridge Parkway. It seemed to follow the ridge of the Smoky Mountains.

"Got it, I think," she said. "There's a points-of-interest box here and a bloom schedule."

"What are we going to see?"

"Catawba rhododendron . . . a purple variety that blooms from early June . . . rosebay rhododendron, a white or pink variety; flame azalea and pinxter flower and mountain laurel; redbud and trillium and tulip trees . . . oh, Charlie, it will be stunning."

"If we're not too early."

"No, we should be okay. It says it depends on elevation and microclimates. A feast for the eye, it says."

"My eyes aren't hungry," he said and squeezed her hand.

Was this really happening? she wondered. Was she traveling through a new part of the world with a man she cared about, with wind coming in and carrying the scent of spring, with nothing to do or care about except their mutual pleasure? A pang of guilt tried to slip into her thoughts, but she pressed it away, shook her head no, and concentrated on the map. She would be a good navigator, she decided. She would give herself to the trip. And when Charlie tapped her knee and pointed to the sky she looked up and saw they drove beneath a wedge of geese. She might not have seen them except for the darkening sky. They resembled black stitches zippered against the clouds. Their sound reached them only intermittently; once or twice she heard them calling when the traffic relented enough to permit sounds beyond the road. The geese flew north. Margaret tilted her head back and gazed up and felt such a moment of joy that she could not tell if she rode in the Jeep or traveled in the sky beside them.

In the silence of sunset, Margaret gazed out at the passing scenery, her mind floating and empty, time fading in and out like wind over grass. She felt Charlie's hand in hers, but he was quiet, too, his concentration on driving. They were on the right route now; she felt confident of that; she had done her job. The first wave of talking, of adrenaline and excitement at leaving, had passed. In its place she felt content and quiet, and thoughts, untethered by the changing countryside, by the foreign Jeep, even by Charlie, came and went, holding to no logic or continuity. For a moment, a round of blood through her veins, she was in the procession with Thomas, driving him from the airport to the hospital the first day he returned from Germany, Grandpa Ben beside her, the police running a flashing light to make way through the sparse Bangor traffic. Then the car became her parents' car, and they were on the way to Rangeley Lake, to the summer cottage they rented for a week each August, and in an instant her memory turned to images of Blake playing wing on the high school lacrosse team, dear Blake who was determined and strong, a tricky player, and they were young and cleated on fresh green grass, autumn stirring around them, both of them in mouthpieces, plaid skirts over running shorts. She watched Blake take a shot on goal, and then the goal no longer belonged to a lacrosse field, but was instead a span of netting over an acre of corn, and she walked through the rows on a transcendent evening, midsummer, full moon, fireflies, the rustle of corn husks like a procession of kings and queens coming down a long stairway, their gowns whispering. This was after Thomas had returned, she remembered, and she had stretched out on the soil, deciding once and for all that this was her land, too, her farm, and she had looked up at the sky boxed by the tasseled heads of corn, and she had vowed to keep the farm, to work until her hands grew stunted with arthritis, because Gordon belonged on the land. The stars had just begun to come out and she heard the cows lowing, and then she was in the middle of a lake, Rangeley Lake, on a small Boston Whaler, her dad driving, her mom trailing a hand through the water. It all mixed together, every life did, and she felt a sudden stab, a painful throb thinking of the sweetness of her boy, his soft sideburns, his T-shirts and his soldier men, the way he played on the front steps, arranging the soldiers and cowboys and space creatures, his lips moving with dialogue only he heard. Then Thomas's eyelids flickering, his hand twitching, and he walked toward her on a spring morning, a cup of coffee in his hand, a gash of motor oil across his right forearm, his smile broadening at the sight of her, of his wife, of his home. The wind that passed over the farm was the wind that came across the Jeep top now, and she suddenly felt she had no substance at all. She was a white sheet flapping on a line in summer sunlight, and the mail delivery car came by and opened the mailbox and dropped in the day's delivery, and she saw the vehicle drive off, then Blake was in it at a drive-in movie, a boy's arm around her in the front seat while she, Margaret, watched the light play out across her friend's cheek.

"You okay?" Charlie whispered.

She shook her head no. Then yes. She was not sure of the proper response. But she could not break the stream of images. She squeezed his hand. She snapped and flew in the wind above the Jeep, the white sheet, the summer day, the drizzle of a spring rain falling softly on the wide leaves of a waiting hosta.

It was a beautiful room. Margaret put her shopping bags down on the bed and turned and smiled at Charlie, who followed her in with their suitcases. Exquisite, really. It had been one of the inns suggested by Terry. The Ruggles, it was called, named after a bend in the river outside. It had been built in the 1800s, not long after the Civil War, and it had worn its age well. Margaret took in the features: a small beehive fireplace on the south wall; deep, comfortable-looking chairs; a wide, handsome bed, with what looked like a handmade coverlet; a floor-to-ceiling bank of windows overlooking the river. It was luxurious, Margaret decided, without being fussy or pretentious. A casual elegance. She felt welcomed and comfortable.

Charlie set down the suitcases. Margaret slipped past him and closed the door.

"Do you like it?" Charlie asked, turning to her.

"It's gorgeous! It's perfect."

"Well, we're lucky it's a little early in the season or it would be booked. And it's a Sunday night."

"It's so good to be here with you, Charlie."

"No regrets? No second-guessing?"

She smiled. She crossed to him and kissed his cheek.

"None whatsoever," she said.

"I think if we open these windows we'll hear the river," Charlie said and slipped his arms around her. "The fellow at the desk said they have good fishing here."

"Are you much of a fisherman, Charlie?"

"Fair. I had a friend growing up—Pete, he's my best friend—who fished the bass ponds around our area and I did some of that with him. I learned to fly-fish about a year ago at a weekend clinic type of thing up in Boston. I can cast all right, but a lot of it escapes me. But I guess there's no hurry. No fisherman like an old fisherman."

Charlie moved to the windows and cranked the right-hand one open. Immediately the sound of the river filled the room and the air became fresher. Margaret took a deep breath.

"Is that the Shenandoah?" Margaret asked.

"I think so. We'll be able to sort it out better in the daylight. Would you like a fire?"

"I'd love a fire."

"That's something I can do fairly well. I haven't told you I'm an Eagle Scout."

"Were you really?" Margaret asked and felt her heart melt a little.

"I was. I am. You don't think it's terribly dorky?"

"Not at all. You're the all-American boy."

"A little bit," he said and began working at the fireplace. "Corn-fed Iowa boy, West Point, the army . . . Maybe I ought to grow out my hair and get a Harley or something."

"Absolutely," Margaret said and began emptying the shopping bags onto the bed.

How natural it felt, Margaret realized, to have Charlie making a fire while she unpacked. It had been ages since she had spent time with a man other than Grandpa Ben and Gordon. She had forgotten what it was like to divide labor, to work in complementary ways, to feel the pleasure of teamwork. She stopped for a moment to watch Charlie making the fire. True to his word, he did it expertly: two fire dogs, a bit of paper, and then the fire started. He knelt beside it and waited, adding a few sticks. For a moment the flames appeared to move with his hands.

"Not really fair to use fatwood," he said, his eyes on the fire. "But they put it here, so we might as well make use of it."

"An Eagle Scout should rub two sticks together, shouldn't he?"

"You laugh, but I can do it. I have the badge to prove it."

She wanted a picture of him there, to stop time and lock it into her memory. The evening light fell softly into the room and she heard the river passing by, its course full-throated this early in spring. Dear Charlie. She observed the outline of his prosthetic; his trouser leg sagged around it. Firelight moved and caused his skin to change colors. She liked watching his patience with the fire. Some men seemed always in a rush, but Charlie moved with a measured confidence so that his presence reassured her.

"I'm very lucky to be here with you," she said softly, a pair of jeans half folded in her hands.

He looked over and smiled. Yes, just like that, she thought. Remember him. Remember him like this.

———

As he walked down the hallway from their room to the grill, Charlie felt happy and buoyant. He liked this place, the Ruggles Inn. The room was exactly right and the atmosphere inside the inn was relaxed and comfortable. Charlie admitted to himself that he liked inns and hotels. Always had. Heck, he even liked motels. Maybe it was the transient nature of such places, but he felt a genuine spring in his step, a sense of well-being as his shoes moved over the thick weave of carpet in the hallway. It was the cocktail hour. His parents had always talked about a cocktail hour and he had thought such an idea old-fashioned and somewhat quaint, but here he was anticipating a good drink and a good meal in a pleasant inn. Why not? Cocktails separated the day from the night, his dad always said. And now the day had given way and it felt good to be inside and looking forward to Margaret's company.

He found the grill by a combination of following his nose and making logical deductions about its likely location. When he pushed through the large, padded doors, he spotted the bar and headed toward it. You couldn't miss it. It was the good kind of bar, dark and hospitable, with heavy stools arranged beside it and a glistening rack of wineglasses above. The river ran outside in the ghost of the dying sunshine, its gray curl running quiet and muted in the faded twilight. A large, mullioned window cut the river into squares as it passed.

"Evening," the bartender said.

The bartender was a short, broad man, dressed in a black wool vest and a clean blue shirt. He had a monk's tonsure, a reddish rim of hair that reminded Charlie of a baseball diamond. His eyes had a merry cast; he seemed to find life humorous, which was probably a good trait in a bartender, Charlie decided.

"Evening," Charlie said and slid onto the bar stool closest to the window. "I'd like a beer, please . . . what do you have on tap?"

The bartender—Hans, Charlie saw by his name tag—went through a list of beers and Charlie stopped him on Bass.

"A pint of Bass then," Hans said.

"Please," Charlie said and looked around the grill.

Three couples sat at a table beside a large fieldstone fireplace. Otherwise, the place was empty.

"Early in the season?" Charlie asked when Hans slid his Bass in front of him.

"A little," Hans said. "A couple warm days and people will

come out of hibernation. It's supposed to be great weather this week."

"Any blooms?" Charlie asked.

"Some. Just starting in places," Hans said. "The warm weather will make them pop."

Charlie sipped his beer. It tasted great. He reached for a bowl of Goldfish and realized he was hungry. He ate a few Goldfish and turned to watch the river running by. The group at the table behind him laughed at someone's comment, and Hans cocked his hip against the bar and watched a baseball game with the volume off.

Margaret came in when Charlie had finished half his beer. She wore her new jeans and a navy sweater but she had changed her hair somehow and Charlie admired it. She was under-stated; that was what he loved about her appearance. She was like a brown paper package—not a great analogy, and not a flattering one, Charlie decided, but one he could build on—that he valued for its lack of ostentation. Her beauty did not depend on clothes or on jewelry, and Charlie stood and put his arm on her chair back to guide her into the place next to him.

"You're beautiful," he whispered and kissed her cheek.

"Hardly glamorous attire," she said, "jeans and a sweater."

"On you they work."

"Well, you're easily impressed, but thank you. Isn't this a pretty room?" she said and turned to see the fireplace and the window. "I like this inn."

"So do I," Charlie said and smiled at Hans, who came over to take their order.

"You're having a beer?" she asked.

"Guilty."

"I think I'd like a glass of wine or maybe a scotch. Would you think I'm a complete lush if I had a scotch?"

"On the rocks?" Hans asked.

"Yes, please. Dewar's if you have it."

"We do," Hans said and went to fix her drink.

"My father of all people taught me to drink scotch," she said. "It was his one small vice. He said it was like visiting a thoughtful friend as long as you didn't do it too often."

"Funny you should say that, because I was just thinking about the cocktail hour," Charlie said. "My parents called it the cocktail hour, but I'm not sure people call it that anymore."

"Shame to lose an important tradition," Margaret said and smiled.

"I'm enjoying this place," Charlie said. "The Ruggles Inn. It has a good feeling."

"It's really lovely, Charlie. I've told you before, but you're spoiling me. I'm a cowherd. A dairy woman."

"Is a shepherd only a shepherd if he herds sheep? Or can you be a shepherd if you drive cattle?"

"Either way I'd have to be a shepherdess, wouldn't I?"

"I suppose so."

Hans brought Margaret's scotch and set it before her.

"Cheers," Margaret said and lifted her glass.

"Something witty, witty, witty," Charlie said.

Margaret raised her eyebrow, questioning.

"Sorry," Charlie said. "Cheers. That was my brother's

little joke. Whenever you were supposed to observe a social nicety, he would simply say the thing instead. Like, if he went up to new people, he might say, 'Icebreaker, icebreaker, icebreaker.' Always three times."

"I like it," Margaret said.

"His favorite was 'Meaningful good-bye, meaningful good-bye, meaningful good-bye.' People thought he was a little crazy."

"Obviously this was before the accident at the quarry?"

Charlie nodded. He tapped her glass and took a drink. Margaret followed.

"Sounds like a fun guy," Margaret said. "We haven't talked much about him. All I know is that he was injured."

"He was a good guy. It sounds a little strange, but he was the most balanced person I ever met. He should have been a tightrope walker. You give him just about anything to do that involved balance and he could do it before anyone else. It was a little uncanny. Skateboards, bikes, even just walking on the railing of a fence . . . he was wizard at it."

"You say wizard?"

"I do," Charlie said and then decided he wanted to change subjects. "Are you hungry?"

"Getting there."

"We need to plan our day tomorrow."

"Let's do that tomorrow. Right now I just want to enjoy being with you."

"I'm glad."

"I called home. Everything's good there. Gordon was a

little cross with his grandfather about something or other, but no emergencies. Blake came over and peeked in on them. You think you can't step out of your life, but surprise, you can."

"Did Blake tell them we were having a wild, illicit getaway?"

"Yes, absolutely."

"Good."

Margaret turned slightly and slid her leg against his. She gave him a look, a look he had begun to recognize as *that* look. He smiled and dangled his leg against hers.

"How's your scotch?" he whispered.

"Whiskey, whiskey, whiskey," she answered.

He leaned across the short distance between them and kissed her lips.

—⁏⁊

In the eighth inning, the Red Sox rallied from behind to take the lead against the Orioles. Something in the satellite reception had gone fuzzy—a storm over the Midwest and sun flares nine million miles away had caused the transmission to turn slightly ghostly. It made no difference to Benjamin Kennedy, who slept in his La-Z-Boy in front of the television, his head tilted to one side, his feet, encased in saggy white socks, extended forward on the footrest. It was 9:32. In eight hours he would rise and slip back into his boots and walk out to the milking parlor and he would stand amid the pooling cattle, guiding them, hooking them to the suck machines, glancing out the door frame to check the weather. But for now he slept.

He slept in the same room where his father had slept before him, and his father before him, and once again, another father before that. His own son, Thomas, would not sleep in this room again, because his son now slept in a white bed suspended on a turn-wheel that the nurses could move to prevent bedsores. At this passing thought, Benjamin drew in a sharp breath, a strangled snore, and it scared the cat, Wink, who had gone to sleep on the rug beside the old chimney. The cat turned and saw the channel changer slide off Benjamin's lap, and for an instant the cat believed it was a mouse, or some other small creature, running down Benjamin's leg. The cat's pupils dilated sharply, and its body gathered, but then its vision clarified, and it tucked its chin against its white chest and returned to sleep, its ears cocked to the wall in case a mouse should enter there, deep in the lath work and horsehair that had clung to the wall since the moment the house had risen from the ground.

Chapter
Sixteen

At dessert, well after the dining room had filled, Marco showed up. He wore a black tuxedo with a frilly white shirt, and for a moment Charlie mistook him for a sommelier arriving to make a late wine suggestion. He stood in front of the table, a little chubby and frazzled, and then he shucked his cuffs back and made a cigarette appear in his fingers.

"Oh, perfect," Margaret said, laughing and clapping.

"I'm Marco," the man said in what may have been a fake Italian accent.

He made the cigarette disappear, then reappear in his other hand.

"So you're not a waiter?" Charlie asked, teasing him.

"I am the world's greatest magician," Marco said, deadpan. "Isn't it obvious?"

He made the cigarette disappear again. Then he drew a deck of cards out of his breast pocket.

"Can you shuffle?" he asked Margaret.

She took the cards and scrambled them together. Charlie watched. He enjoyed seeing her delight. Nothing threw her; nothing disappointed her. Clearly, she had needed a little break from her routine, and Charlie felt pleased and honored that he had a part in it. Now as she handed the cards back to Marco, he watched her gaze up at the magician, her eyes filled with light, her expression asking to be dazzled.

To be honest, Charlie hardly followed the trick. It was of the "pick a card, any card" variety, and though Marco carried it off with adequate aplomb, Charlie concentrated on watching the trick reflect in Margaret's pleasure. She laughed at Marco's jokes and took every request seriously. She did not try to hold back, or to trick Marco at his own game, but obliged him by taking his magic seriously. When Marco finally revealed her chosen cards, she bubbled up in a happy murmur, clapping and smiling. A glance at Marco let Charlie understand he seldom found a more appreciative audience.

"Anything after Marco is going to be a disappointment," Charlie said as Marco moved to the next table. "Talk about spoiling you."

"Wasn't he fabulous?"

"The greatest magician in the world, no less."

"I don't think we can prove that he wasn't, do you?"

"He is in my book."

"I'd love to sneak out and get a breath of air," Margaret said, her face still glowing with excitement. "Would you mind? It's so cold in Maine and it feels so wonderful here. I can't get enough of this spring air. Let me just run back to the room for my coat. I'll meet you in the lobby. Is that okay?"

Charlie held her chair back and she hurried off while he walked to the lobby. Someone had started a woodstove that was hooked into the backside of the grill chimney. The woodstove pushed a deep, soothing heat and Charlie stood with his back to it. He wondered again if they weren't too early for the spring buds. It could fluctuate, he imagined, but the plants required a certain level of light without which they would remain curled in their casings, waiting. He imagined someone could identify a metaphor in the annual blooms, but he hadn't the energy for the moment. He turned and faced the woodstove, then smiled when he saw Marco appear out of the dining room, obviously warm from performing. A line of sweat had bisected his temple.

"How did it go?" Charlie asked.

"Same old, same old," Marco said, stopping for a moment to stand by the stove. He appeared out of breath.

"Margaret loved your work," Charlie said. "It made her night."

"People either love magic or they don't. You'd be surprised how sharply divided people can be. I show up at some tables, and I'm a guest of honor. At other tables . . . you can tell they want me to bug off."

"How long have you been doing it?"

"Oh, years, really. Not here, but magic, most of my life. The management here thought it might liven the place up during the slow season."

"So what's your guess as to why some people like magic and some don't?"

Marco shrugged.

"You really want to know?" he asked and patted his forehead with a white handkerchief.

"Sure."

"People who don't like magic don't think life has any more surprises for them," he said. "They see everything as a con. Magic is simply theater and you have to let yourself go to enter it. So it's a good trait in your girlfriend that she likes it. At least that's what I think. That's what I've observed, anyway."

"Sounds right to me."

"You down here for the rhododendron?"

"That's part of it."

"A little early, I'm afraid. But you never know. Magic, right?"

Marco left and a moment later Margaret appeared. She handed Charlie a sweater and stood beside him while he slipped it over his head. When he had the sweater on, she reached across and straightened it a little at the back. It was such an intimate thing to do, such a wifely thing to do, that Charlie couldn't help smiling.

"Marco says people who like magic still have the capacity to be surprised," Charlie said as he held the door for her. "He says it's a good trait that you like magic."

"If Marco says it, then it must be true."

"I think I'm getting jealous of Marco."

She took his arm and pressed her body against his. The air, Charlie admitted, felt wonderful. The river made a deep, restful hum as it passed. Somewhere above the inn Charlie heard the rapids that gave the place its name.

"Thank you for dinner," Margaret said. "It was delicious."

"Was it all right?"

"It was great, Charlie. I could have eaten anything, I was so hungry, but it was well prepared. And the wine was excellent. You're turning me into a lush. I don't usually drink this much. There's no real occasion except with Blake."

"We're on vacation, so vacation rules apply."

"Is that what Marco says?"

He nodded. She leaned toward him and kissed a spot beneath his ear. They continued to walk. The night felt chilly, but occasionally Charlie felt a fold of warmer air that moderated things. Now and then through the trees a cat's paw moon raked the branches.

"I had one of those moments as I was getting my jacket that made me stop," Margaret said. "I realized that for plenty of women it's not so completely out of the realm of possibility to visit a nice country inn with a man she cares about. Do you know what I mean? This has been an extraordinary couple of days, but it makes me realize I have set the bar pretty low for myself. I've been asleep, a little. Or maybe numb. You're waking me up and I'm a little worried about that."

"Numb?"

"Well, not to Gordon. Not to my responsibilities. But to my own journey, as Blake would say. She's big on the journey thing. I guess I've grown a little bit of a shell. It's safe and dry in the shell, but it's also a little dull."

"Did you ever consider dating anyone at all?"

She shook her head.

"Not that kind of gal," she said, "although I've often wondered if it would be easier if I were."

"Marco would say you've been waiting for me."

"Oh, really?" she said and bumped her shoulder into his. "Is that what you think?"

"That's what I know."

"You think we were destined to meet?"

"Star-crossed lovers, no doubt."

They arrived at a small turnout with a view of the rapids. Charlie steered her to a bench and sat beside her. He tasted moisture in the air from what he guessed must be the Ruggles. An old willow, bent and misshapen, leaned over the river and dangled a few of its tendrils into the water. Margaret moved closer.

"So what's Blake going to say about all this?" Charlie asked.

"Oh, she'll be crazy to hear all the details. She'll want to know about you, though I've already told her some of it. Her marriage . . . I think I mentioned . . . is not going great at the moment. Her husband is gone a lot, trying to build his business, and Blake is left holding the bag pretty often. Donny's a good guy, but he seems a little surprised to find himself married with a child. I don't know. Then Blake puts pressure on him and that only chases him away more and more. It's complicated, but that's why she'll want to hear about you so much. You are a delicious little story that doesn't come along every day. A nice distraction."

"So that's what I am? A distraction, huh?"

"You are a glorious distraction," she said and held his arm. "What is it about men and women that makes it so difficult? A lot of my friends are struggling in their marriages. All this yearning we do, men and women. We all hope for something to be dramatic, but it usually isn't, is it?"

"There's that old poem when the narrator says he isn't Hamlet. He's just a small actor to swell a scene. I think that's the line. We act like we're center stage, but really we aren't."

"Do you know a lot about poems, Charlie?"

"Actually, no. I have a good memory, though, and I retain things. I know movie lines, too. My mother always said I had flypaper between my ears."

"One of the things you've made me remember is that it can be easy between a man and woman. It doesn't have to be wrapped in a hundred things. I know we don't have all the usual concerns on a trip like this, but still it feels natural and simple."

"How about for you and Thomas?"

"You mean before everything? I don't know what to think about him right now. It's a little like a movie star dying young, you know? We remember them for what they were. It's hard to imagine him around today, being a husband, a father, all of that. Maybe we would have grown in different directions. You never know. But we felt solid at the time. That's one of the things I see in Blake's situation. She's a good person and so is Donny, but they have this battlefield over the house and work and who does what and who should be doing more. I think they have their heads down and don't see each other clearly anymore. Maybe I'll try to say that to her when I get home."

"Will she listen?"

"Blake is very open. Donny, not so much. They're like Chevy Chase in the *Vacation* movie when they're driving past everything without slowing down to look. The good stuff is on the pull-outs and the side roads. But they keep thinking they have to get someplace and you want to remind them there isn't anyplace to go. They're there already."

"How did you get so smart?" Charlie asked.

"Oh, I'm far from smart. Maybe the cows slow me down, that's all. It sounds funny, but I'm grateful to them. You can't rush a cow."

"That should be a bumper sticker."

She slid her hands up under his sweater for warmth. He leaned down and kissed her cheek. She squeezed tighter against him.

"You make me want to talk," she said. "Sorry if I'm going on. I spend all my time talking to Gordon and Grandpa Ben, so I don't use these particular muscles very often."

"Not at all. I like hearing your thoughts."

"What about you, though? Why aren't you married, Charlie? That's what I can't understand. Women must have tried to snatch you up."

"A few have, maybe. But then I was in the service and I was injured and all of that took time. And at West Point, well, that's just a crazy place. I feel like I'm ready now. Or getting ready. And now Marco made you appear, presto chango."

"I sure appeared, all right."

"I'm glad you did."

A wind came down the river and made the willow move. Charlie felt her shiver next to him. He used his arm to tuck her closer.

"Ready to go back?" he asked, his lips against her hair.

"To our beautiful room overlooking a beautiful river?"

"Yes, that room."

"And will the Eagle Scout make another fire?"

"The Eagle Scout is yours to command."

"Okay, three quick breaths," she said and pushed away from him for a second. She stood and took a deep breath. She let the air out slowly.

"Spring, spring, spring," she said.

—⟨⟩

She listened to the river late at night, her ear against Charlie's chest, her skin on his skin. She slept in little fits and starts, but she didn't mind. She liked being awake, because she didn't want this day, these few days, to end quickly. The fireplace had died down and the last coals burned with a red glow. Occasionally she smelled smoke, and it reminded her of bonfires outside, burning off the spring clippings around the dairy barn, brush piles pushing green smoke into the May air.

She sent her thoughts to Gordon, wishing him gentle sleep; she thought of her husband, Thomas, and her eyes moved a little beneath their lids. *Forgive me,* she thought, but that was wrong, that was incorrect. She had left with Charlie deliberately. It had been a choice. And if it was a sin, as the old priests would have told her in childhood, then she accepted it. But she did not believe it was a sin. Charlie was a joy. He was a welcome, kind spirit who had crossed his life with hers. She vowed not to regret a moment of her time with him.

A little later in the night she woke to find herself worried. The fire had gone out and the room had become chilly. She reached for his hand and he settled around her, spooning her, his heat perfect and comforting. The world tried to push in: details about the cows, the decision to spray biosolids on the apple orchard, Blake and her marriage, a health plan change-over for Thomas, the ongoing but stalled renovations on the second farmhouse, but she resisted such thinking. *Not now,* she thought. She pushed back into Charlie's arms and he tightened his body around her, and she admitted she liked feeling a man beside her in the small hours. Yes, it was a fact. It was a luxury. And as she settled into him she heard his breathing change and then his lips touched her ear.

"I'm here," he said, apparently sensing her restlessness.

She took his arm and tightened it around her. Maybe light began to appear in the east, a mere glimmer, but she felt her body give way. And she took his heat and kept his arm over her chest, and for a while she slept as she hadn't slept in years, deep and full, the wind calling her to come outside, to fly with it, to see the morning sun chase its reflection across the river.

Chapter
Seventeen

Margaret turned her face to get the early morning sun directly on it. The air felt luscious. It was still early; the inn provided a buffet breakfast. Charlie had already said he would fish only a half hour or so, just to try his luck. Margaret felt hungry and content and part of her wanted to sit like a tortoise in the sun and think about nothing. But Blake needed her and she straightened a little on the boulder, making herself concentrate on her friend's situation. It was not a story she hadn't heard before, but perhaps Blake's voice sounded more fatigued and dispirited than in any previous recounting.

"Did you talk to Donny this morning?" Margaret asked.

"No, he was out of here before it was even light. He works hard, I'll always give him that. He might get a new contract doing the government offices in Bangor . . . the grounds, the arbor work. He's put a bid in and he feels like he has a good shot at it. We'll see."

"I'm sorry it's going that way, Blake."

"You make your own bed, I suppose. It's weird, but hearing you talk about getting away from here, I keep thinking if Donny and I could go somewhere and reconnect a little it would help. Just spend time as a man and woman instead of a husband and wife and parents . . . you know what I mean."

"I'll watch Phillip anytime you say."

"I know you would. What's your soldier boy doing now?"

"Still casting. He hasn't caught anything."

"You're crazy about him, aren't you?"

"Yes. To my toes."

"Be careful, sweetie. I know I've said that, but it bears repeating."

"I'm being as careful as I can be. But it's not easy."

"I should run. I'll swing by this evening and check on your boys. What's Gordon think of this whole thing?"

"He doesn't really know what's going on, but he's good about it. I think it lodges somewhere in his head in the 'for Dad' category, but what that means the Lord only knows."

Margaret hung up a moment later. A small wave of worry started in the pit of her stomach, but she pushed it down. *Not now,* she told herself again. Not while there is sun and a sparkling river and a man you are crazy about fishing and enjoying himself fifty yards away. Not when he is going to come back and you are going to have a good breakfast, and maybe you will see spectacular blossoms and you will travel on the Blue Ridge Parkway and take in the delicious air. *Not now.*

Charlie fished a hare's ear nymph through the tailwater at the base of the Ruggles Rapid. He was not very good at this, he decided, and he felt slightly pretentious in his waders and fly jacket, waving a fly rod at innocent fish. But he liked being out; he liked standing in water, studying the currents, deciding how to replicate whatever happened naturally on the river. A hare's ear, he knew, was as close to a universal fly as an angler could choose. He let it plunk in the white water above him, then chatter down gracefully into the swirls and eddies of the deeper pools below.

His leg hurt. Through the months of rehabilitation, that had been the most singular thing about his injury. His foot and ankle and a portion of his shin had disappeared, shredded to strings of confetti by the blast, and yet he still felt pain in the missing area. Phantom limb syndrome, he comprehended, but no matter how he worked his mind around it the concept refused to make sense to him. It should have been the single advantage of losing a limb, the lack of pain, but instead it had become a troublesome annoyance, one that bothered him as much for its irrational underpinnings as it did for the actual sensation. It had something to do with the mind-nerve transfer, he had read, and doctors currently experimented with mirrors: it seemed if a patient could visualize the missing limb, see its absence reflected through the eye to the brain, then the brain would begin to let the limb recede and disappear. That was the coming thing.

It was all too confusing, Charlie decided. He did not want to think about it now, although his missing foot, remarkably, felt cold with the river water. He deliberately waded a few steps downstream, careful to keep his balance, and he turned to Margaret for a moment and called to her softly across the water.

"Getting hungry?" he asked.

"Famished."

"I won't be long. They don't seem to be biting."

"You look like you know what you're doing, Charlie."

"Looks can be deceiving."

"How's the water?"

"Cold."

"It's wonderful in the sun here."

"How do I know you're not a mermaid?"

"No tail."

He felt a small quiver on the end of his line.

"I may have just had a hit," he said, turning back to the water. He cast again, trying to place the fly in the same patter of water where he had experienced the quiver.

"A fish?"

"Maybe. It's hard to tell. It might have just been a little snag on the bottom, or a twig. . . ."

But then he raised his rod tip and he saw a fish fly up and out of the water. He tightened the line with his right hand and kept a steady pressure on the fish. It was not big. He knew that from the weight in his hands and the bend in the rod. He backed a little out of the stream and led the fish toward him, playing the fish quickly so that he wouldn't tire or injure it. The fish pulled and ran, darting back to the faster water, but Charlie checked it and moved it back. When it was within reach, he bent down and removed the hook easily. The fish hovered for a moment, stunned, then drifted away with the current.

"Did you have one, Charlie? I wanted to see!"

"It was a little brookie."

"You're my hero," she called, her voice teasing.

"You're easily impressed," he said, smiling.

He turned and began winding in the line. He was not paying attention to his footing, and he felt his balance shift, his foot slip on something on the riverbed. He lunged sideways, feeling drunken, and he tried to catch himself. He succeeded partially, but he knew he was going down, and he lowered himself onto his knee rather than take the full fall. Water rushed in over the top of his waders and he jerked himself back onto his feet, annoyed and embarrassed. He nearly lost the fly rod when he opened his arms and tried to regain his balance. He knew he looked clumsy because he felt clumsy.

"Damn it," he said as he finally got his stance squared on the bottom.

"Are you okay?"

"I think the fish is taking revenge. But I'm okay. I got some water down my waders."

He saw her stand and come to the edge of the river, her face concerned. He couldn't help it; he felt annoyed with his leg, with the stupid awkwardness it spread to his body at inopportune times. He felt like Caliban from *The Tempest*, a humpbacked, misshapen child of the devil, a hoofed creature stumping through life with a loss of grace. He did not give in to such feelings often, but he felt it rise in him now and he despised seeing concern on her face. He would rather see anything else, he thought, but pity.

"Are you cold?" Margaret asked. "You must be freezing."

"A little. I've got a bunch of water in my waders."

"I thought you were going under."

"So did I, frankly," he said and felt himself gain the shallows.

He turned the fly rod around and held it out for her to take. Then he slipped the waders' suspenders off his shoulders and pulled down the bib. Water rose up and spilled out, dripping down into the stream. His shirt and trousers were wet.

"I told you I wasn't much of a fisherman," he said.

"You caught one. That's not bad."

"Are you always this nice, Margaret?" he asked, and he felt a small snake of his own frustration loaded onto the question. Why was he taking out his clumsiness on her? But he still felt annoyed at his leg's betrayal, at his own feebleness. He climbed out of the water and deliberately took his time fixing his waders, getting the water out. He felt flushed and cold and his blood was stirred.

She stood to one side with the fly rod.

"I'm sorry. I was just frustrated with my leg," he said when he finished stripping off his waders. "I have a little temper from time to time. The leg . . ."

"Okay."

"You've done nothing wrong. Not a thing. It was all on me."

"I get it."

"Irked. I was irked," he said, trying to bend the silly word into a joke.

She stood on her toes and kissed him. She smelled like soap and lotion. He swung his arm down around the small of her back and pulled her to him. Her sweater gave off heat collected from the sun. He kissed her again, and he knew that he wanted her. He wanted her now, and he wanted her in the days to come, and he wanted her a dozen years from this moment. He wanted to tell her that, but it was better to kiss her, better to feel the sun in her hair, to smell the warmth of her sweater and feel her soft body beneath it.

Blake carried the wicker basket toward Donny's truck, the sun warm for so early in spring. She felt self-conscious. She had dressed with particular care and had packed a turkey club and salt & vinegar chips and a huge dill pickle from Diebler's Deli—Donny's favorite restaurant, probably his favorite meal—but she felt herself losing confidence in her idea with each step she took. She doubted, frankly, that he would see the visit for what she intended it to be: a reminder that they were married, that they had been in love, that they did not have to give up. She had even put on special underwear in case, she didn't know, in case they could sneak away in his truck, do something wild and different, be a little naughty. There had been a time, she remembered, when he could not get enough of her, when he had made a thousand excuses to get her alone, in the dark, in a secluded parking spot. But now it had been a long time—she did not want to attach a number to the interval, did not want to be that specific—since they had made love.

When she reached the truck, a diesel F-250, big enough for a plow, she put the sandwich basket on the lowered tailgate and took a breath. The truck smelled of Donny, she realized: lubricating oil and grass clippings and soil. It was a familiar smell, not a bad one at all, and she put her hand to her eyes for shade while she scanned the grounds of the state DMV office. She saw Donny and Little Jim shoveling cedar mulch onto a row of hedges near the front door of the DMV building. The mulch looked orange and artificial, but it was probably all right for a government building. She watched as Donny upended a wheel-barrow full of mulch; Little Jim forked it out with the edge of his shovel. They worked well in unison, Blake knew, and did twice the work of the other crew Donny had in his business.

Little Jim spotted her first. He was big and strong, a man who looked like a cartoon version of a Native American, frankly, whose broad cheekbones and impenetrable silence never failed to unsettle her. She watched as he said something to Donny, then she saw Donny's head swivel. Donny seemed to take a moment to put the elements together: wife, work, what was she doing here? Then he tossed the shovel to one side and she worried that he had jumped to the conclusion that Phillip was in some kind of danger.

"Everything okay?" was the first thing he said.

"Hi, Donny," she answered, trying to be soft. Trying to be feminine and warm. "I just wanted to see you is all. Nothing's wrong."

He stopped when she said that. She saw the wheels spinning, his brow furrowed in distrust. And why shouldn't he distrust her? she wondered. She never visited him at his jobs, never brought him a turkey sandwich, much less wore special underwear for him. She tried to chase those thoughts from her head and turned slightly so he could see the wicker basket. He didn't advance and he didn't seem to tie the facts together.

"I brought you a sandwich from the deli," she said, "and some chips and a pickle."

"I ate already," he said.

"Oh, so early?"

"I get hungry," he said, his voice slightly defiant.

"I meant, I'm sorry. I would have gotten here earlier if I knew."

"What's going on, Blake?"

"Nothing, Donny. We've just been missing each other. You know. I'm not your enemy, I mean. I just . . ."

She felt her eyes get damp and she turned to the basket and picked it up. How stupid had she been? How idiotic could one woman be? *Abracadabra* and everything was supposed to be okay on the strength of a deli sandwich?

"Sorry," she said.

"Hold on, Blake," he said. "Just wait a second."

But she kept going. Maybe she should have stopped, she couldn't tell, but she knew one thing: he didn't follow her.

She watched through the windshield as Donny went back to work beside Little Jim. She saw him raking the mulch into an even bed. Somewhere, she decided, somewhere down inside him was her husband, but she could not see him, could not even know if he was still alive.

Chapter
Eighteen

It was the old dream. Charlie sensed it coming and he tried to wake, his eyes moving quickly, frantically beneath his slammed lids, but the dream did not permit it. The dream did not allow it and never would. He felt himself falling through a rabbit hole of memory, and part of it made sense, and part of it was cobweb and dream. He lay in the sun on an old blanket, Margaret beside him, asleep, but none of that made a difference. It never made a difference when the dream visited, because in the dream the addled logic of his foot—his limb was there for a moment, then gone, then returned, then turned into a hoof and a forked spatula like a dinosaur's three-fingered claw—defied explanation. Mostly the dream approached with heat. It had been an exceedingly hot day, he remembered, he dreamed, and the heat had been white light, had fallen on everything, casting diamonds even from the corner frame of the Humvee. Every piece of metal or glass or bucket of water caught the sun and juggled it, tossing it upward and letting it fall again, and Charlie recalled seeing a chicken sitting in the shade of a mud wall, its beak open, its tongue a tag of pink between the yellow beak halves. The chicken held its wings out to let air find its breasts and it appeared to Charlie, in the dream, in reality, that the chicken had decided it could not fly. The chicken struck him as hesitant, as if all the heat of the day had collected in its black feathers, and Charlie turned to say something to the Humvee driver, Erich, but when he opened his mouth only feathers came out. Just feathers, black and coiled, and the feathers turned into lightning bugs, blinking summer bugs on a quiet Iowa evening, and he suddenly found himself looking past Erich to the cornfield behind his childhood home and he smiled and felt great warmth and kindness and welcome.

He always saw it before he saw the boy.

Because when he turned his head back, he saw the boy for the first time. It was all that sickening slow motion, that terrible swivel of the head, then he watched as the boy came through the crowd. Why did he see him? Why was he so easy to pick out now, though he had snuck into the roadside crowd without a worry? A boy on the edge of puberty. A boy with a soft, fuzzy beard, a goat in his arms. He had seen the boy's eyes and the goat's eyes at the same time: the goat had been alive, wiggling in the boy's arms, and Charlie had felt a moment's pleasure at that domestic detail. A boy carrying a goat. It was the kind of thing that registered, remained in your memory long after all the horrible details of war and occupation dissipated. He turned to tell Erich about the boy, a detail, a point of conversation, nothing else, when he heard the eruption form underneath the Humvee. The dirt road had not erupted; it had been the cornfield, after all, the backyard of his childhood home, and he watched as the boy and the goat went sideways. He observed dispassionately as the pair of living creatures vaporized, became sand, their life force swept away as easily as one might clear crumbs from a counter. *Here today, gone tamale,* he thought. It was an old joke, one told by Bugs Bunny, he thought, a play on the Mexican dish. *Here today, gone tamale.* Because the boy and the goat had disappeared, had become wall and roof and road, had vanished in gouts of blood and gristle.

Here today, gone tamale.

That was what Charlie dreamed.

And when it came time to lose his own foot, his own injury, it took place in the cornfield. He walked toward his home, his parents turning on lights to welcome him, black crows rising from the sleeping heads of tasseled corn. *Home,* he thought. It had been something different in reality, but in his dream he lost his foot on a clod of dirt. He stepped on it, as he had stepped on a million dirt clods in his childhood, and an enormous gopher, a comic gopher, had suddenly popped up through the soil. He had stepped on the gopher's head, it appeared, and the gopher turned, annoyed, and Charlie's foot dangled from the rodent's mouth. Gophers did not eat feet; they were vegetarians as far as Charlie knew, but in dreams anything could happen. Charlie had tilted sideways, the gopher coming out of the hole toward him, growing as it approached, and the foot disappeared down the wobbly gullet of the animal. He wanted more. Charlie saw the gopher's rapacious gaze, his hunger, and as he fell Charlie kicked at the animal and his foot had been replaced by a bird's foot, a dinosaur's toes, and the gopher tore at those appendages, too. The corn husks fell around them, and Charlie's vision went into the sky so that he could see a black-backed animal climbing over him, watch as the corn husks moved and swayed like a miniature forest. Then he saw the boy, the boy with the goat, and he watched as the boy scattered again, became flying blood, and the dream ended there, ended with him rising and sitting up, his panic pushing like splinters into an ungloved hand.

"Charlie?" Margaret whispered, her body next to his. "Charlie, wake up. Charlie, you're dreaming."

He mumbled. His face contorted and twisted as if flinching from something horrible.

"Charlie, it's okay."

He woke suddenly. Margaret watched him become conscious and she felt something dark and shadowy had slipped away. She felt cold; it was afternoon and the sun had put its bottom edge on the mountaintops as if testing water with a toe. Charlie put a hand on his eyes. She wondered for a moment if she saw tears on his cheeks. She kissed his cheeks. She kissed him over and over until he moved his hand down and pulled her to him.

"What is it?" she asked. "Where do you go, Charlie?"

"My foot . . . ," he said.

"In the dream?" she asked, still kissing him.

He nodded.

What was worth saying in those moments? She didn't try to say anything, but put her body closer, held him, and kissed him. In time she felt him return. She didn't understand how she knew he had returned, but she felt certain of it. The slithery dream fell away. She looked around. They lay on a blanket in a small hollow near a stream. The trees above them had tentative green leaves. The sound of the stream filled everything. Depending on the wind, she felt the coolness from the water seep close to them.

"Is it something you have a lot?" she whispered.

"Not really. It comes for a while, then it leaves."

"Is it the same dream?"

He nodded.

"Can I do anything?"

He pulled her closer.

"You're doing it," he said.

"I hate the war. The wars," she said. "I hate what they do to people. They kill people, but it might even be worse for the people who don't die."

"I'm okay."

"I know you are."

"The dream . . . it's not even accurate. I mean, it doesn't even follow the events. It collapses things and makes them wild and strange. I can't even make sense of it, really. It's more about sensation."

"If it were rational you might be able to think it through and disarm it."

He nodded.

"If I had a magic wand, Charlie, I would make it go away."

"I know you would."

"The sun's going down."

"Are you cold?"

"A little."

He sat up. Margaret ran her fingers through her hair. She couldn't guess what she looked like. Probably sleep marks on her face, leaves in her hair. But it didn't matter.

"Want to go skinny-dipping?" Charlie asked, teasing.

He smiled. Yes, he was back. He stood and extended his hand and pulled her to her feet.

"We're a pair of Rip Van Winkles," he said.

"How long did we sleep?"

"Gosh, I don't know. It must be around six. We need to get to the next town, wherever that is. Are you hungry?"

"Starving. I'm always hungry around you. And sleepy. I think maybe I'm relaxed."

He put his arms around her. She leaned into him and put her forehead against his shoulder.

"You don't have to worry about the dreams," he whispered. "I'm okay, honestly. They come on their own and I usually have them in succession, then they go away. I don't know why. Maybe anxiety, maybe a change of venue. I've talked with a counselor. I've gone all through it. It's pretty normal for someone with my type of injury to dream about it."

She nodded.

"You know," he said, his voice lighter, his arms moving

her back while he bent to grab the blanket, "we better get moving. We're at elevation. It could get pretty cold."

"I need to call Gordon. I meant to call him after school, but we slept. . . ."

"We must have needed it."

"You're turning me into a hedonist."

She went to the stream and splashed water on her face. The water felt icy and bright. She splashed it on her face until her skin felt tight and chilled. Charlie squatted beside her and performed the same washup. A bright blue bird hopped in the branches across the stream. It was a bluebird, Margaret realized with something like wonder. She had never seen a bluebird, but this one was unmistakable.

"That's a bluebird, isn't it, Charlie?" she whispered, pointing her chin across the stream.

"Yes. It has to be."

"I've never seen one."

"I've seen a few. But that one is brilliant."

"It doesn't seem possible. I can't believe that's what they look like. So blue."

"They're making a comeback. Up where you live, you probably don't get many. That's likely to be the edge of their range."

Margaret watched the bird hop from branch to branch. It appeared to be the size of a robin. No, smaller, she corrected. The last of the sun found it in small pulses, bringing the blue color out in tiny flashes. It had black eyes and a sharp beak. As she watched, it dropped down into the leaf litter and pushed things around, looking for insects.

"Isn't it some kind of omen . . . a bluebird?" she asked.

"The bluebird of happiness."

"I can't believe there's a bird that color. It's bluer than a jay, even."

"Probably nesting. They like nests near the edge of a meadow. They're active at sunset."

Then it flew off. Just like that. Its wings made a beating sound and it disappeared into the forest, its brightness improbable and visible long after the sound of its wings had evaporated.

—☙

Gordon pushed back into the couch cushion, lifting the saw-chuck guy up with his left hand while his right hand guided the meerkat forward. The saw-chuck guy fired a dozen shots at the meerkat, hitting him each time, but the meerkat absorbed the shots and showed no indication of pain. Then the saw-chuck guy didn't move fast enough and the meerkat squashed him with one large, furry paw. The saw-chuck guy screamed a long, painful scream, but he didn't die. The saw-chuck guy never died, that was a fact, and when the meerkat moved forward, stumbling a little at a jujitsu move from the saw-chuck guy, the tiny soldier sprang up and delivered a karate chop to the meerkat's neck. *Ayyyyyy,* the soldier said, but whether he said it aloud or only in Gordon's head, the boy couldn't tell.

The phone rang. Gordon listened to Grandpa Ben pick it up in the kitchen. Gordon knew it was his mother, but he didn't really want to talk to her. He felt shy and quiet and he preferred to march the meerkat forward into combat with the saw-chuck guy.

At the same time, he thought about Charlie. He had been thinking about Charlie a lot since the day he had come and taken his mother away. The boy did not know what to make of the man. For one thing, he couldn't tell if the man was a soldier, like his dad, or a regular guy. His grandfather was a regular guy, and so was Mr. Raymond, the school principal, because neither of them had ever been in army clothes. But one of the teachers at school, Mrs. Mudge, had been an army guy, but she was a girl and that didn't make sense.

The other thing Gordon wondered about was Charlie's leg.

It didn't look like a leg, he recalled. It had had a strange shoe on it at the bottom, and his pants flapped around too much. Nothing in his experience gave him anything to go on in trying to understand the leg. He wondered if he could ask Charlie about it, but his mother had told him many times that too many questions were rude. But, he thought, if he had the right moment he might ask Charlie about the leg, and what was under the pant leg, and why when he walked he looked like a zombie man on one side.

"Gordon, it's your mom," Grandpa Ben called from the kitchen.

Gordon kept marching the meerkat at the saw-chuck guy, ignoring his grandpa.

"Gordon?" Grandpa Ben said and came into the TV room. He wore a towel over his shoulder and his hands looked wet when he held the phone forward. "It's your mom."

Gordon accepted the phone, put it to his ear, but did not say anything. It was silent on the other end, too, then he heard his mother say something. Probably to Charlie. Gordon made the saw-chuck guy deliver another kick to the meerkat's pointed snout. The meerkat fell back in slow motion.

"Are you there, sweetie? Gordon?" came his mother's voice.

"Mom?"

"So you are there. I couldn't tell. How are you? You doing okay?"

"Yeah."

"What have you been doing? Have you and Grandpa Ben been having fun?"

Gordon nodded. He had the saw-chuck guy on top of the meerkat now, grinding him down. Gordon's jaw muscles worked in tandem with the saw-chuck guy's boots.

"Gordon?" his mother said. "Gordon, when I ask you something, I need you to respond."

"Okay."

"School was okay? Did Blake pick you up?"

Gordon nodded, then realized he needed to speak.

"Yes."

"That's good, honey. I'll be home day after tomorrow. That means not tomorrow, but the next day, okay?"

"Yes."

"I love you and miss you, sweetie. You're being a good boy, right?"

Gordon nodded but didn't speak.

"Okay, I'm going to hang up now. I told Grandpa Ben that I wouldn't talk to him again, so you can just push the button when we finish, okay? Like I've shown you?"

"Okay."

"I'm sending lots of love to you. Charlie says hi, too."

"Does he have a robot foot?" Gordon asked in the last silence before hanging up.

"No, sweetie," his mom said. "Why don't we talk about that when I get home? We'll have lots to talk about, I promise."

Gordon nodded. His mother said good-bye again and hung up. Gordon let the phone drop on the couch, then realized the size and shape of it made it a perfect bomb. He picked it up and launched it at the meerkat, the bomb exploding just as the meerkat started to run away. The force of the explosion shot the meerkat into the air, somersaulting, and Gordon made the poor animal fall in slow motion, the impact of his landing a puff in the boy's round cheeks.

Chapter
Nineteen

Motel sex. That was all Margaret could think about, and it astonished her that she didn't care. It felt good and exciting and a little illicit. She liked the sound of the cars outside the window, the flimsy walls, the temporary quality of every aspect of the place. She couldn't even remember the building's name. If she called the police at that moment and had to tell them where to come to save her, she couldn't have done it. The entire building was dedicated to quick exchanges, to namelessness, to a tiny interruption in a day's travel. Under other circumstances she might have felt less drawn in by it, but Charlie made it right.

She wanted him. In the last tiny bit of failing light they made love on the king-size bed, more directly now, more hungrily, and she found herself responding to everything in a fierce, eager fashion. Sex had been good before, it had, she told herself, but now something had changed. She realized that time had changed her; she had not been with a man in a half decade, and the slightly nervous, shy girl of her early marriage was a woman now. A motel woman, she amended, and she liked thinking that, liked the way Charlie moved with her, orchestrated their lovemaking. This was a land she didn't get to visit any longer, and she found she could not deny herself any pleasure. Where before she might have been too timid, worried that a demonstration of deliberate passion was defeminizing, now she answered specifically to her body. It was all good. Everything was good and she liked the way the last daylight caught the edge of the bed, the way the bathroom door moved ever so slightly to a wind she could not even sense, the way the nubbled ceiling reminded her of sand, or clouds, beyond Charlie's back.

She kissed him. The kiss burned through her body.

When they finished, she did not allow their bodies to separate. She climbed on him and fit her body exactly to his and she let his breath become her breath. He took her hands and held them out to the sides so that every inch was every inch of them both. For a long time neither spoke.

"I'm falling in love with you," he whispered. "You know that, right?"

She nodded.

"Okay," he said.

She kissed his neck. She kissed him over and over, moving across his shoulders, his throat, his lips. Afterward she stayed directly on top of him, skin to skin. She felt sleep closing in, but she didn't want to sleep. She inched up on him so she could whisper into his ear.

"Charlie," she said.

"Yes."

"I'm not saying thank you. I don't mean it like that. But thank you. Thank you for coming and taking me away. At least for now, at least so far. Thank you."

He nodded.

"I'm in love with you, Charlie, but I don't want to say it yet. Not freely and easily. It's too much. I won't be able to come back if I say it too much. Do you understand?"

He nodded.

"I have to come back," she whispered. "I do. Don't make me go too far away."

"I understand."

"This has meant so much to me."

"I'm glad. It has to me, too."

"And our bodies," she said.

"I know."

He kissed her. She put her ear to his chest and listened to his heart beating. For a moment a drip from the bathroom sink echoed on the beat, but in time it separated and the two sounds broke apart. She listened for a while until her stomach gave an enormous growl. It was incredibly loud and she rolled off him and started laughing.

"Did I just hear someone say pizza?" Charlie asked.

"Yes," Margaret said, scrambling out of bed, her voice light and happy, "that's exactly what you heard."

Ben ran hot water over his left hand in the kitchen sink until his fingers slowly began to move again. They froze up from time to time; they went on vacation, he thought when it happened, and refused to return until the hot water soaked down into the bones. He slowly closed his hand, opened it, repeated the action until his hand closed somewhat normally. Afterward he put both hands under the stream and began washing the day's dirt from his skin.

It was suppertime. He smelled the casserole—tuna casserole, one of the ones Margaret had left for them—warming in the oven. He heard Gordon in the television room, listening to a show that starred a character with a high, squeaky voice speaking rapidly. Ben leaned back a little, his hands still under the water flow, and checked to make sure the boy didn't sit too close to the screen. He wondered, absently, if that was a matter of concern; sitting close to the screen was not supposed to be good for you, but honestly he didn't know what harm it could do.

"Gordon," he called, "you come and clean up now. Dinner's almost ready."

The boy didn't answer. Ben hadn't really expected him to answer, but you had to throw a line to catch a fish. He finished with his hands and dried them on a paper towel. He checked the dinner table to make sure it was properly set. If he had one pet peeve in the world, it was getting up to get more things once you had sat down to eat your supper.

"Gordie," Ben said as he stepped into the television room, "you're going to fall into the picture screen if you're not careful."

The boy stood but kept looking at the screen.

"Okay, buddy, time to clean up. You ready?"

A great stroke of luck: the show ended. The annoying voice disappeared and Ben heard a commercial about dish soap come on in its place. Gordon pointed the remote at the television and the sound went dead altogether.

"Horse ride," Gordon said, tossing the remote onto the couch.

"No horse rides right now. You need to get ready for dinner. Come on and clean up."

But the boy bounced and leaped and caught Ben's left hand. The pain caused a bright shower of sparks to skitter in Ben's brain. The boy swung on his hand, lifting his feet and trying to get airborne, and Ben had to hold him so he wouldn't fall. The pain grew and then became something dull and manageable, and Ben lifted the boy a little higher, accepting the bargain, and then he lowered him and made sure he was properly on his feet.

"Come eat," Ben said, his voice carrying a little more weight.

And Gordon complied. He ran to the kitchen and stepped up on the stool near the sink and Ben followed him, flexing his hand, his fingers thick as apple cores.

―⟡―

Charlie put a half dozen quarters on top of a pinball machine and fed three into the coin slot while they waited for the pizza. He felt good. He felt happy. He held out his arm and invited

Margaret to stand in front of him, both of their hands on the flippers.

"Ready?" he asked when she stood with him.

"I'm warning you. I'm bad at this."

He kissed the side of her neck.

"You're good at other things," he said.

"Am I?"

"Yes, very, very good."

"You're pretty good, too, you know?"

"It's a pleasure to practice. I know that much."

She bumped back into him. Then he pulled the spring-loaded ball shooter and let it go. A plump steel ball shot up to the top of the machine and began its inevitable fall.

"Here it comes," Charlie said.

Together they used their fingers to send the ball rocketing all the way back to the top. The machine liked that and rewarded them with a ton of points. The picture on the front board, Charlie noticed, had something to do with girls on motorcycles, gang girls, and behind them stood Harley-looking fellows holding pool cues. Evidently the game had something to do with pool, or motorcycles, but Charlie couldn't say for certain.

They did better with the second ball, keeping it alive for a minute at least. But when the second ball died Margaret pulled back the spring-loaded delivery rod and sent the last ball into the game immediately.

"A little competitive, are we?" Charlie asked.

"Women's lacrosse, Charlie. I was a jock for a couple years

in high school. Blake and I were teammates on the deadly Lady Pirates."

"Good for you."

"Here it comes."

She went after the game this time. Charlie felt her determination, her concentration on each moment that promised termination. Twice she rescued them from the brink of elimination. But then the ball drifted lazily to one side, to a lane they could do nothing to protect, and the ball settled into the killer slot and the game ended.

Margaret leaned back into his arms.

"Get me away from this machine, Charlie, or I'll be here all night."

"We're learning a little bit about this Margaret from Maine."

"My sister gave up playing games with me when we were about twelve. I was cowabunga about games."

"That's Annie, right?" he said and opened his arms and followed her back toward their small booth. The one couple who had been eating when they had come in was gone. Apparently the place relied on take-out business.

"Yep, Annie. The one in Oregon."

"Your pizza's ready," a kid behind the counter said before either of them sat.

Charlie veered off and grabbed the pizza. It looked good— deep cheese, a crisp crust, and a nice layer of tomato sauce. Margaret collected napkins, paper plates, and two Diet Cokes. Charlie slid the pizza onto the table and waited while Margaret scooted into the booth. He felt wonderfully hungry.

"My father used to say he was so hungry he might bite off a finger in his hurry," Margaret said, serving them both. The pizza steamed.

"So you were saying about Annie . . . ?"

"Oh, nothing really. She didn't like games with me, that's all. She was always a little bit of a hippie. That was her big regret. She wanted to live in the 1960s. She romanticized the whole thing. So she kind of followed the Dead even after they were over and done, and then she followed Phish. I don't know. Annie's complicated."

"Not to change subjects, but are you worried the pizza's too hot?"

"You're going to burn your mouth, Charlie. Don't do it."

"The pain might be worth it," he said, holding off. "So Annie has a tumultuous marriage?"

"I'm not sure I'd say tumultuous. They fight over money and life choices. He's with the Forest Service, so they don't make a lot . . . and he's out doing things all day, and when he comes home she wants to have her turn. I think she's underengaged, if you know what I mean. She needs more to do, but they're in a rural area, so work isn't easy to come by."

"I have to try the pizza now. I'll sacrifice the roof of my mouth for the greater good."

"Still too early, Charlie. I promise you. Don't do it."

"Do they have kids?"

"One girl. Charlotte."

Charlie lifted the slice of pizza from his plate and folded it so it would fit in his mouth. He waited until Margaret copied him.

"Ready?" he asked.

"We're pushing it. It's still too hot."

"Go for the gusto."

"Did you just use an old beer slogan to get me to burn my mouth?"

"I guess I did."

She nodded. They both took a bite and both reached for their sodas at the same time, their mouths opened like monkeys hooting through the forest. Charlie felt the top of his mouth come close to burning, but it was okay. He couldn't remember tasting anything better in a long time.

"Hot?" she asked.

"Manageable."

"I'm going to wait a second. You can live dangerously if you like."

"Do you think they will stay married?" he asked as he took another bite. It was not as hot as the first one, and Charlie wondered if he hadn't happened on an important property of thermodynamics: pizza is hottest at its center.

"I hope they do. They both like the outdoors, so they have that in common. Annie has always wanted to be wherever she isn't, if that makes sense. Yearning, kind of. When she received presents as a kid, they were never quite right. I suppose I'm making her sound awful, and she really isn't."

"Do they have a good kid?"

"A great kid. I love being an auntie. You can zoom in, spoil the brat rotten, then zoom away. Charlotte is a sweet child. I hate to say it, but she takes after her dad more than her mom.

She's easier to please. I must sound like a horrible sister. I'm going to eat now, then I'll probably be struck by lightning."

"Family is complicated, that's all. Right? My brother and I got along okay, but who knows what it would be like today if he hadn't had the accident? Life is tricky."

"I'm supposed to go out and see her sometime this summer," Margaret said, taking a bite. She put her napkin to her lips. "They live in a beautiful area and they go canoeing and kayaking all the time. It's a treat to visit."

"Will you take Gordon?"

"He loves it there. They dote on him. Especially after Thomas."

"How's your pizza?"

"Probably the greatest pizza I've ever eaten."

"Isn't it?" he said and took another bite.

Chapter
Twenty

Sometimes it goes right. That was what Ben thought when he hooked up the last cow, her sagging sack as full as a tick. *Sometimes it goes right.* It wasn't a great morning weatherwise, but Ben liked the quiet the fog brought. The cows seemed to like it, too, because they had settled into their milking stations like graphite bearings into a proper gear. Click, click, click, and they were done. Ben stood, stretched his back, then went to the sink for his coffee.

He carried the coffee to the open door of the barn and watched the morning find the farm. He loved this moment, although, asked to define it, he would fail. But he knew the fall of sunlight in this season, the slow crouch of it across the fire pond, then the chicken yard, then the red of the barn. He could tell the hour by holding out his hand and watching the light rest on it, each finger five minutes. He took a deep breath, sipped the coffee, and permitted himself rest.

He let his eyes go where they liked, his thoughts trailing

after them. Gordon was still asleep and would be another hour, hour and a half. The Red Sox had lost the night before, and that put them only a half game ahead of the Yankees, three ahead of Tampa Bay. But they had a good team and he wasn't worried. As he thought this, he spotted a dead limb, no, make that three, hanging from the oak above the porch. They weren't large, which was why he had missed them, but they hung nearly vertical, ready to stab down and pierce the shingles, swing in and crack a window. It was always something, and that did not necessarily upset him, because he liked being busy, liked the contest the farm imposed on him. Everything tried to break down, it was just a fact, and everything shedded, broke, trimmed away. He felt a warm satisfaction in his stomach at the prospect of the branches: ladder onto the roof, careful walk across the front slant, a bow saw, maybe a tree saw, the wiggle back and forth like a tooth giving way in a child's mouth, then the toss down to the ground. Afterward he would work the branches up, measured for the fireplace, not the stove, though they were oak and they would burn as hot as any wood except apple or ash. It would be done easily and quickly, and it would be one thing he could point to, a finished project, and from that he would draw satisfaction.

He took another sip and tasted sugar marching forward onto his tongue. One of the cows shook her gear, rattling hard against the head pipes, and he turned to look. She was okay. He turned back and watched the sun crawl onto the toe of his boot, the light smoky from the outline of a spiderweb that strained it as it passed. He lifted his boot and jiggled it softly in the sunlight. As he watched, he thought of Margaret. She had delayed her return and he didn't doubt for a moment why. It was plain as paint. He had seen the way they looked at each other, Margaret and the young officer, and it didn't take a genius to figure where it went from there. He couldn't blame her. She was young and she was locked to her husband's breath, to Tom's life, and she had not bargained for that. He didn't blame her a bit. She was a wonderful wife and a good daughter-in-law, and he had seen her come to love the farm as clearly as he did. She was like the sun this morning, slowly working her way across the mud and buildings and equipment until she possessed it all.

He tilted his cup to finish it. A few coffee grains followed the sugar and left his tongue with a bitter taste that wasn't entirely unpleasant. He flicked the cup forward and dashed the dregs out of it. The drops landed on the ground and made a straight line in the dirt, and he thought of the sun drawing the liquid up, all things rising in the spring soil.

It was foggy. It was the first poor weather they had experienced, and Margaret tried not to take it as an omen. Last day. No, she corrected herself, last *full* day. They still had tomorrow morning. She looked out the window of the small breakfast café and watched the fog curl and wrap around the trees. *The fog comes on little cat feet,* she remembered from the Sandburg poem, but that was all she could remember. Teachers had always used it as an example of metaphor and she realized, studying the fog, that fog was not feline at all. It did not creep but swam instead, pooling and moving like a horror monster, like Dracula spinning and slipping beneath a door.

"Penny for your thoughts," Charlie said.

He sat in front of a large bowl of oatmeal. She had an English muffin and pomegranate-orange juice.

"I was watching the fog," she said. "Empty-headed right now. Not worth a penny, really."

"It's going to cut off a little of our sightseeing."

She smiled and reached across the table and took his hand.

"I just like being with you, Charlie."

"You okay?"

"Oh, I'm fine. I'm starting to think about the outside world intruding. We've been in our bubble and I don't want to leave it."

"I thought you said it was the basket of an air balloon."

"I did say that, didn't I?"

"And you said no wishing time away, so shake it off. Be right here with me now."

"I am. I guess I'm a little sleepy."

"We haven't found any blooms. We're slacking."

"We will today. I can feel it. This fog is an omen."

"It might burn off later. But they're calling for rain, too."

She squeezed his hand. The waitress came by with more coffee. She was an older woman, gray and slightly bullet-backed, and her hands, Margaret noticed, had been twisted by arthritis. She appeared fierce at first: angular and sharp, with bright blue eyes that seemed to focus best when she glanced sideways. But she had a friendly way and the café was not crowded and she apparently enjoyed visiting with customers. She had already asked where they were from, were they down for the parkway, and so forth. Her name tag said *June*.

"You know, the cook told me the rhododendron was out over his way," she said, topping off their coffee. "A big forest of it. Would you be interested if I could get you directions?"

"Absolutely," Charlie said.

"At the higher elevation, you're going to have trouble finding it . . . but down in the hollows, you should come across some banks. He said the azaleas are out, too. Could be real pretty."

"We'd appreciate it," Charlie said.

"Easiest thing in the world."

Margaret finished her muffin and drank some juice. For a moment she pictured the morning routine back in Maine: Gordon waking, sleepy and soft, and Grandpa Ben tiptoeing in to check on him. It was Tuesday, so Blake would swing by to pick up Gordon and Ben, likely, would use the morning hours to patch or repair something. A piece of machinery was always down or up on the farm; fences needed perpetual mending; and water troughs collapsed and broke, sprung leaks, the cows stropping their heavy bodies against them to scrape away winter coats. She imagined the light finding the oak tree, climbing it slowly, and she could see the phoebe bobbing its tail in the early air. She would be back there tomorrow. It would be evening by the time she returned, but still she would know she'd returned by the smells and sounds. *Home,* she thought. Yes, it was Gordon's home, and her home, too, although deep down it felt like Ben's land. The property and houses would pass on to Gordon, but at times, when she felt down or blue, she wondered if she wasn't an intermediary, a caretaker for a line of men. She wondered if most women didn't feel that way: as onlookers somehow, not quite team members but managers instead, the outsider kid who was quick with a water bucket and a dry towel who did not get to play, precisely, but waited in attendance on those who did.

Gloomy thoughts, she decided, and shook herself. When June came back with a piece of paper Margaret was glad to get out of her own head.

"Gary got this for you off Google Maps," June said, putting the paper down and offering more coffee. "He's a big computer enthusiast, is Gary. It's about five miles from here. You follow these directions and it will take you right there."

"Thank you," Charlie said. "And thank Gary for us, too."

"I'll do that. Now, here's your check. You need anything else?"

"We should be all set."

"Well, you two enjoy the rest of your trip. We might get lucky and get a little sun later. You never know this time of year."

She moved on and Margaret finished her juice.

"We winning or losing?" Charlie asked.

"Winning."

"You okay?"

"I'm fine, Charlie. I'm feeling a little sentimental about you already."

"That's a good thing, right?"

"Yes, a very good thing. You know what I was remembering a little while ago? The music at the ball. When we got out of the cab you could hear it, and the lights were on in the embassy, and everyone was dressed so beautifully. The music made everything soar. I know that sounds ridiculous, but that's how I remember it. See, I'm already nostalgic over us."

He lifted her hand and kissed the back.

"Let's find some rhododendrons," he said.

"Yes, let's."

⌒

Charlie saw the glow of azaleas through the fog. It did not quite seem possible. Margaret's concentration was fixed on the map in her lap, and Charlie, at first glance, thought they had come across an old sign, or a building, buried on the side road. He could not initially believe in the colors. Then the truth of what he saw came to him: a forest of pink and red blooms, pale and shimmering in the early fog.

"Margaret," he said, "look."

She looked up and instinctively reached across the console and put her hand on his knee.

"Awesome," she said.

"There must be a pull-off."

She sat up on the edge of her seat. The map slid partially off her lap.

"It doesn't look real," she said.

"I thought it was a building at first."

"Oh, does it really look like this?"

"Here, I can pull off here."

And he did. He eased the Jeep onto a dirt turnout and then switched off the ignition and did not move for a moment. He wasn't sure what he had expected, but it wasn't this. He had not anticipated anything this vast. Margaret took the Google map and slid it onto the dash. She alternated between looking at the azaleas and looking at him. Each time their eyes met, their smiles grew broader.

"I had no idea," she said, emphasizing the "no."

"Do you think we're finally getting far enough south? Is that it?"

"I don't know. Come on, let's get out. There's a path."

He followed her. Whatever had gripped her for a moment at breakfast fell away. She kept turning and smiling, amazed and wanting to share her amazement with him.

"The fog makes it better, doesn't it?" she said. "It's muted but more beautiful. Oh, Charlie, look at what we've found!"

"The mountains could be covered with these."

"I read that azaleas and rhododendrons are both rhododendron. I know that sounds confusing, but it's what I read."

"I'm not sure the name matters."

She took his hand and led him down the path. It was not a park or a prescribed path; it was a path made by people's interest in the plants. At the edge, Charlie saw a few plastic soda bottles and the inevitable beer cans, but as they went farther the debris disappeared. In its place a cape of flowers covered the forest floor. Though it was foggy, Charlie imagined dappled light would find the plants in most weather. It was exquisite. He pulled Margaret to him and kissed her softly.

"I'm glad I'm seeing this with you," he said.

"It's beautiful, Charlie."

"Every spring this happens. It's hard to believe."

He let her go and followed her deeper into the plants. *Azaleas*, he thought. How strange to discover these plants existed on such a scale, that springtime for people in the area meant this profusion of beauty. He closed his eyes for a moment and let the scent of the blooms come to him. It reminded him of the poppy field in *The Wizard of Oz*. Snow on poppies, he remembered, that was what woke Dorothy and the others. The plants went on for acres. If the rest of the mountains held entire forests of rhododendron, it would be nearly too much to take in. He wondered how he had never had a sense of this before.

"This is crazy," Margaret said and turned and laughed. "This is way more than I ever guessed."

"You're right about the fog. It makes them even more beautiful."

"Sometimes the fog covers the entire plant and all you can see is the bloom. It looks like a floor covered with beautiful flowers."

Then for a moment they stopped. Charlie felt an overwhelming love—yes, he could call it love now—for her. For Margaret. For this kind, good woman from Maine.

"This can't be the end," he said.

"Shhhhh," she whispered and came into his arms. "Shhh, not now. Not now. Flowers, just be here."

⎯ৎ

Blake found Grandpa Ben in the dooryard, the innards of his old Farmall tractor spread around him like an oily skirt. Oil covered his hands, too, and his cheek had a single slash of gunk that he probably hadn't noticed. Blake didn't know much about tractors, but she knew this one was famous for breaking down. When Margaret wanted to be a little naughty, she referred to it as Ben's hobby. They needed a new tractor, of course, but the financing on farm equipment was paralyzing.

"See you're working on your race car," Blake said, climbing out of her Civic.

"Going to take it down to Daytona and make my fortune," Ben said, looking up, his hands picking up a nut and trying to fit it to a bolt that didn't want to receive it.

Blake stepped over the muddy dooryard and gradually gained better ground. The sun had worked clear of the morning fog and she found a blade of light and stood in it. She was greedy for sunlight. Everyone in Maine was greedy for it at this point of the year, but in a couple weeks, Blake knew, they would be complaining about the heat.

"Just checking in," Blake said, "and Donny wanted me to ask you about that biosolids deal. He thought he might be able to use it on a field he has under contract up to the Davidsons' place."

"Emmett Davidson?"

"The one and only."

"That northern pasture?"

"I guess. You'd know better."

Grandpa Ben put down the nut and bolt he was fiddling with and pulled a rag out of his back pocket. He wiped his hands.

"What's he want to do with that pasture?" Ben asked.

"Turf, I guess. Donny has the idea he can grow turf up here and sell it down in the Boston area or over to Portland. Suburbs, I suppose."

"Well, people from Boston will buy just about anything."

"That so?"

"It's what I hear," Ben said, giving her a dry smile. "But the biosolids might work on the Davidson place. It would make the turf grow pretty thick."

"That's what Donny was thinking. He figures it's free fertilizer."

"There's a lot of that around here."

"You guys doing okay? Is Gordon getting excited for Margaret's return?"

"Oh, he's pretty pleased. He has trouble calculating the time, but he knows it's tomorrow. I haven't talked to her much. How's she doing?"

"She's fine. She's ready to come home, I guess."

She watched him try the nut on the bolt once more. He wanted to be in the sun, too, she saw, and she marveled to realize that Ben, Grandpa Ben, had been a boy once, had been a young man, had had his days. Why had she never seen him in that light before? she wondered. When he looked at her again, he smiled.

"I'm glad she got away," he said. "Life on a farm can wear you out unless you get away from time to time."

"When do you get away, Ben?" Blake asked, seeing him clearly for a moment.

"Oh, not much. You take on livestock and it takes on you."

"If you could go away, where would you go?"

"I don't think about it much."

"Where would you go, though? If you could get away?"

He shrugged and turned a little in the sun. Blake realized she saw the source of the great kindness in the Kennedy men. They did not want or yearn after things they couldn't have. Gordon was the same way, just as Thomas had been. Was it contentment, she wondered, or philosophy? She couldn't say in any final way, but she smiled to see it and she watched him fiddle with the bolt. She wished she could borrow some of his acceptance.

"You'd go see the Red Sox, wouldn't you?" she said.

"I wouldn't mind."

"You know, we could make that happen, Ben," she said and felt a moment of great tenderness toward him.

"I've always liked a ball game."

She smiled. She moved a little to remain in the sun. How funny the world was, she thought. How pretty in its unfathomable way. How good it was to have the warmth of the sunlight and to talk to Ben. She made a small promise to herself that she would see about Red Sox tickets. Donny knew someone who had an angle on them. She would mention it to Margaret, she decided, and she would volunteer to babysit if they needed her to. Or maybe, she thought, Ben would want Gordon with him. It was a male ritual to see a game with your dad, and Ben was as close to a dad as Gordon would have anytime soon.

"I should run," she said, "and I'll drop Gordon by later. So you're saying the biosolids deal might work on that field?"

"If we're talking about the same one, it'll be right as rain."

"Good luck with the tractor, Ben. When I come back I expect to see it running."

"You can expect frogs to be princes, but that doesn't make it so."

He smiled and she smiled back. Then he picked up his bolt and turned and tried to fit it into the engine block. Blake walked slowly back to her car. She hardly wanted to move out of the sun. When she climbed in behind the driver's wheel she was surprised to find the vehicle had grown hot in the short time it had been parked. Spring, then summer, she knew. For no reason she could pinpoint, she cried as she pulled down the driveway. For Ben, mostly. And for all of them, Gordon and Phillip and Margaret and Donny. And for Thomas living out his days in the home. Plants bending to the sun. That's all anyone was.

Chapter
Twenty-one

"Do you have any idea what kind of house you'll have when you get posted?" Margaret asked.

They had been driving most of the morning, their journey marked by stops to see more and more blooms. It was as if, Margaret felt, they had unlocked the secret of the blooms by finding the first pocket. Now, through the rest of the morning, they saw them everywhere, most of them held by gray fog. Occasionally they spotted them on a hillside or down in a hollow, their individuality blurred by the fog until they appeared as clouds of impossible hues. *Little low heavens,* she remembered. Informally, she was responsible for the passenger-side outlook, while he watched on the driver's side.

"They have pretty nice housing, I guess," he said. "And I think most places come with a guard and a gardener and sometimes a cook."

"How long is a post?"

"Depends, I imagine. A couple years. Sometimes less. They don't like to go to the expense to get you over there, then move you right away. It's a whole world, I guess, the politics of moving and posting."

"That should be exciting."

"I'm looking forward to it. I'm pretty stoked. I like travel. That's one benefit of the war. I learned I like to travel."

"Even under the circumstances?"

"Well, not for the war, of course. But I like the perspective of seeing America from a foreign country. It sounds crazy, but it feels like a big vacation to me. I don't know why. I guess part of it is in America everyone is running around after money and promotions, but when you step out of it you see it isn't particularly important after all. The whole mall culture we've developed, the television shows, I don't know. There's something I enjoy about stepping out of it. It feels more real overseas sometimes. I think a lot of soldiers feel that way and they don't know what to do with it."

"I think I know what you mean."

"Have you been overseas?"

"No. I've wanted to go, but I haven't done it. Thomas always said if you say you want to do something, but then don't do it, maybe you didn't want to do it in the first place. You think that's true?"

"My dad used to say we all get exactly what we want. He said that's a much more frightening proposition than the other way around. I never knew if I agreed with him, but sometimes I see what he means."

"So I guess I have to accept that I didn't want it as much as I thought I did."

"Maybe, maybe not. Who knows?"

"I think we're too high for blooms now."

"It would be beautiful up here without the fog."

"I feel like it's our own little world. Like we're living in a cloud."

"Do you want to call Gordon soon?"

"Yes, next time we get cell reception I should."

"He'll be crazy to see you."

"It's good, though, to have a little separation. This trip has taught me that. I don't want to smother him and it's important that he learn independence. He's fine without me and now he *knows* he'll be fine without me. Most of the parenting books advocate adequate separation. That's my guilty vice. I read a ton of those parenting books."

"That's a good thing, isn't it?"

"Mostly. Sometimes they contradict one another, and then what do you do? But they're helpful. I lean on Ben a lot. He's been wonderful and he adores Gordon. In the end, though, I'm a single parent. I wish Thomas could sit up and talk to me about discipline and a dozen other topics, but he can't. So I read books when I have time."

"Do you and Blake have similar parenting styles?"

"Oh, more or less. She may be a tiny bit more lenient than I am. I'm a tyrant. My grandma always said there is nothing worse than a poorly trained dog or child, and I think she may be right."

"Let me pull over here and you can see if you have enough bars."

Where were they? Margaret wondered as she dug in her purse for her cell phone. The fog had removed landmarks and made the entire day's journey feel dreamy and unreal. Even now she could discern that they were parked near an overlook, but the fog joined with the clouds and held the afternoon light hostage. She pushed the button on her phone and stepped out of the car as she did so. She leaned against the rear fender and waited while the connection rang through to the farm. She watched Charlie move off down a small trail that apparently led to an overlook. He had the binoculars in his free hand.

"Hello," she said when Gordon picked up. "Who is that on the phone?"

"Mom?" Gordon said.

"Hi, sweetheart. How are you doing? You home from school?"

"Mm-hmm," he agreed.

"Is Grandpa Ben cooking dinner?"

"Not yet. He said he will later."

"Good. Did you have a good treat?"

A good treat meant an apple or piece of fruit as opposed to a cookie. She listened while her son tried to think of a way to dodge the question.

"A cookie," he said.

"Okay, but you'll lose a star for that. It's important to eat good food, right?"

She heard the phone move and guessed he had nodded.

"I'm going to be home tomorrow and I can't wait to see you. I won't make you a special dinner tomorrow night because I'll be home too late to shop, but the night after . . . what would you like?"

"Shepherd's pie," he said instantly.

"Okay, shepherd's pie it is. Will you help me mash the potatoes?"

"Yes."

"Do you know how much I love you, sweetheart? I love you like corn," she said, playing an old game with him.

"I love you like salt."

"Like . . . potato chips with peanut butter."

Then he was gone. Just like that. Either he had inadvertently hung up or the satellite connection had fuzzed out, but regardless of what happened he was gone. She considered trying to call back, but then figured there wasn't any point. Ben would know she had called; Blake had doubtless told him the itinerary. Let it go, she told herself. Gordon is fine and the house is fine and you are fine, she reminded herself. She slipped the phone into her purse in the car, then followed Charlie's track down toward the overlook.

And what happened next? She wondered that a thousand times afterward, but when she saw him standing beside a railing, his face staring down at the banks of fog spooling and purling away from the mountainside, she called him by her husband's name.

"Tom?" she called and the word was out of her mouth before she could stop it.

A bright red wave of embarrassment torched her face. She saw him turn—and it had happened too quickly for him to conceal anything—and watched the hurt cross his face. It all passed in an instant, less than an instant, and yet it had crossed his features. It was natural, she told herself, to think of her husband after a call home. Her brain wires had merely crossed, and the form of a man standing in the fog, going to him, had somehow touched the wrong memory cord. No one could blame her for that and she felt their eyes meet, his expression going from shock and pain to understanding, and she shook her head, trying to make it all go away. He smiled. His wonderful, warm smile, and she felt tears fill her eyes and she would have done anything, anything at all, to erase the memory of his initial hurt, the flash of pain she had seen there. He said something, *It's okay,* then a joke, *No, I'm Charlie,* and when she reached him he took her in his arms. But huddled next to his chest, the fog like a deep cloud around them, she knew something had slipped away, something had returned to remind them that all the king's horses, and all the king's men, could never put Humpty Dumpty back together again.

Charlie watched the redtail hawks float on the spring thermals above them. He had imagined they would run into redtails— they were predictable travelers, migrating merely by floating on wind that carried them northward—but he was pleased to see them anyway. He had never stood at elevation to watch them pass, however, and now, watching them float and glide by, their wingtips bent back with the uprising thermals, he took pleasure in their travel. He liked redtails; they had always been his father's favorite bird. His dad had purchased a taxidermy redtail, its chest mottled and slightly jaundiced, its beak fiercely turned in stillness, and it had remained on the kitchen mantel for years. It was probably there still, Charlie thought, though he didn't have a clear memory of it from his last trip home.

He lowered the binoculars and turned to check the rest stop ladies' room. Margaret had disappeared a moment earlier, before he had spotted the hawks. As he trained the binoculars on the hawks again, watching them effortlessly hover in the wind, he remembered the look on her face when she called him Tom. How quickly things had changed by that small slip. It was not a big deal, they had both said, but underneath they understood that it was. It was the pebble in the shoe. Thomas was alive and she was a married woman, and the fact that she had called him, Charlie, by her husband's name merely highlighted those central truths. That could not be erased or pushed to one side, and he could not think of the moment without wondering if Thomas had not been present for a moment in their company. Absurd, of course. Thomas lived in a bed near Bangor, Maine; he was not a phantom or shade who wafted in the foggy hollows of North Carolina like Hamlet's father patrolling the battlements in Denmark. Yet how heavily his presence had suddenly asserted itself into their exchanges! Margaret had been drawn back to her world by her son's voice, and in the fog for an instant he had reminded her of her husband. Charlie could not help thinking that all their words, all their passion, had been trumped by this small moment.

He put down his binoculars and called Terry.

"Hello, Charlie," she said, her voice bright. "I was wondering when I would hear from you. How's everything going?"

"It's going great."

"Are the rhododendrons out?"

"Maybe not in full force, but they're here."

"Where's Margaret? Is she there with you?"

"Yes, but I thought I'd give you a call."

"You okay? You sound a little punk."

"No, I'm fine. We're in North Carolina now. She's going to fly out of Asheville tomorrow."

"That makes sense. Then you can pop onto the interstate and make it home in a jiffy."

"She's a wonderful woman," Charlie said.

"I think so, too. From the little time I spent with her, I really do."

"I've fallen for her a little bit, you know? I guess you knew that would happen."

Charlie heard Terry become still on the other end. She had been doing something—he heard water running, and something clink—but gradually the background noise ceased.

"Oh, Charlie," she said. "I was afraid of this."

"Afraid of what?"

"Don't pretend you don't know what I'm talking about, Charlie. Did something happen?"

"No, not really. I just kind of came up against a reminder that she's married, that's all. Nothing she did."

"That was the risk going in, wasn't it?"

"Yes, I know."

"What are we going to do with you, Charlie?"

"I'm okay. Just wanted to hear a friendly voice."

"Will you come by tomorrow for dinner? You'll be back in time, won't you? The kids would love to see you and I'll buy you a drink. How does that sound?"

"That sounds great, actually."

"Okay, that's a plan. Now, I hate to shoo you off, but I'm out the door and I've got to run. Keep your hands up, Charlie. Don't lead with your chin."

"Thanks, Terry."

"You're both good people, Charlie. Just keep that in mind."

She clicked off. Charlie started to raise the binoculars again but paused when he saw Margaret crossing the parking lot toward him. His eyes met hers. Then it was there again, the former warmth, the woman he had taken to the French Embassy. He smiled and kept his eyes on hers. She smiled in return, and it was okay again, at least for this minute, for now, for the moment it took her to cross the last of the parking lot and step into his arms.

Chapter
Twenty-two

It was the final perfection. Margaret sat up on her passenger seat and felt she couldn't breathe for excitement. She turned and started to say something to Charlie, but he shook his head and shrugged and she decided she would not protest. Not now. She had never heard of it before, but the Inn on Biltmore Estate was the most dazzling residence she had ever seen in person. Charlie slowed to let her take it in. A thousand flowers, a million flowers stood scattered around the welcoming meadow. In the late afternoon light, the flowers nearly choked her with beauty. And the meadow, in turn, gave way to a gravel drive, and the drive then spread into the warm canvas-colored walls of the estate.

"Charlie . . . ," she said, but she couldn't stop looking.

"The Vanderbilts built it. It's the biggest residence ever constructed in America, I think. It has wonderful grounds and hiking trails and we're staying here."

"In the house?" she asked, not quite believing it.

"No, that's pretty much a museum, but there's an associated inn on the grounds. Is it all too stuffy? I worried it might be."

"Oh, Charlie, it's amazing!"

"I wasn't sure you would like a place like this, but the grounds are supposed to be wonderful . . . azaleas and tulips. This time of year, I suppose the flowers are changing. I've always wanted to visit it."

"Charlie, it's so extravagant! You've never been?"

"I drove past it once and promised myself I'd be back. That's how I knew about it. This seems like the perfect occasion."

Margaret felt her heart racing. How glorious and how gallant of him to find such a romantic hotel! Was it possible a small wedge of sun had worked itself free to send a single curtain of light across the building's facade? The setting was beyond anything she could imagine. A building like this, she thought, could become a horrible tourist cliché, but a glance told her that the estate had escaped such a fate. The setting had kept it pure and lovely; the tall spires—it wanted to be a castle, she realized—gave it a grandeur that maintained its dignity. It resembled the castle at the beginning of the Disney program years ago, the one with Tinker Bell darting above, only this was real and present and situated perfectly on the land.

Charlie eased the Jeep forward, following signs for the inn. She unsnapped her seat belt and crawled on top of him.

"Thank you," she said and kissed him, once, twice, fifty times.

"I wasn't sure you would like it. It might be fussy."

"Charlie, most women will like a thing like this no matter what," she said, scrambling back into her seat.

"Cornelia Vanderbilt was born here, I think."

"You're extraordinary, Charlie, do you know that?"

Then they arrived, the Jeep's tires crunching gravel. Margaret stared up at the enormous building. It required no imagination at all to picture horses arriving, old cars, carriages. The women would have worn long skirts, clothes from the early 1900s if she had it right, and the men in solid breeches and tweed jackets. And dogs. Dogs would have been everywhere, and workmen, too, everything bustling and gracious. She watched as the sun glinted off one of the glass panes; it blinked like a star. She suddenly felt absurdly, ridiculously underdressed, but there was no help for it.

"We have a reservation here, Charlie?" she asked when he pulled the Jeep into a slot. "Are you serious? Or is this some kind of a joke?"

"Looks like we do have a reservation. If we missed it somehow, I guess we'll sleep in the car."

"You're crazy, Charlie. I can't help you—"

He leaned over and kissed her to cut her off. She wanted to say something about the cost, about the ongoing expense, but what was there to say? In reality, she didn't have the funds to cover their travel. She tried when she could to pass along a little money, but it was not an even contest. She closed her eyes and reminded herself to accept things, to not resist, to permit the world to bring things to her. That was what Blake would have advised.

A doorman came and handed her out. He was a young blond man, thin and slightly overwhelmed by his uniform, but he smiled broadly and tipped his hat. Again, she began to feel embarrassed about her clothing, and then she let that go, too. Who cared? She squared her shoulders and tried not to gawk like a complete tourist. But the residence was undeniably grand. Everywhere her eye fell, she discovered new details: a row of summer chairs under a long portico, a stone column made of granite, acres of rich, worn mulch lining the flower beds. It was all delicious. She wanted to see everything, to tour it all, but for now she stepped away from the car and let Charlie handle things.

And she liked—she freely admitted it to herself—to see Charlie's command of the situation. Where Thomas might have been shy and deferential and ill at ease, where she would have felt she was imposing, Charlie moved with quiet assurance. The doorman who had handed her out inquired if they had more bags, and Charlie pointed to the back, allowing the doorman to empty the Jeep into a luggage cart. How simple it was, really, she decided, when you let people do what they were paid to do. Charlie was perfectly friendly and kind, but he did not try to help or to second-guess the doorman's effort. He took her arm and led her inside, and Margaret snapped mental pictures of every detail.

"I love this kind of thing, Charlie," she said. "I feel like I've stepped into a PBS movie . . . with Dame Judy Dench and a bunch of other vaguely identifiable stars. You should be wearing a top hat and I should have an Empire gown."

"You'll like this, then. But I suppose it's Edwardian, isn't it?"

"I guess. I want to know everything about this place."

"Let's check in, then we can poke around."

They walked into a luscious lobby and Charlie moved confidently to check them in while the doorman tagged behind with their luggage cart. Margaret walked a slow tour of the lobby, letting her eye run over everything. The lobby had tall ceilings and bright windows everywhere, the expanse broken only by small seating islands for the guests. How wonderful, she thought, to spend their last night together here. It didn't truly matter, because she had loved their night in a motel, too, but this was something special. It struck her as she moved slowly around the lobby—a wood fire burning in the oversized chimney, its andirons fashioned like Hessian soldiers—that life with Charlie would be like this, filled with surprises and small moments of delight. He was not a show-off, and she didn't believe he was rich, but he knew how to spend money in ways that brought pleasure. That was a talent, an enviable one, and she made a mental note to become more adept at it in her own life. Use money; don't allow it to use you, she told herself. That was Charlie's simple message.

"Ready?" he said when he finished with the desk clerk. "We have a nice room overlooking the back grounds. It has a small terrace. It's called the King's . . ."

Charlie glanced at the doorman.

"King's Terrace Room," the doorman supplied. He was just a young boy, Margaret saw now, underneath his formal uniform.

"Makes sense to me," Charlie said.

They followed the young doorman through the inn. Margaret could not help thinking of Blake, how she would love seeing a place like this. At the same time, she cautioned herself against saying too much to Blake. Things were not going well with Donny, and to take too much pleasure in the details of the trip wouldn't be fair. But she did wish Blake could see the lobby and the long hallway they followed to the King's Terrace Room. It would have been a little orgy of details, each of them greedily marking things for further discussion. The upholstery, the glassware, the ashtray stand, the tiebacks holding the thick folds of gray-green material in tiny fists. How lovely it all was; how much care had been lavished on the smallest elements of the inn. She tried to observe everything.

As soon as the doorman pushed back the door to their room, she spotted the tiny terrace, the sweet fountain table set up overlooking the gray grounds. She couldn't help passing by the doorman and Charlie and opening the French doors that communicated to the terrace. How sweet! She turned and smiled at Charlie as he passed a bill to the young doorman—how did he know what to give as a tip, she wondered, how did he know how to do these things so effortlessly?—and she walked into his arms.

"This is beyond lovely," she whispered as the doorman slipped out. "Charlie, this is a dream. I know it's just a room, but it's such a sweet room. You're very thoughtful to arrange this. It means the world to me."

"I'm glad you like it," he said. "What's the view like?"

"Come here," she said and took his hand and led him out.

The grounds swept away from them. Fog made the early evening darker, but here and there she spotted beds of azaleas and rhododendrons. And peonies. She had never seen so many peonies, nor so many varieties and colors, and they saturated the lingering fog and pierced the grayness with muted tones. Charlie put his arm around her. Gradually, shade by shade, she felt evening win over the day and calmness settle over the grounds. She slid deeper under Charlie's arm.

"How do you know to do these things?" she asked. "Most men don't, you know?"

"Don't they?"

"No," she said, her eyes watching the light fail on the gardens, "they don't. It's not their fault. Most women don't know, either. I certainly don't. But you . . . you see how things might be and you aren't afraid to risk something to have it. I admire that."

"Well, if it's worked these last few days, then I'm grateful. My father taught me some of it. I guess it was my father, if I understand what you are saying. He called it living with flair, but he didn't mean it in a boasting way. He always said you could make something festive and pretty nearly as easily as boring and normal. He had a knack and he made things fun. I never really thought about it much, but I guess he made things nice for my mom. I remember one time as a kid he created a drive-in movie in our backyard. It was a date for my mom and he took her out and he made us promise to let them have some privacy . . . anyway, I remember looking out in our backyard and there was our old Dodge Dakota pickup and mom and dad sat in the front seat looking out at an old movie screen. It was Iowa, so we didn't really have drive-ins nearby, heck, by then they were mostly gone anyway, but Dad pulled it off. Mom used to laugh and tell him he was a kook—that was her big word—but he did things anyway and she liked it deep down. I remember seeing moths flash back and forth in the light of the projector. I haven't thought about that in years. . . ."

She turned and kissed him. It was a different kiss than any of the others that came before it. It was a kiss of gratitude and understanding and something else Margaret couldn't name. It had something to do with the quiet night, the gentle crickets, the memory of bright flowers drifting down a hillside wrapped in layers of drifting fog.

With his window cracked, Gordon heard the spring peepers calling from the fire pond beyond the barn. It was early still and he did not feel sleepy, but Grandpa Ben had read him a story and turned out the lights and so it was time to rest. Secretly Gordon thought Grandpa Ben needed sleep: that was what adults did. They took their own moods or needs and projected them onto kids. Gordon didn't have words for these concepts, but he understood why he was in bed and why it was still twilight outside.

He danced the saw-chuck guy across his stomach and let him begin a fight with the meerkat. But the fight felt half-hearted. The saw-chuck guy paused once or twice, then decided to ride on the meerkat's shoulder. Lately they had become friends, although occasionally the meerkat still posed a threat—he was wild and unpredictable, like King Kong, Gordon thought—and the saw-chuck guy needed to be vigilant. But they walked around the bed a little bit, coming close to the edge and nearly falling off, then climbing back to the safety of his stomach with the soldier happily whispering into the meerkat's ear.

Then for a while Gordon puzzled over the spring peepers. What he wondered about, particularly, was the idea of frogs watching him. They were *peepers*, after all, and the notion of hundreds of frogs resting in the pond grass, their eyes trained on the house, weirded him out. Why would they watch? The only reason to watch, Gordon figured, was to plan an attack. But he couldn't quite get his mind around the idea of frogs marching on a house, so as he listened he involuntarily moved the saw-chuck soldier into a defensive position, getting him ready for karate chops if the peepers sprang into action.

In small pulses, sleep stole up on him. He heard his grandfather's radio, the broadcast from Fenway Park, and he listened as Grandpa Ben cleared his throat. An empty spot existed where his mother's sounds should be, but that was okay. She would be home tomorrow, he reminded himself. He did not think of her arrival with anything resembling clarity. His mother represented warmth and comfort, and his blood grew quieter remembering her. A breeze came off the pond and he smelled cows and mud and water. Then the curtains lifted and waved good night, and the saw-chuck guy slid from his hand and landed at the meerkat's feet. The meerkat had a chance to devour the saw-chuck guy at last, but the larger animal ignored him. In the tall grass the peepers called for mates, their tiny clouds of vaporous breath on the cool evening setting around the house.

—☙

Charlie sat on the terrace and smoked a cigar. It was a small luxury to smoke a cigar, one he did not indulge in often. He liked the weight of the cigar in his hand, the sweetness of the smoke as it curled and rose to the night's heavy moisture. He had asked Margaret if she minded, and she had answered by lighting the cigar for him, her leg suggestively draped over his for a moment, then calling room service for two good scotches. She was still waiting for it while he smoked, and he didn't mind the moment alone, the chance to clear his head and consider the next day.

It was coming to an end. That was clear. It was not something he wanted or desired, but he felt powerless to change what was inevitable. He squinted against the smoke and reminded himself that he had known it all at the outset. It did no good to pretend otherwise. She had not misled him nor had she pretended to be anything but what she was: a devoted wife. He understood how difficult these couple days had been for Margaret. She was not prissy or prudish—quite the contrary—but she had a genuine decency and he knew she felt troubled going against her innate sense of fairness. Ultimately, it was not even about Thomas any longer. She answered to something deeper, something foundational in her nature, and she could not escape those moral considerations. It reminded him of a Shakespearean tragedy, a character born with a fatal flaw, except in Margaret's instance it was not a flaw but an unassailable strength. But the strength was the wounding flaw, and vice versa, and he let the thought go as he blew a large circle of smoke into the air and watched it drift and settle away from the building.

But time would tell. He did not mean to be cunning, nor to plan too well, but he was willing to wait to see what would happen. He loved her, he realized. He understood it with a brutal simplicity, with a pure, painful comprehension. He wondered if most men didn't reach toward love faster than they truly understood it. Yet it was here now. He loved Margaret and wanted her for his own. He did not delude himself that he couldn't live without her. That was the damnable thing: people could always live without one another. The movies pretended otherwise, but it simply wasn't so. Life moved on and one went with it. It might have been easier, frankly, if it had been some crazy affair. He might have let that go and moved on without too much pain, but with Margaret it was different. He knew he had discovered something solid and honest and he knew unquestionably that he could live beside her for the rest of his life. He did not have to think twice about that, and as he rolled his cigar ash gently on the edge of the table, letting the white flakes fall to the stone floor, he saw what a wonder it was to know without doubt that he had met the woman he had searched for all his life. No, that made it sound too grand, he decided. But she was the one. That was as simple as he could frame it in his mind, and he took a tiny whiff of smoke into his lungs and coughed gently, the smoke mixing with the scent of flowers and the rich earth and the mossy sky above.

What now, he thought. Did they wake up tomorrow and say good-bye? One final night in bed together? He knew he wouldn't—he couldn't, was more accurate—pursue her in Maine unless she permitted it and he doubted she would. It would make things too hard, and so they would go apart when everything he understood about the world told them to stay together. He could take on Gordon, it would be an honor, and they could come with him overseas, and they would live together as they had these past days and life would be simple and beautiful. That could be done and the only thing standing in the way of it was not Thomas but Margaret.

He blew another cloud of smoke, a thin, hot stream that rubbed his lip as it left his mouth, and a moment later she appeared on the terrace with their drinks. She smiled, obviously pleased. She swung her leg over his and reached back and put one drink down on the small table. She sat on his lap, facing him. She gave him a small sip of scotch and took a small sip herself, then kissed him deeply.

"Oh, Charlie," she whispered, her body and breath close, "I'm so happy right now."

"I am, too."

"I like you out here and I like coming out to you. And I like that you have a cigar now and then . . . not many, for your health, I mean, but I like it. My father smoked a cigar once in a great while and I always knew he was happy when he did it just as I knew you were happy out here."

He kissed her again. He started to pull back, but she tucked closer to him and kissed him hard. She put her lips next to his ear.

"I had been sleepwalking when I met you, Charlie. I had. I know I've told you some of this already, but it's true. You woke me up. You're my Prince Charming."

"I get to keep you, then, and to live happily ever after."

She kissed his neck, his cheek, his lips. The cigar smoke licked across the side of the chair and drifted across the lawn.

"People go to sleep all the time and don't even know it," she said. "That's what you taught me."

"You weren't asleep, really, Margaret. You have your son and the farm work and your husband. You had too much to do to be asleep."

"I love the farm, it's true. But deep down I was numb in a way I didn't realize. I had given up on having small joys like these. Not all the way, not completely, but I had given a big shrug to everything. But I see now it was wrong to do that. You have to keep trying, don't you? That's the whole game, to keep trying. I see that with you."

He took a deep breath and reached around her to put the cigar away. She started to get up, perhaps thinking she was too heavy on his legs, but he gathered her closer. She reached over and put the glass on the table and curled into him. He smelled the earth and watched the sun sink through the trees.

Chapter
Twenty-three

From the shower, Margaret peeked out to watch Charlie shave. He stood in the foggy bathroom, his chin poked forward, his hand dragging a razor over his cheek. How quickly, she thought, they had become intimate. They could share a bathroom, sleep beside each other, navigate a trip. They had made love every day, discovering new, pleasurable things, each of them growing bolder with practice. Margaret realized again that she had missed living with a man. It seemed a peculiar yearning to her, living as she did with two men, but that was different. She liked the thumps and heavy footsteps a man made; she liked the cigar and the scotch and the firm way Charlie handled the doorman. She liked his strength, his force, his steadiness. It felt as if she were a slightly tippy canoe that now had an outrigger.

"What are you looking at?" he asked, his eyes crinkling a little to see her through the fog.

"You, Charlie. Is it strange that this feels so easy?"

"Yes, a little bit."

"I can't believe how it is between us."

"Should we have a fight? An experimental fight just to sample the waters?"

"I can't imagine fighting with you right now."

"Give it time. Now, why don't you pull back the shower curtain and let me see you naked?"

"You're a horrible man."

But he turned and stepped across the tub. She ducked back into the stream of water, squealing a little as she went. A second later he had stepped out of his boxer shorts and climbed in with her. A little shaving cream ran off his cheek. He kissed her. His lips still tasted of cigar and scotch.

"You're beautiful," he said, still holding her in his arms.

"You have to say that. We're in the shower."

"I'm going to buy you a really big steak or a lamb chop or something that requires a bib."

"I'm starving."

"Then we'll go for an evening walk like proper ladies and gentlemen."

"I'd love to go for a walk. All right, you finish here and let me dress," she said. "I'm showered out."

She kissed him again and stepped out of the tub. Steam covered the bathroom. She wrapped her hair in a towel, wrapped a larger towel over her body, then walked outside. The change in temperature between the two rooms made her slightly light-headed. She lifted her small suitcase onto the bed and tried to think of something new to wear. But the cupboard was bare, she admitted, and Charlie would have to be satisfied with a variation on the same old outfits.

Before she could decide what to wear, her cell phone rang. It took her a moment to find it among the jumble of clothes and odds and ends scattered around the room. She glanced at the incoming number—Blake—and almost let it ring unanswered. But then she thought about Gordon, and she thought about Blake herself, and she flipped it open and said, "Hello?"

Nothing came back to her except the strangled breath of a sob.

"Blake?" Margaret asked, stopping everything to listen. "Blake, what is it?"

But Blake couldn't speak. Behind her, Margaret heard Charlie turn off the shower. Margaret took a step outside and snatched her scotch glass off the table.

"What is it, honey?" Margaret asked. "What's wrong?"

"Donny," Blake said, but Margaret could tell there was more.

"What about Donny? He isn't hurt, is he?"

"No," Blake answered, her breath stuttering and punching holes in the next thing she said. "He wants a divorce."

"Oh, Blake, I'm so sorry."

"He said," Blake said, and Margaret pictured her friend squaring her shoulders, slowly getting control of herself, "that he doesn't have any feelings for me. None. He said we were just roommates."

"Oh, I'm sorry, Blake."

"He said he wants to be free to pursue other options. Those were his words. 'Other options.' "

"Where are you?"

"I'm in the car in the driveway. I didn't want to talk around Phillip."

"And where is Donny?"

"He left."

"For good?"

"I don't know. He took a bag and drove off."

"Do you think he's seeing someone?"

"That was the first thing that came to mind. Donny's too lazy to fend for himself without a woman. Do you know what I mean? He's not going to live in a motel and go to a Laundromat and do all of that. He needs a woman. He wouldn't have the guts to leave unless he had another situation lined up."

"Do you have any suspicions?"

"No, not one."

"Well, we shouldn't jump to conclusions, should we? It's all raw and new. Give him the benefit of the doubt for the time being."

Margaret saw Charlie step out of the bathroom. For an instant her eyes fell on his leg, the mechanical foot. She covered the mouthpiece of the phone and said, *Blake*. Charlie nodded and started to dress. Margaret sat on a chair near the door to the terrace. Water dripped out of her hair onto her shoulders.

"Is he right there?" Blake said. "I'm sorry. I'll let you go."

"No, you will not, Blake. Charlie's going to go to the bar and have a nice big scotch and wait for me. Or maybe he'll sit out on the terrace and finish his cigar. And I'm going to talk to you as long as you need me to talk to you."

"He smokes cigars?" Blake asked, her voice slightly brighter.

"Yes, it turns out he does."

"I like cigar smoke at ball games."

"I do, too."

"I'm sorry to bother you with all this. It just took me by surprise. I mean, I knew we weren't Ozzie and Harriet, but I didn't think we were on the edge of a divorce. I don't know what I thought. Maybe Donny is smarter than I am. Maybe he's more willing to see it clearly."

"Little by little, Blake. Just take a deep breath. There's nothing you can do right now. He's not going to leave his business."

"No, he likes that too much. He likes building it. That's one good thing about him."

"And he's going to continue being a dad to Phillip."

"Yes, when it's easy for him."

"Okay."

"I could kill him right now, you know that? I could. Then in the next instant I think I love him so much it's going to kill me. I'm all turned around."

"What did he say exactly? How did it happen?"

"He came in early. From work. He didn't look as dirty as he usually does and it's not like him to knock off early at this time of year. This time of year he's going flat-out. Maybe he was trying to get home before Phillip. I figured he had just stopped in for a second on his way out to someplace else. Back in the day he would do that just to say hello. But he sat at the kitchen table and he announced that he needed a change. Simple as that. No big preamble. He said he didn't feel the same way about me. . . ."

Blake broke off and started to cry. Charlie stepped over, leaned down, and kissed the side of Margaret's neck, and she reached with her hand and touched his cheek. He nodded, understanding, then he went outside onto the terrace. Margaret leaned forward and saw him light a match and puff at his cigar. She smiled, but then turned her attention back to Blake.

"So he said he didn't feel the same way," Margaret prompted Blake.

"He said he was sorry if he hadn't been very attentive—he used some other word; Donny wouldn't use 'attentive'—but that was the idea of it. Then he said he had given it thought and he didn't feel like we were a couple anymore. That was it. I asked him if he was sure, if it meant he wanted a divorce, and he stopped at that. He said he needed some time to figure things out, then he marched upstairs, packed a bag, and headed through the door. He tried to kiss me good-bye, you know, kind of on the cheek, but I turned away. Big dramatic me."

"I'm so sorry, honey. I know it's hard right now, but take it easy. Don't jump to any conclusions. Just listen and take it in and hold off on doing anything rash."

"You know what I was thinking as he left? That no guy has ever broken up with me. I'm not sure if that's accurate, but I think I was always the one to break up with the guy. Donny's a first that way."

"That's because you're a beautiful, wonderful woman."

"To everyone but Donny, I guess."

"Don't get down on yourself, sweetie."

"I know. Okay, thanks for listening. You go back to your lover boy there. Everything you've said about him, he sounds terrific."

"He's a good guy. We click so far."

"I'm happy for you, Margaret. I'm sorry to rain on your sunny day. I didn't know who else to call."

"Blake, call me anytime you need me. Now, why don't you get out of the house? Maybe take Phillip out to a movie . . . something to take your mind off things."

"Maybe I will."

"I love you, Blake. I'm sorry this is happening."

"Into every life a little rain must fall, right?"

"I guess that's true."

"Okay, thanks for listening. Say hello to Charlie for me. Tell him I hope to meet him someday."

Margaret said good-bye and hung up. Out on the terrace, Charlie talked on his cell phone. Margaret sat for a moment, playing the conversation over in her head. Poor Blake. And poor Donny, too, who yearned for something he probably didn't understand himself. Phillip, of course, would get trapped in the middle and he would carry anger at Donny for leaving. Maybe not, Margaret chided herself. Who knew?

She shook herself and then stood and dressed. Life was strange, she thought as she pulled on jeans and tucked a white blouse into them. Here she was deliberating about what a new man meant in her life, while Blake, married for years, suddenly found herself alone. You could never know what would happen, and she wondered, briefly, if making plans made any sense whatsoever. You only had the present; the past and future were illusory. Thomas had proven that, and so did Charlie's miraculous appearance in her life, and now Donny had brought a dark note to everything, but the point was still the same. We lived in a small spotlight, and beyond the light, in the wings of the stage, people moved scenery and made costume changes, but we could not be aware of them. We had to play our part, as Shakespeare said, and the role was always fresh, always current, never past or future.

"How was Blake?" Charlie asked when she stepped out on the terrace.

"Donny left Blake and she's all broken up."

"Oh, I'm sorry to hear that."

"Saying it aloud like that, it sounds clinical. Doesn't it? You need to cheer me up."

"Let's go to dinner and you can tell me about it."

"Same old story."

"The fight for love and glory," Charlie said, rising.

"Yes, all that. You don't want to leave and drive off in your pickup like Donny, do you?"

"No," Charlie said, drinking off the last of his scotch and taking her hand. "I don't even have a pickup."

"Blake thinks he might be seeing someone else."

"Wouldn't be the first man to do that."

"I wish I could do something for her. Something nice."

"It sounds like you're a good friend to her, Margaret."

"I try to be. She's a good friend to me."

Charlie closed the door to the terrace and then helped her on with her sweater. She turned in his arms for a moment and put her forehead against his chest. He put his arms around her and she didn't move for a ten count.

⌒⌒

Charlie watched the waitress—a thin, toned young woman who might have been a dancer, given the way she moved—slide a plate of chocolate cheesecake onto the table between them.

"Enjoy," the waitress said. "I'll be back to freshen your coffee in a minute."

"I never eat desserts," Margaret said, grimacing and smiling at once, if that was possible. "You're going to turn me into the circus fat woman."

"It's supposed to be the best cheesecake in the universe. They're famous for it."

"Take the other fork," Margaret said, handing him one. "Ready?"

He cut into the cheesecake and lifted the fork slowly to his mouth, watching her as she did the same. She nodded a little to tell him she was ready, then she put her mouth around the forkful of cake. She closed her eyes almost instantly. He mirrored her movement and in an instant confirmed that the reputation was deserved: the cheesecake was flawless. He let it roost for a moment near the top of his mouth.

"Oh, my," she said.

"It's ridiculously good."

"It's exquisite. It's incredibly smooth, isn't it?"

"I'm not sure. I think we need another bite to know for certain."

"I'm not going to eat for a week when I get home."

"You can spare the calories."

"Pretty to think so, Charlie, but I can't. I guess on the farm the cows give me a workout, but I'm being luxuriously lazy on this trip. Except for certain exercise."

She smiled and let her eyes find his. Charlie smiled in return and took another forkful of cheesecake.

"Okay, we have to try the crust," she said.

"I love crust. Are you a good baker, Margaret?"

"Not really. Basic stuff. I'm sort of a low-grade Betty Crocker."

"I bet you're not telling the whole truth."

He took a bite and watched her match him. The crust was delicious. Graham cracker, he thought, but with a twist of some sort. The chocolate came across as dark and sweet.

"It's marvelous," she said.

"Mm-hmm."

"Promise me we'll go for a walk before we go to bed."

"It's on the schedule."

"You know, Charlie, home feels so far away."

"Maybe we've got it all wrong. Maybe this is all about vacation sex."

She laughed. He liked making her laugh. The waitress came back with coffee and warmed their cups. Charlie asked her for the check and signed it to the room.

"So what will you do after you drop me at the airport?" Margaret asked.

She motioned for Charlie to join her in another bite of cheesecake.

"You mean after I finish gnashing my teeth and pulling out chunks of hair?"

"Yes, after that."

"Terry asked me to come by. I'll probably stop there for dinner."

"Good. I'm glad."

"Then the next day I should make some phone calls, catch up on a few things. I'm supposed to take Fritz birding. He wants to see the hawk migration. But we haven't made any solid plans. How about you?"

"Cows. And I have to make Gordon shepherd's pie. It's his favorite."

"Do you make it with beef or lamb?"

"Beef. Hamburger. It's really like a glorified hamburger, but he doesn't know that. Ben likes it, too."

"You're looking forward to seeing him, aren't you? Gordon, I mean."

"It's not even conscious, really. It's just a whole big thing in my gut. It's hard to explain."

"And will you go see Thomas?"

"Yes," she said, "I'll go see Thomas."

"How often do you see him?"

"I try to do it every other day at least."

"Is it a long drive?"

"Half hour, door to door."

"Do you bring Gordon?"

"Not very often. He understands Thomas is his dad, but I don't know. I've wrestled with it, the pros and cons of exposing him to it all. Ben goes over every now and then, more to give me a break, I think, than anything else. A few other family members drop in around the holidays. That kind of thing."

"Gordon will remember it when he's older."

"I hope so. I hope he remembers it in a good way. I mean, there's no *good* about it, really, but I don't want it to be a guilty thing, either. Do you visit your brother very often?"

"Whenever I'm home I do. My mom and dad go pretty often to see him, but it's hard, as you know. He doesn't register that they're there, so you start asking yourself what the point of it is. Mom's a trouper about it. She does his birthday every year. Paper hats and cake. She does it mostly for the nurses and to remind them all that he's her son."

"It must be very touching."

"It is, actually. My parents are good people."

"They call Thomas's wing the Greenhouse, because that's where all the vegetables live. They don't say it when we're around, naturally, but I've overheard it a couple times. It hurts to hear it, especially the first time, but I suppose it's a gallows humor for people who have to tend the . . . what do we call them these days?"

"I'm not even sure anymore."

"It's just day-to-day work for the nurses, so you can't get in an uproar. Thomas receives good care and that's all I can concern myself with. They do the best they can."

Margaret broke the last small piece of cheesecake in two with the edge of her fork.

"Sorry," she said, looking at him levelly, "how did we get off on this track? Gloomy topics. Eat that and then please take me for a walk. I'm so full it's absurd."

"It's good cheesecake."

"It's a new benchmark in cheesecake," she said, lifting the last little bit to her mouth. "It is the cheesecake by which all other cheesecakes will be judged hereafter."

He reached out and clinked her fork with his. Then he took the tiny bite on his side of the plate and put it on his tongue. She nodded as she chewed her last taste, and he nodded with her.

—◌⁀

Gordon woke and it was late. He knew it was late because the darkness grew at night like a balloon swelling, and then the sun came and drew it down again. But now, on his waking, the balloon was ready to burst, and he felt nervous and alone. He missed his mother. He ran his hands around the edge of the bed, looking for the saw-chuck guy. The saw-chuck guy protected him at night and even if he sometimes couldn't find him, Gordon knew, at least, that the saw-chuck guy set perimeters and went on scouting missions, and that no one got through the line without taking fire.

After Gordon found the soldier beside the meerkat, he slipped out of his bed and went to the bathroom. He followed two night-lights in the hallway. He heard Grandpa Ben snoring, and it was a good sound after all. He wanted to talk to Grandpa Ben about the saw-chuck guy, and setting perimeters, and he would do that in the morning first thing. For now he let Grandpa Ben's snore set a perimeter around the house. His snores sounded like ropes.

He peed into the toilet and felt cold and shivered as he finished. He ran back to bed, his feet dancing a little on the ox-blood boards to keep his toes from freezing. He spotted the meerkat on the side of his bed and he grabbed him quickly and tucked him under one arm. In a flash he got under the covers again and he felt the bed's warmth reach up to meet him. He put the meerkat beside him, cheek to cheek, and together they examined the night's dark balloon. Soon, he knew, the sun would come up and it would be the day his mother came home, but what that meant, what demands the day would make on him, he couldn't say. He pictured Charlie for just a second, a man living in a city that was somehow higher than his own house, a place where you needed a plane to bring you, and he thought that was odd, one of the oddest things he had ever thought about. Slowly he marched the saw-chuck guy up to rest on top of the meerkat. Maybe, he thought, his mind returning seamlessly to earlier propositions, he could ask for a dog, one like the dog in the movie, with white fur on its chest and a bark that sounded like cans falling. He would teach the dog to stay in bed with him, he decided. It could stay down by his feet and it would be another snore, a rope he could follow when he felt nervous at night. For now, he shivered farther down into the bed and found the phantom of his former spot, still warm, still waiting, and he clutched the meerkat to his chest, the creature's beady eyes dancing with merriment in the spring moonlight.

A few miles away, Blake reached across her bed for Donny but he wasn't there. She had already cried, so Donny's absence did not jar her as it might have an hour before. It merely felt strange to have him absent. She wondered if her equilibrium had become so accustomed to the motion produced by another body on the mattress that it was like sleeping at sea. She had never been to sea, and did not particularly care to go, but the thought stuck in her head and she could not shake it.

She sat up slowly and grabbed a water bottle from her bedside stand. The water felt cool from sitting near the window. She drank a long time, feeling that the cells of her body required replenishing. Donny was gone, she told herself. Just like that. Gone to another woman, gone to his rattletrap pickup, gone to his lawn mowers and gas-covered truck upholstery. She wondered if he hadn't been going their entire married life, his life orbiting around her own, ready to fling off like a slinging comet. She wondered, too, what she would tell Phillip. *Daddy's gone,* she said inside her head. It sounded like a bad blues lyric and she promised herself never to utter it.

She replaced the water bottle on the bedside stand and slid down into the fold of covers again. Without Donny, the bed felt crisp and even. Maybe that was one advantage to having him gone. There would be other advantages, she imagined, but she could not think of them right now. Things about staying clean, being organized, the house in order. But she rested in the neat envelope of her bed like a letter unsent. Return to sender, she thought. Donny didn't want her anymore.

She watched the wind move the tree branches beyond the window, the shadows from the branches dancing. *Here I begin again*, she thought. *Here I return to myself.* She rested in bed with her arms outside the blankets, her feet snug against the tightly tucked sheet at the bottom of the bed. A handkerchief folded and left in a man's suit pocket, she thought. An arrow in a quiver, resting, not drawn out and nocked on a string, never sent on its way.

───❦───

And in the last stroke before midnight, Margaret turned and felt Charlie follow her, his hand coming across her hip, then hanging like a counterweight of comfort and quiet. Awakened at that moment, she would not have been able to express exactly what the hand meant across her hip, could not have raised an answer to consciousness. But in the small hours with the crickets calling, the sheets crisp, the pillows luxurious, she settled beneath his arm with a deep animal contentment.

She did not dream. At least she had no memory of dreaming the next morning, though she pushed back into his arms, feeling safe and warm, his breath a steady metronome on her neck. For a time she ran in her sleep, her legs moving slightly. She did not move in panic, but in an attempt to arrive someplace. Then his hand tightened on her waist and pulled her closer—was he asleep?—and her legs settled and went slack.

Far away, in Maine, Sgt. Thomas Kennedy continued to breathe, his breath as steady as a broom sweep. He felt nothing, thought nothing. His body continued to function even as his brain, inactive, turned slowly softer. Night and day made no difference to him; only a full moon, with its pull on tides, affected him now. The interior of his body had become a sea, an ocean following the dictates of gravity. Whatever had been the essence of Thomas Kennedy had long since drifted away or ceased or become part of the gentle sway of liquid that washed with the light from the moon.

Chapter
Twenty-four

Margaret called Blake. She sat on a bench by herself, her carry-on bag at her feet. Blake picked up on the third ring. They had talked twice that morning already, but it had been about details of traveling.

"Hi, honey," Blake said, her voice raised and happy, "is this my southern girl?"

"It is indeed."

"I can't wait to see you, honey. Where are you now?"

"At the airport."

"You sound a little off, darling. Are you okay?" Blake asked, then she said something to Phillip, her son, and added, "Sorry. They had a half day today so he's home. A teachers' service day, I guess."

"Everything is okay," Margaret said. "He's parking the car."

"Your fella?"

"He's not my fella, Blake," Margaret said, and she felt a sharp, grinding pain in her gut.

"Oh, sweetie, you're sad," Blake said, her voice moving with the phone away from somewhere—her kitchen, probably, Margaret guessed. "Oh, Margaret, what's wrong?"

"I'm just an idiot," Margaret said and began to cry.

"What, what, what is it?"

"I was crazy to let it get so out of hand," Margaret said. "So stupid. He's perfect, Blake. He's a perfect man."

"No one is perfect, Margaret."

"You haven't met him. No, of course not, of course no one is perfect," Margaret conceded, feeling a deep, sad sob growing inside her. "But everything that was so sealed up and shut down . . ."

Then she couldn't help it. She turned and faced the window, trying to keep her sobs private. She put her hand over her face and for a long time she couldn't breathe. She heard Blake say something, but her friend's voice had no weight or substance. Sadness came in like a bright, scalding log falling slowly out of the fireplace. Such sadness felt dangerous and she let it build and burn for a moment before she decided she needed to put it back among the other logs. But it didn't go back easily, and she felt her need for breath building and searching her lungs, and then the sob she had anticipated broke through and forced out of her a sharp, anguished cry.

"Oh, sweetheart, I'm so sorry. I'm sorry. It's okay, though," Blake said. "It's okay, it's just big feelings. It's just your heart thawing in a way it hasn't in a long, long time."

Margaret nodded, her hand still over her face. She felt horrible crying on the phone to Blake when Blake had her own problems to deal with. Her own huge problems. It was selfish, horrible behavior, but she couldn't help it right now. She held still for a second, then let out something that was closer to a laugh than a sob.

"Oh, boy, I've got it bad," she said. "And I'm being so self-involved I'm not even asking about you and Donny."

"Donny and I can wait. Nothing is changing there. Right now we have to help you leave things the way you want them to go. It's so new to you, that's all," Blake said. "You're having positive thoughts, Margaret. There's nothing wrong. You met a terrific guy, that's all. That's a good thing, right? Just take everything in time."

"I know, I know, I know you're right," Margaret said. Then she whispered into the phone, "I have such feelings for him."

"Good," Blake said. "Good for you. If you couldn't feel, you might as well be dead. Or married to Donny!"

Margaret laughed, her face feeling wet and stretched and unsettled. She took a deep breath and squared her shoulders. What a strange, mixed-up day it felt to be.

"No word from the Donn-a-nator today?" she asked Blake, trying to lighten things.

"Nope, not a word. It almost feels like a relief."

"I'm sorry, Blake."

"Listen, right now just collect yourself and see where things go. You don't have to make any definitive plans this moment. This doesn't have to be the whole shebang one way or the other. Just take it easy."

"Thanks, Blake," she said. "I called just to touch base and tell you we were at the airport. . . . I don't know where that all came from. I should hop off. Charlie will be here in a minute."

"I've got your itinerary, so don't worry. I'll be there to meet you."

"You haven't told anyone else about this weekend, have you, Blake?"

"No. I thought about it, to be honest. I saw Maryanne in the Shop 'n Save and she asked about you, and I started to say something, and then the good angels told me it was none of my business to be telling, and it sure as heck wasn't any of Maryanne's business to know."

"Maybe down the road I can talk about it, but not right now. Not with anyone but you."

"Okay, we'll do it just that way. Now, I should go back and make sure Phillip eats some mac and peas. I'll be right on time, don't worry. Can I bring you anything?"

"If you're stopping at Dunkin' Donuts, how about a coffee?"

"Done."

"Thank you, Blake. Thanks for listening."

"I wish I had some poetic thing to say to you that would make it all right, but I don't, honey. It's all good. You're entitled to a little happiness."

Margaret closed her phone. She looked out the window and realized it had begun to rain. She watched water streak down the window and she felt Charlie's presence return more than saw it. His hand touched her shoulder and she reached up

and covered his fingers with her own. He smelled of the outdoors and soap, and when he kissed the side of her neck she
leaned away from his mouth and held his head close to her, and
she opened herself, gave access to her neck as she would to a
vampire, to a lover, to a husband.

—ᶜ

It felt like a movie. Margaret couldn't escape the sensation. She
saw the security station in front of them, and she understood—
in a way she had never considered before—why filmmakers
relied on departure scenes. It was the big show, only it didn't
feel like a big show. It felt quiet and sad and lonely. She did not
want to leave; she did not want to say good-bye. But it was
time to go, and momentum carried her forward. She knew,
without question, that she could lose herself in the busy details
of air travel, but that would be a cheat. She needed to concentrate, to record these last moments. They had time, not much,
but some.

"Do you think we just let everything get out of hand?" she
asked Charlie quickly, her voice choked. "Was this real, Charlie?"

"Yes, it was real. It still is."

"I'm afraid when I get home it won't feel real."

"We had good days together. It was exactly what you think
it was, Margaret."

"But the rest of it . . ."

"Trust it," Charlie said simply. "Whatever you were feeling, so was I. It was true."

"And now it's over and we're going to go back to our separate lives."

"Nothing's over, Margaret."

"You'll be leaving soon."

"Who knows what will happen?"

"I do," she said. "I know what will happen. You'll be this
wonderful memory that I will visit each spring. When the lilacs come out, and when the apple blossoms bloom. I'll never
smell a lilac again without calling you to mind."

"Come here," he said and he turned her body toward his.

He held her in his arms. She wanted to crawl into his
pocket and stay there. She put her forehead against his chest
and nodded. She felt her eyes begin to grow glassy. She rubbed
her fingers against them and nodded again.

Then, a few steps later, it was time to check in. The first
security guard asked to see her boarding pass and Margaret
showed it to her. The guard read it and handed it back.

"Go ahead," the guard said. "Have your ID out."

"We just want to say good-bye."

The guard nodded and took boarding passes from a couple
behind Margaret.

"Good-bye, Margaret," Charlie said.

"Good-bye, Charlie."

"I'm not going to try to say anything clever or memorable,
if that's okay."

"Me neither. *Meaningful good-bye, meaningful good-bye,
meaningful good-bye.*"

"My brother was smarter than I realized."

"Thank you for everything."

He kissed her. At first it started as a calm, rational kiss, but then it grew. She felt herself falling into him, losing herself, and she thought it was impossible that she would never kiss him, never do *this*, again. She shook when the kiss reached its climax.

When they broke apart, she stepped immediately into the security line. She did not look back and she did not try to cover her tears.

—☙

"I wanted to make sure you're okay," Terry said over the phone. "Are you all right, Charlie?"

"I'm okay."

"Where are you?"

"Coming back from the airport."

"Will you swing by?" Terry asked. "We're just eating leftovers, but there's a plate for you if you want it."

"I think I'm going to go home, if you don't mind. I'm sorry. I just don't think I'd be good company right now."

"And lick your wounds?"

"And lick my wounds."

"Do you think she'll relent?"

"I don't think so. She's loyal to her husband."

"That's commendable."

"But . . . ?"

"But he isn't conscious, is he?"

"Apparently not."

"It's a tough decision. From outside it seems like an easy thing, but not when you're inside it. It's a house of mirrors when you're inside it."

"I can't push. I want to, but I can't."

"Are you sure?"

"She wouldn't want me to. I'd just make things harder for her. It wouldn't be fair to put that kind of pressure on her."

"Fortune favors the brave."

"I'm not sure it does in this case."

"Okay, are you sure you won't come back over? Henry says he'll beat you at Scrabble."

"I'm going to go home, Terry, but thanks. Thanks for everything. She had a good couple days, I hope. You made her feel welcome, so thanks for that. She liked you a great deal."

"Well, the feeling was mutual."

"I may bring Fritz out Saturday if that's okay. The birds are incredibly active right now."

"No problem. He's always welcome. And so are you."

Charlie hung up. It felt strange being in the Jeep alone. Twice, as he drove home, he pushed his hand over toward Margaret's knee, but she was not there.

"So, talk," Blake said when they had navigated the airport traffic and made it safely onto the interchange. "When you're ready, go ahead and talk. I'm all ears."

"First tell me about Donny. Has he been in touch?"

"He's with Phillip now. He came back home around the

time I was set to leave. I guess he remembered he promised to watch him."

"Did he say anything?"

"Donny? He hasn't yet acquired language."

"Seriously."

Blake shook her head and then insisted she wanted to hear about Charlie.

Margaret didn't know where to begin. She held the coffee Blake had given her against her belly. She liked the warmth of the coffee, but she wasn't sure she could drink it after all. She felt jittery and out of sorts; travel always did that to her in any case, but it felt more unsettling in this instance.

"What was Grandpa Ben like when you went to the house?" Margaret asked, thinking if she could listen to Blake for a while she could follow her friend's voice.

"Oh, he was fine. He was asleep in the chair watching the Red Sox when I went over. He had a big bowl of strawberry ice cream beside him . . . empty, I mean. He's fine. And I guess the cows are doing something good. . . . I forget what he said, but he seemed pleased."

"Thanks for looking in on him."

"My pleasure. So tell me about the ball at least. I want to hear about it. Was it what you thought it would be like?"

"It was beautiful, Blake."

"I'm so stinking jealous. And the gown?"

"It was fine. I looked passable."

"Passable? I bet you were stunning."

"I looked okay, Blake. We made a nice-looking couple."

"You have pictures somewhere, right?"

"A few. Not many."

"And Charlie . . . he's how tall?"

"Six-two or so, I think. He's a perfect size. I wouldn't wish him any other way."

"And you danced?"

"We did. And we kissed on the veranda. It smelled of lilacs. Everything about this weekend, this time away, had lilacs or apple blossoms underscoring it. It was a little weird that way."

"So freaking dreamy."

"It actually was. You know, I was thinking about it. It was one of the few times in my life where the reality matched the anticipation. Childbirth was one occasion like that. I can't think of many others."

Blake drank her coffee and took an exit off to the right. Margaret heard spring peepers calling from marshland as they merged onto Highway 157. She rolled down the window a little to get more of the sound. Then she realized it might be cold on Blake, so she wound it up again.

"And so he was terrific?" Blake asked.

"He's a good man. A truly good man. His friend, Terry, she adores him. Did I tell you Charlie is an Eagle Scout? And the thing is, he *is* an Eagle Scout. I guess a lot of the women in that circle of friends in Washington have shown interest, but he's not the sort to tip a bunch of women into bed. He's not a conquest sort of guy."

"And he's in the diplomatic corps?"

"He's going to Africa. He's excited about it."

"So you could travel the world with him?"

"I could travel the world with him, yes. If we decided we wanted to stay together. And if I didn't have a husband in Bangor. And if a thousand other things fell into place."

"Are you going to see him again?"

"I don't think so, Blake."

"Are you serious? Give me his number and I'll call him."

It was meant as a joke but it didn't quite work. Blake sipped her coffee. Then she reached over and touched Margaret's hand.

"Sorry. I meant it to be funny, but it wasn't really, was it?"

"I guess it's all too fresh to be funny."

"But you don't think you'll see him again?"

"I don't know. I'm tired of thinking about it. It gets complicated pretty quickly. I saw that happening. Then there's Thomas to think of, and a whole bunch of practical concerns. But mostly it's Thomas. I don't want to put us all into a big blender if there's no resolution to it. Do you know what I mean?"

"I do, honey."

"If I was the only one in the equation? I wouldn't let him go."

Margaret smiled. She reached across and touched Blake's hand, wanting her to know everything was okay.

"If anyone deserves a little fun in her life, it's you," Blake said.

"That's the thing. A little fun would be one thing, but this felt like more than that. You know all those clichés about true love and a soul mate . . . I never put much stock in any of it, but now I don't know. It's crazy, and I'm hoping a little distance will give me perspective, but we matched. We just did. In every way."

"And . . . ?"

Margaret saw Blake's face. Blake sipped her coffee, but Margaret saw her lip curl in a little smile.

"And, yes," Margaret said, "the bed part was good, too. Really good. You're such a little voyeur, Blake."

"I'm glad, honey."

"Actually, if it had been lousy it might have helped the situation."

Blake smiled hard at that.

"Could you keep it casual?" Blake asked. "Just a thing you could visit now and then down in Washington? At least until he leaves."

The car passed another acre or two of marshland. Margaret heard the peepers pushing their voices out into the chilly spring air even harder than before. She sipped her coffee, which was lukewarm now and tasted of cream.

"I guess I could propose it, but I like him too much for that. And maybe he likes me too much. He's a decent man. And if I feel this way after one little getaway, I can't imagine what it would be like if I had a steady diet of him."

"Can you put it on a shelf and not decide right away? I mean, why does it have to be all one thing or another?"

"Time will eventually settle it. Maybe he'll meet someone.

We didn't talk about it, but he wants to have a family, I'm sure. He was so good with Gordon, Blake, in just the little time he had with him. And he was good with other kids. He played with them."

Blake nodded.

"The world's a funny place, isn't it?" Blake said.

Margaret let out a long sigh.

"Anyway, we met the president. President Obama was very personable and sweet. Now tell me about the Donny situation. We've just glossed over it. Tell me what you're thinking."

Margaret let herself relax back into the seat and took a sip of coffee. She listened to Blake, hearing the old domestic litany: Donny working too much, not attending the soccer games, being distant, plopping down in front of the television. In time, Margaret's mind wandered, pushed by the intermittent sounds of the peepers, by the steady drone of the car tires on the asphalt. Safe inside her friend's voice, she imagined what it would be like if Charlie were waiting at home for her. She imagined him pushing open the door and stepping onto the porch, his arms opening, his smile wide and welcoming. *Oh, Charlie,* she thought, and then made her attention return to her friend, and she nodded, and made the appropriate sounds of bewilderment, of incomprehension at Donny's actions, but in her heart she called to Charlie.

In the first light of morning, Margaret wept into her pillow. At last she could let it come: she heaved deep, heavy sobs into her pillow and felt her body clench and release, clench and release. *Mercy*, she thought. She should have been a turtle, a lumbering, gentle creature buried in the pond mud, waiting for the turn of the calendar to wake her. *To have a shell*, she thought. She wept for Thomas and she wept for Charlie, and she wept for herself. She wept for the oak tree, the tree she loved, as it sifted the first light of dawn through its many fingers. She wondered how deep the tree's roots went, how far they had traveled in the darkness of soil, only to retrieve this spark of beauty for one hundred and more years. She felt, in her deepest crying, that if she saw the phoebe on the walk to the barn she might dissolve like vapor, like mist, and the bird would carry her away on its wings.

Eventually she rolled over and studied the light piercing the window, the familiar shadow of the oak as it warmed in the sun. A few minutes later she heard Grandpa Ben make his way downstairs, his heavy tread met finally by the *sprong* of the screen door as it opened and swung quietly shut. And what about tears for Benjamin, father to her husband, a plain, simple man who loved the cattle and brought white milk into the world with his two hands and his careful husbandry? When did his day come? When did his son return to him, his brave boy, and promise that his father's youth and energy had not been wasted?

She nearly began to cry again, but she was from Maine, deep Maine, so she swung her legs over the edge of the bed and went into the bathroom. She used the toilet, then washed her face, and then she dressed in jeans and heavy socks and slid quietly downstairs.

Benjamin had left the back door open and she followed him out, blinking a little at the new sun. And for an instant the scent of lilacs assaulted her. The fragrance entered her heart and made her grip the banister railing to steady herself. Common lilacs, she remembered, common as she herself was, and she held up two great heads from the dooryard bush and breathed in the scent of sweetness and pleasure and springs remembered even as they were lost.

Daisies

Chapter
Twenty-five

Margaret did not remember driving to the hospital, but suddenly she arrived. It unnerved her to travel the distance without being fully conscious. She remembered picking up groceries for shepherd's pie at the Shop 'n Save, and she remembered dropping a quilt—a family heirloom, probably past saving—at the dry cleaner's, but the final quarter hour had passed automatically, a hum of time without any resonance. She had been like that since she had returned: the reunion with Gordon, the early morning with the cows, the gentle questions from Ben had all been somehow removed from her full comprehension. She was aware of making phrases, responding properly, but her heart was somewhere else. Even the lusciousness of Gordon—and, yes, she had kissed him and hugged him and made him understand he had been missed—had not fully penetrated the hangover left by Charlie. And now her preoccupation had pinched her consciousness shut while she drove, and she did not like knowing that.

She shook herself and climbed out of the old pickup, then reached across the front seat for the bundle of lilacs she had cut for Thomas. It had astonished her to find them still fragrant, still in the middle of their blossoming. She felt as though she had been away for a year, but it had only been a long weekend and the lilac heads, slightly gone by, still sent a marvelous fragrance into the air.

"Hi, Margaret," Julie, the hospital receptionist, said when she entered. Julie wore a flowered smock and she had done something new to her hair, but Margaret couldn't focus to see it. Margaret stiffened her shoulders, trying to pay attention. She took a deep breath and stopped for a moment. *Julie,* she reminded herself. Margaret nearly squinted with concentration. She stared at Julie's round face, her round eyes, the bead of a telephone mouthpiece suspended under her chin. A perm? A color change? Margaret couldn't quite put her finger on the change. Her eyes glazed over and Julie could not swim out of the fog that surrounded her.

"How was your trip?" Julie asked, filling in the conversational gap. "Washington, right?"

"It was wonderful. Thanks. I can't believe I'm back."

"Lilacs, huh?"

"The last of them, I think."

"They're so amazing," Julie said and lifted from her seat to smell the bundle that Margaret held over the reception console. Margaret saw Julie clearly for a moment.

"You went blonder?" Margaret asked.

"I did. Life is more fun as a blonde. Isn't that what they say? Do you like it?"

"I do. It's flattering for you."

"Ronny said I look like Jean Harlow, the old movie actress. I didn't even know who it was. I had to Google her name. I don't see the resemblance, but Ronny thinks I look sort of sassy."

"Then it's worth it."

"People think it's a perm, but it's not."

"It's very becoming," Margaret said and realized that word sounded hopelessly old-lady-ish.

"So you must be eager to see Tom."

"I am."

"Those lilacs are just the thing."

For a man who won't even know I'm there. Margaret finished the thought for Julie.

"Well, I should head up," Margaret said instead. "I'll see you on the way out."

Julie nodded. The phone had buzzed and she began speaking with her official voice.

Margaret walked through the hallway and stopped at the elevator. A few people smiled at the lilacs. She smiled back, her face pasted on.

⁓ℭ

Gordon stood between his grandfather's knees and drove the Farmall tractor. He liked driving it better than just about anything, but he didn't get to do it often. Today felt a little like a holiday, though, because his mom was home and the milking was finished and they had shepherd's pie scheduled for dinner. Gordon loved shepherd's pie; it was his favorite dinner, although he liked certain desserts better than any meal in the world. Still, driving the tractor, his hands on the large wheel in front of him, his grandfather's thick shirt behind him, made him jiggle a little in his legs. For a moment he thought he had to pee, but then his body calmed and he felt warm and happy and centered.

They drove up to the apple orchards, where they planned to meet Noel Grummond and the boys with the biosolids truck. Gordon didn't know what "biosolids" meant, nor did he fully understand the project, but he knew his grandfather needed the tractor up in the apple meadows. Gordon was aware of the apple meadows; the trees were in late bloom and they appeared to be a white cloud beneath the white clouds in the sky. His grandfather often talked about restoring the orchards, pruning the old trees, but that work was best done in late winter and Grandpa Ben never got around to it.

Halfway up to the meadows, they drove through a pocket of cows that had wandered into the dirt path. Gordon felt the tractor gear down and brake a bit. The cows didn't seem frightened or worried by the tractor, but they slowly split, like wood leaning into a maul, and he heard his grandpa yelp a little to get them moving faster. Gordon steered carefully, aware of his grandfather's hands next to his. Mud covered the cows, dotting them and turning their tails into weighted bells of liquid, and they smelled—even on this good early summer morning— of hay and clotted manure and milk.

Gordon released one hand from the steering wheel and dug into his right hip pocket for the saw-chuck guy. He took him out and propped him on the steering wheel, shooting at the cows. And he wasn't sure what happened next, but suddenly the saw-chuck guy spun free of his hand and tumbled down. The tiny plastic man slapped against the deck of the tractor and continued spinning, hurtling down to the back left wheel and disappearing. Gordon's stomach wrenched. He leaned to the left, trying to see, and he felt Grandpa Ben pull him back straight behind the wheel.

"Pay attention, Gordon," Grandpa Ben said, but the saw-chuck guy was gone, buried in grass and cow imprints and the swollen soil of early summer.

Blake had just returned from dropping Phillip at swim class when she saw Donny's truck pull into the driveway. Her stomach flip-flopped. She opened the cupboard to the right of the sink and glanced at herself in the note-card-size mirror some housewife had placed there long before they owned the house. She had always been grateful for the mirror, wondering why more houses didn't have one. She pushed at her hair quickly, then closed the cupboard door and turned on the water in the sink to have noise. For a passing instant she felt she might be sick, and she wondered what Donny would think if he walked through the door to find his wife heaving in the sink.

"Morning," Donny said, coming through the door.

"Morning."

"Just grabbing some stuff. Where's Phillip?"

"Swim class, then he has a playdate with Maryanne's boy."

"How was Margaret?"

"Fine."

"She have a good time?"

Blake nodded.

"So we're going with one-word answers today?"

"I guess."

"That's two words."

"What do you want me to say, Donny?" Blake asked and turned.

He stood in the doorway, brown and slightly grassy. She hated to admit it, but he looked good. Detestable, really, that he would thrive under the current circumstances. She felt her face flush. He might have been a stranger standing there. Whatever she felt, he seemed to feel it, too, because in two steps he came across the room and then his hands roamed everywhere. It was nearly violent. She couldn't pretend it wasn't, but it was exciting beyond anything that had happened to her in months, and she met his hands and met his requests, and before long they both stood leaning against the sink, their pants absurdly down on their legs, their breathing hard and fast and stunned. Her limbs quivered. The water still ran in the sink.

He didn't kiss me, she thought.

"I don't hate you," he said, slowly dressing. "I hope you know that."

"I know that."

"I'd like it if you didn't hate me."

"I don't, Donny."

"It's for the best."

"What is?"

He shrugged.

"Is there someone else?" she asked.

"No."

"Are you sure?"

He made a little sideways motion and finished buttoning his jeans.

"I'll make all the payments," he said. "You don't have to worry about that."

"This is really what you want?"

He shrugged again. She waited, wondering if he would answer.

"Go ahead," she said, "get what you came for."

He nodded. When she turned the water in the sink off, she heard him upstairs, going through their bedroom, removing more of his clothes. She kept both hands on the sink, listening. Drawer, closet, closet, closet, drawer, bathroom, under the bed, closet. She followed his movements and did not move until he came back downstairs, whatever he had taken shoved into a large duffel.

"If Phillip asks," she said, her eyes locked on the window over the sink, "where should I say you're staying?"

"I'm staying at Billy's right now."

She nodded. He paused a moment, and then he went out. She listened to his truck door slam and he drove off.

Margaret's hands trembled as she placed the stem ends of the lilacs in a vase she had requested at the nurses' station. Her stomach felt buoyant and troubled in her body and she still found it difficult to concentrate on the task at hand. One of the nurses—Gloria, an older woman who was competent but all business—looked up from her paperwork and smiled softly. Margaret smiled in return and finally slid the stem ends inside the vase.

"It's never easy," Gloria said, but whether she referred to fitting the flowers in the vase or life in general, Margaret couldn't say.

"No, I guess not."

"Still," Gloria said and looked back down at her paperwork.

Margaret smiled. Then she nodded, more to herself than to Gloria, and carried the lilacs toward the Greenhouse. She could not stop the trembling in her hands. Did she feel shy? Was she ashamed? She couldn't pinpoint her emotion. She felt young and girlish, but in an insecure way, like a teen walking into a dance. She put her nose to the lilacs, trying to take strength from them. They were nearly gone by entirely, she saw now. She hadn't seen it clearly before, but she saw it now. She had misjudged them.

She counted the beds as she always did. One, two, three, and the fifth bed was Thomas's. She walked slowly around the bottom of the bed, giving the lilacs more attention than they deserved, her eyes staying away from Thomas's face. She trailed her free hand across his feet, let it dangle as she stepped up to the bedside table. She placed the lilacs on the table, the glass vase chattering slightly as she settled it. She took a deep breath. Then she turned and looked at Thomas.

Her eyes clouded. She bent down and kissed his forehead. She left her lips on him a long time. She reached and smoothed the skin on his cheek and gently brushed back his hair. He needed a haircut, she realized. A glance told her his nails needed trimming. She was glad to see that; it gave her something to do. She pulled a chair around to the side of the bed and opened the bedside drawer for clippers. When she had them out she sat and drew his hand over the edge of the bed. She turned his hand this way and that to get the proper angle for the nails, then suddenly she dropped the clippers and brought his hand to her face. She held it against her eyes and wept. Then she surged forward and she leaned across the bed, her body joined with her husband's, her head at last on his shoulder. She cried into his neck, sobbing, and she told herself to stop, that these tears served nothing, but she couldn't prevent them. She pressed more of her body against his, aware of his fragility, his thin ribs, his sharp chin. She felt his arms—those arms that had been so strong but had now become two dull hoses shrunken by atrophy—and she lifted one to cover herself. But the arm dropped and returned to the bed, and she lifted it again, once more, and each time the arm fell like snow casting away from an eave on a warm winter day.

"How are we?" a nurse said behind her.

Margaret had not seen the woman approach, but she shook her head. She tucked herself closer into her husband's body, and then she let the nurse slowly lift her away, let her pull her back, the woman's voice murmuring, "It will be okay, it will be all right." But it wasn't okay, and Margaret sank to the side of the bed and knelt and held her husband's hand, and she asked forgiveness, and she asked for mercy, and she expected neither.

"IT IS NOT OKAY!" Margaret screamed. "IT IS NOT OKAY."

Then things happened quickly. Her voice carried down the hallways. Margaret heard footsteps coming. She had caused a scene and she didn't care. She kept repeating the phrase—*it is not okay, it is not okay*—her voice raspy and broken, and when they came to her and tried to lift her she slapped at the hands. Then more footsteps. A male orderly appeared and she refused to cooperate. She clung to her husband's hand and she leaned down, taking refuge under the bed railing. She was aware of everything. It fascinated her; she felt divided. She was aware of losing control, and in being aware of it she wondered if that didn't prove it a counterfeit. In a tiny wedge of her mind she wondered what they would do, what anyone *could* do, if she decided to keep screaming. How long would they put up with it? And another part of her mind felt satisfied that she had finally done this, finally stepped over a line, finally told them all the truth, because it wasn't fine. No more pretend. No more noble wife. She wanted her husband back and she kicked twice at the male orderly before a woman in a gray pantsuit arrived and squatted next to her. It was Mrs. McCafferty, the hospital administrator. Margaret had had a thousand conversations with her about bills and government programs and

veteran benefits. She was a small, blue-eyed woman, unquestionably of Irish ancestry, who was thin and reddish and close
to retirement.

"Everyone step away, all right?" Mrs. McCafferty said,
her voice oddly calm. "Just leave us alone for a second, if you
will. We all know Mrs. Kennedy here. Let's give her a moment
to collect herself."

Margaret kept her eyes away. She didn't want to meet the
eyes of anyone circling her. She clung to her husband's hand.
If she let go of her husband's hand, she felt she might perish.
She might drift away or never find another breath of air. Meanwhile, Mrs. McCafferty said nothing. She changed positions
slightly to be more comfortable. She put one hand out to steady
herself against the bed.

"Hi, Margaret," she said quietly when the rest of the staff
had backed away.

Margaret nodded.

"I don't want to pretend to know what you're feeling,"
Mrs. McCafferty said, her voice slightly flattened with a
Maine accent. "No one can know that. I've watched you come
here faithfully all these years, and you've never raised your
voice, never caused us any problem, and so I know something
has hurt you. Or maybe you've finally reached a point . . . we
all have points, don't we? We have a place that fills us too much
and then we give in, we can't help it, we're saturated. You and
I both know I have nothing good to say here. You know it. I
won't try. But I promise you I will defend you to the last moment I work here because I have seen what you have been

through. And if you've just had a little collapse, so what? How do you not deserve that? I'm going to stay here for a few minutes and let you decide when you're ready to rejoin the world. I'll help you, so don't worry. And we can go have a nice cup of tea, or a glass of whiskey, I don't care, because I see your husband there and I know a little of it."

Margaret placed her husband's hand against her eyes. She held it there. Slowly, breath by breath, the world came back into focus. She flushed with embarrassment. Had she really gone crazy that way? Had she kicked at people? She kissed the back of her husband's hand and slowly lifted it to the bed. Then she uncurled from under the bed, moving gradually into a sitting position. She could not bring herself to meet Mrs. McCafferty's eyes.

"I'm sorry," she whispered.

"Don't worry a second about it. We all have days. You've never been anything but a pleasure to be around, so don't give it another thought. You just take your time. We have lots of time around here."

"It's childish."

"Not a bit of it. Would you like a hand up? Have pity on an old lady. I can't squat like this much longer."

Between the bed and Mrs. McCafferty's hand, Margaret stood. She felt shaky. She sensed that the others—the orderly and the nurses—watched from the nurses' station. The lilacs had fallen from the table; a glass of water had tipped over.

"I'm so sorry," Margaret whispered.

"You can make your apologies another day. I'll have a word

with them. You go home and get a good rest. We'll see to everything here. Or would you like to stay and have a cup of tea?"

"I'll go home."

Margaret touched Thomas's hand once more, then she allowed Mrs. McCafferty to walk her slowly out. Margaret did not look closely where she was going, but trusted Mrs. McCafferty. Mrs. McCafferty walked her all the way out to her car.

"Will you be okay to drive? Would you like me to call someone?"

"I'm going to sit for a few minutes. Maybe I'll close my eyes."

"That's a good idea. It's shady here. I used to take a nap sometimes at lunch in the parking lot. Better than eating and putting on more weight I didn't need."

"Thank you for your help."

"Margaret, you've broken my heart many times in these last years. You've made me a better wife to my husband, believe it or not. I go home and I see him and, as crazy as he sometimes makes me, I remember your circumstances and I thank God for what I have. You're brave, Margaret. Tremendously brave."

Margaret hugged Mrs. McCafferty and didn't let go. Not for a while. Finally she folded herself into her car and put her head back against the seat rest. Mrs. McCafferty left. Margaret felt sleep steal over her. Shade pushed and pulled in the spring breeze and when she woke, a little later, she felt cold.

Chapter
Twenty-six

The daisies had come at last. Margaret noted them as she pulled out of the driveway, amazed that it could be July, mid-July, already. She was not sure who had planted them, if anyone at all, but they clung to either side of the driveway in great sweeps, extending from the bare earth of the tire tracks to the dull gleam of the fire pond higher on the hill. Simple daisies. They arrived every year, their march unobtrusive and silent, and they carried the Maine summer into its full expression. She slowed to watch them move in the afternoon breeze. Wind went through them and bent back the heads like a child blowing on dandelion seeds.

She drove Blake's car, a secondhand Civic, because Grandpa Ben needed the truck. It was one of those impossibly complicated domestic confusions that meant nothing at all except that two people needed the same thing at the same time. Grandpa Ben had gone off to a dairy farmers' symposium, of all things, sponsored by the Maine Department of Agriculture. The local agent, Tim Oberman, had insisted Ben attend; north-central Maine dairymen needed to discuss pricing, and that was one of the few things that would draw Ben away for so much as a day. So he was off to Bangor in the truck, and John Walt, the son of one of Ben's closest friends, had volunteered to watch after the cattle, and now for the first time in memory the house was going to be empty. It felt strange to drive away, and she glanced in the mirror several times to watch the house disappear.

"You looking forward to playing with Phillip?" she asked Gordon, who sat in the backseat buckled in and obviously out of sorts. He did not want to go to Blake's; he had protested, asking if he couldn't simply go with his grandfather, but the arrangements had already been made.

He nodded anyway and looked out the window.

"Did you see the daisies are here?" she asked. "Right up to the pond."

"Yes."

"What do they look like to you?"

"Like daisies."

"But if you had to imagine they looked like something else? What then?"

He shrugged, then said, "Water."

She met his eyes in the mirror and smiled. She made a face; he returned it. Ten minutes later they pulled into Blake's driveway. Blake had the lawn mower going. Phillip watered something near the house, but mostly he sprayed water into arcs and bullets, occasionally drawing a fine rainbow out of the late afternoon sunlight. Margaret pulled up and turned off the car. She climbed out and waved to catch Blake's attention.

"You look nice," Blake said when she had spotted them and turned off the lawn mower. "Hi, Gordon. You want to help Phillip water the pumpkins?"

Margaret held the door for Gordon. He climbed out like an old man. He was shy. That was another element of the Kennedy men, for better or worse, Margaret thought.

"Go ahead, sweetie," she whispered, squatting to kiss him. "I'm going to be leaving in a second. Be a good boy, okay?"

He nodded.

"I'll be over to get you first thing in the morning."

He walked off, raising his hand in greeting to Phillip. Phillip turned with the water hose and nearly got him.

"So, you ready for this?" Blake asked.

"As I'm going to be, I guess."

"What do you think he wants to say?"

"I don't know. Maybe nothing. Maybe just good-bye."

"Margaret, he could have flown out of Washington, for Pete's sake. He wanted to see you, so he made his flight from Portland."

"I suppose."

"Are you going to spend the night?"

"No, I'm not going to spend the night."

"Just asking."

"I guess we left it a little unresolved, that's all. The whole affair, I mean. This is about closure."

"Oh, aren't you Miss Clear Thinker?"

Blake laughed. Margaret began to be cross, but then realized she was wound too tight.

"Really," Blake said, "you look beautiful. You're going to dinner?"

"A lobster place or something. I don't know. I won't be able to eat, that's for sure."

"Well, you better get a move on if you're going to make Portland in time. You all set with the car?"

"Yes, and thanks again."

"I'd hug you, sweetheart, but I'm covered in sweat and grass. Do me a favor, okay? I know it's complicated, but just listen to everything he has to say, all right? Just hear him out."

"I will."

"And don't worry about Gordon. He'll be fine once you're out of here. He always is."

Margaret nodded and blew a kiss at Blake. Blake blew one back. Margaret called to Gordon and said good-bye, and Gordon waved but didn't leave Phillip. They both stared into a plastic bucket, amazed at what water could do.

─ C ─

Charlie rode the elevator down, his hand jingling change in his pocket. He glanced at himself twice in the mirrors lining the interior of the elevator, wondering if mirrors were supposed to make the elevator column feel more spacious. It failed, if that was what was intended, but Charlie studied himself anyway. He felt good, he admitted. He was on his way to Africa, to his first diplomatic posting, and as he looked at his reflection, he felt that something had been settled. Probably his professional life, he decided. The military had been one thing, and service in Iraq another, but now he felt ready to open a new chapter, one that had the potential to carry him forward in ways he wouldn't be able to predict. It felt exciting.

When the elevator doors opened, he crossed the hotel lobby and looked out at the parking lot. Margaret had called to say she was fifteen minutes away according to the GPS. Thinking of her made him nervous and fidget more with the change in his pocket. He looked out the window again, then realized he wouldn't know her car anyway. He took a deep breath and found a seat on one of the couches in the center of the lobby. As he reached for a copy of *Sports Illustrated*, his cell phone rang.

"You see the Reds last night?" Pete asked without saying hello.

"I didn't. They win?"

"Came from behind. They scored five in the ninth inning. Where are you anyway?"

"Portland."

"Have you seen her yet?"

"She should be here any second."

"What are you going to say?"

"I don't know."

"You don't know what you're going to say?"

"I don't know exactly. I have the general idea."

"You leave tomorrow?"

"Yep."

"All right. I won't hold you. I saw your dad yesterday in

Putter's, by the way. He looked good. He was buying tomato towers."

"I talked to them, too. I'll call when I get there. Take care of yourself, Pete."

Before he could say anything else, he saw Margaret pushing through the revolving door. He whispered, "Got to go," and closed the phone on Pete. He stood and smiled. She smiled back. And the smile grew brighter as he crossed the lobby and took her in his arms. In the first instant of their contact, he understood it was still there. Whatever had been between them was still there, and he held her for a second, feeling something restored, something that had been missing returned.

He held her hand on the walk to the restaurant, and Margaret felt grateful for the steady balance his grip lent to her on the cobblestones that lined the streets of the Old Port. It had been a mistake to wear heels, even modest heels, and she chided herself for forgetting about the cobblestones and the difficulty of walking on them. But it didn't matter. Her concern about her heels was a small pin-light of worry in a typhoon of emotions that churned inside her. *Charlie*. His hand, his height, his kind smile. She hadn't known what it would be like to see him, but the first glance, the first touch, had transported her back to the rhododendrons, to the ball at the French Embassy, to everything that had passed between them. He was in her blood, she admitted, and walking beside him felt natural and inevitable.

She smelled the sea as they walked. The scent was everywhere in the Old Port, carried by fog and rain sometimes, but also by the wind that blew and from the sea that lifted ships and took them away. She had forgotten how much she loved Portland. In a different life, even before she had met Thomas, she had thought about moving to Portland. She had visited with a college friend, Shea, and they had called Realtors and checked the newspapers for apartments before accepting jobs that killed the notion of a Portland life. Still, she admired the city, the proximity of the sea, the cobblestone streets and brick storefronts, the blend of workaday life and tourist luxury.

"This looks like it," Charlie said when they finally reached the bottom of the hill that led from the city, where the hotel was, down to the working port. The restaurant—Growcher's—stood on the corner overlooking the harbor lights. "Terry recommended it. She said to say hello, by the way. She said she still plans to visit you one of these days."

"I hope she will."

"I didn't even ask if you like lobster."

"I love it, actually."

"I didn't grow up with it, obviously. Not many lobsters in Iowa."

"Well, maybe this is one thing I can teach you."

"You'll have to, I'm afraid."

He held the door for her and she walked into a marvelous restaurant, old and established, with white linens and dark wood and the smell of good food cooking. She was happy to see it was not a stuffy place; she had worried that they would have to talk in a quiet, perhaps pretentious restaurant with hovering waiters and judgmental sommeliers. This was better. A waitress passed by carrying a tray on her shoulder, smiled, and told them someone would seat them in a minute. When the waitress pushed into the kitchen, Margaret saw something flame up on the range.

"Two?" a hostess said when she arrived at the small lectern.

Two couples arrived behind them and Margaret stepped forward to make room.

"Two, yes," Charlie said.

"Right this way," the hostess said and led them off.

They did not get the best seat in the house, but it was still a lovely banquet overlooking the harbor. Margaret slid in on one side, while Charlie, Margaret noticed, took a moment to navigate the table with his leg. The hostess informed them the waitress tonight was Barbara, and that Barbara would be over shortly to take drink orders.

"How does this place feel?" Charlie asked. "Is it okay?"

"It's perfect. I was worried it would be a fussy sort of restaurant, but it's fun. Blake had a meal here last winter. I was going to recommend it. I've wanted to eat here."

"How is Blake?" Charlie asked.

He still did not appear entirely comfortable with the position of his leg under the table. He lifted slightly and made an adjustment that apparently settled the matter. Margaret smiled.

"Blake's okay. She's a little sad lately. Donny is gone. He's living with a buddy and doing his lawn business. He's been good with Phillip, at least. That's their boy."

"So they'll go ahead and divorce?"

"Looks like it. Blake will probably keep the house. They're sorting out the details. Blake seems more stunned than angry. She's talking about going to work. She has always done things outside the home, but I guess she has a line on a receptionist slash accountant slash human resource position in a small tech company. I'm not sure what they make, but she feels like she has a pretty good shot at it."

"Well, that's something positive."

The waitress arrived. Her name tag said Barbara. She was a short, wiry young woman with unusually wide eyes and a wild broom of black hair. She wore a black T-shirt and blue jeans and a blue kerchief tied around her throat. Her voice came out of the side of her mouth.

Margaret used the distraction caused by her arrival to study Charlie. He looked the same, she decided. Handsome and quiet. When he asked for her drink order, she requested a scotch, a Dewar's, and he smiled at that, obviously remembering. Before Barbara left, she listed off a half dozen specials, but Margaret couldn't concentrate sufficiently to take them in. He had cut himself shaving, she saw. Or not cut, perhaps, but scraped down under the right side of his jaw. And he had a recent haircut, fresh for his travel and his new position. She found his grooming endearing. He was a boy heading off for the first day of school, but of course he was not a boy.

When the waitress left, Margaret reached across the table and put her hand over his.

"It's splendid to see you, Charlie. I missed you."

"I was nervous to see you. Were you nervous?"

"Yes. Ask Blake. But now I don't feel that way. It's too good to see you to feel anything but satisfied. Or happy. You're still the best date I've had in years."

He smiled and wiggled her hand.

"I liked our date," he said.

"I think about it all the time."

"It felt as though you were suddenly gone. I don't know. Did you feel that way, too?"

She nodded.

"It was tough right afterward," she said. "Adjusting to being back. Adjusting to everything. I wanted to call you so many times."

"But you didn't, did you?"

"I couldn't. Blake called it my Charlie diet. If I gave in to temptation, it would only make it harder."

"Why did you agree to see me now?"

"Because I love you. And because you're going away."

Charlie started to say something, but Barbara came with the drinks. Charlie had ordered a Bass. He asked Barbara for a few minutes before ordering, then he tipped the bottle top and clinked with her glass of scotch.

"Important toast, important toast, important toast," Margaret said.

He smiled and nodded. "You remembered!"

"I remember everything, Charlie."

She sipped her scotch. Charlie had a swallow of beer. She turned and looked out at the harbor. The lights flickered on the water and now and then when the door opened she smelled the sea and something fouler, pollution, maybe, or something gone dead in the lapping tidal wash. Charlie looked out, too. She could see a ghost of his reflection in the window when the light moved in certain ways.

"You're leaving tomorrow," Margaret said and turned back to Charlie. "What time is your flight?"

"Early. A little after five, I think."

"Does it go direct?"

"It goes to Frankfurt, then on to Senegal. Then there's a small plane to Ouagadougou."

"Is there really a town named Ouagadougou? Did I come close to pronouncing that correctly?"

"You did all right. I still don't feel comfortable with the names, but I'm learning. I guess the local tribal language is More."

"You must be excited. And proud. Do you know what your living quarters will be? You didn't know the last time we talked."

"I've been assured it will be comfortable. I don't know for sure. Why don't you come and see it for yourself?"

She took a sip of scotch. She felt the invitation slide into her ears like smoke. What did she want to say? How was she going to reply? She had thought about this moment, this exact instant, a thousand times. Now or never. Yes or no. It could not be more simple. She kept her eyes on his. Her heart thumped and she put down the glass of scotch so that she wouldn't drop it. *Now, it is happening right now,* she told herself. She knew her life could not go in two directions at once.

"I don't think I'm brave enough," she said quietly.

"I think you are."

"I'm not, Charlie. I've had time to think about things. About you. I'm not very brave, it turns out."

"How do you mean that?"

She shrugged. She suddenly felt close to crying. She couldn't even say why. Or she couldn't point to one thing. It was all mixed together. Fortunately Barbara returned to take their order. Margaret sighed, relieved, and bantered back and forth with Charlie about the advisability of a lobster. It was a minishow they put on for the waitress. They decided on one large lobster, with accompanying mussels, and small garden salads on the side. It was far too much food, Margaret imagined, but they were in a restaurant famous for lobsters and so she went with it. Charlie did, too.

"You were saying," Charlie said when Barbara left. He reached and covered her hand.

"I don't know what I'm saying. Every time I think I have things figured out, I have this rush of emotion whoosh through and cloud everything. I've been trying to see myself as your partner."

"And what did that look like?" he asked.

"Well," she said, trying to think and to select her words carefully, "suppose we went in that direction. Let's just say that. I've tried to think it through and I stumble every time. I keep coming back to Tom. I keep coming back to my vow to him. My heart is yours, Charlie. You know that, I think. I'm honored that you're interested in me."

"I'm not interested, Margaret. I love you."

She looked in his eyes. And nodded.

"That you love me, then. I am honored by that, and so, so flattered. Then I sometimes think, Who am I kidding? I'm a simple girl from Maine. What would I be doing running around the world, flying here and there? Am I cut out for it? And deep down I love the farm. I love it. I didn't know I was going to love it, but I do. I love the stupid cows and the never-ending work. It's home."

"You could have a home with me."

She studied him. He squeezed her hand and shook it slightly.

"Okay, maybe you're right. Maybe I could learn what I needed to learn. Maybe I could adapt and change. I would do that to be with you. Gladly. It would be an adventure."

"But Thomas . . ."

She nodded. Her eyes filled.

"You want to hear what I thought about?" he asked.

"Of course."

He peeled the label off the beer. A sign of sexual frustration, she had always heard. She watched him carefully. He took a deep breath and then launched into it.

"All along I thought that I could overcome any objection except Thomas. He was a deal breaker, I knew. And I also knew I couldn't say a word one way or the other about him, or your commitment to him. I admire it. I want that kind of commitment for myself. I want to be able to give that level of commitment. Is this sounding too much like an insurance seminar?"

She laughed. She took a drink, relieved that he could still make a joke under the circumstances.

"No, I understand."

"Fate absolutely rots, you know that? It's unfair. I talked to Pete and I talked to Terry about it and they both said the same thing. The decision is yours, finally. I've done what I could. I'm not being passive. I'm being respectful."

"Yes, you have been, you sweet man."

"There's nobody else in my life, Margaret. I'm not dating, and I'm not looking right now. I want to make a good start with the new post. I want to concentrate on that. I won't contact you or trouble you, but you have to promise me if things change, you'll find me. Do you promise to do that?"

"Yes."

He tilted his beer back and took a long drink.

"You asked me once if what went on between us was real. I know what you meant. Did it really happen? Are we making things more dramatic than they were? But I know now that it's exactly what we thought it was. On my end, it was."

"I feel the same way."

"So . . . Are you okay? You look . . ."

"I need to leave, Charlie. I can't stay here and talk calmly about this. Can we leave? Can we ask them to wrap up the lobster and take it with us?"

"Sure," he said, although he wasn't certain about it at all, she knew.

"Please," she said, and then she slipped out of the banquet. "I'll wait for you outside. I'm sorry. I thought I could do this, but I can't. I can't say good-bye and pretend it isn't killing me. I have to get some air."

She nearly ran to the door and pushed out, happy to have a gush of cool, moist air strike her. She walked to the dock and threw up. Simply and abruptly, she voided her stomach and held on to the dock post with her right hand, while her left held her hair back. Disgusting. The vomit splashed into the seawater. She wretched several times, heaving and beginning to cry. It was all ending, and she knew it was ending, and she was solid in her decision, but he was Charlie, that dear man, and she wretched again, shaking and quivering. He was right. Fate rotted. She wished she had never met him. To have food when you are starving, to have a small taste of it and then see it removed, was crueler than no food at all.

She forced herself to take deep, even breaths. She tried to distract herself with the glimmering water. A few minutes later she heard Charlie step behind her. He carried an insulated bag that smelled of lobster. The odor nearly made her gag again.

"You okay?" he asked, touching her back gently.

She shook her head.

Chapter
Twenty-seven

C harlie handed the lobster to a homeless man. The man nodded and received it.

"You like lobster?" Charlie asked the man. "There are some mussels in there, too. It's all good. We haven't touched it."

The man nodded again.

"Okay then."

Charlie felt Margaret slip her arm through his.

"Sorry," she whispered.

"You owe me a lobster."

"I really do. It's true."

"Do you think it would have been good?"

"It would have been delicious."

"I like thinking of that man eating it. I bet he doesn't get lobster every day."

"I'm sorry."

"It's okay. I guess it was silly to think we would sit and calmly discuss things."

"I love you, Charlie."

He clamped her arm with his elbow. She nestled closer to him. Despite everything that was going on, he liked Portland. He liked the shops and the bright windows and the pubs. Several times on their climb up the hill back to the hotel he heard music and glasses clinking and doors pushing open. He liked the smell of the sea and he liked Margaret's arm on his. It was all out in the open now. That was a relief. He had made his request; she had made her decision. He doubted she would reverse herself in any significant way. She would remain with her husband. He would leave for Africa. It filled him with emptiness to think about it, though he could not help but admire her fortitude. In the end, she had seen things more clearly than he had. Fate had played them a dirty trick, it was true, and there was nothing either of them could do. Star-crossed lovers. It was an old story.

At the hotel he invited her up. She nodded without speaking. And on the ride up in the elevator she kissed him. He led her to his room and swiped the card and they were inside.

"Do you want me to order up some food?" Charlie asked. "Are you starving? You must be."

"I am starving. I think I could eat now. Could we split a BLT?"

"That sounds perfect."

"And I promise to eat. I'm going to wash my face now. I'm sorry about the dinner."

"For one night that guy eats like a king. That's kind of fun to think about."

"It's good karma, Charlie. I'll be right out."

He sat at a small circular table and called down and ordered the sandwich with two Diet Cokes and French fries. The person on the other end of the line said it would be fifteen minutes. Charlie thanked her and hung up.

"It's on its way," Charlie said when Margaret reappeared. "Feel better?"

"Yes, thanks. Much."

"I haven't asked about Gordon. How's he doing?"

She sat. She smiled.

"He's a good boy. He's been more helpful around the farm lately and he loves his grandfather. He's doing great. It's summer and he's tan and full of bug bites."

"I'm glad to hear that."

"By the way, he plays with the meerkat. It's become one of his favorites. He sleeps with it at night."

"That's terrific."

"You're going to have such an exciting life, Charlie," she said, changing subjects. "You know that, don't you?"

"I hope so."

"Think of your bird list. You're going to bag some new birds."

He smiled. She smiled, too.

Charlie signed off for the food at the door when a kid in a hotel uniform brought it up. He carried the tray to the small table. Margaret snitched a French fry as soon as he set it down. She looked beautiful sitting with the window behind her. He bent down and kissed the side of her neck. Then he sat and divided the sandwich and poured half the French fries onto her plate.

"Better than the restaurant?" he asked. "Dig in."

"I was too nervous. Everything was too large."

"I know what you mean."

"Did the people in the restaurant think we had a terrible row?"

"The waitress was sympathetic. I told her you were pregnant."

"You did not!"

"I did. No one can be mad at a pregnant woman."

"You scheming devil."

She ate more fries, but she smiled broadly. Then she took a bite of the sandwich. It was a good sandwich, Charlie saw, built carefully and divided in four triangles. He ate some himself.

"I want a Christmas card from you every year, Charlie. Without fail. I want to know how things turn out for you."

"A card a year?"

She nodded and slipped another French fry into her mouth.

"I can handle that. What do I get in return?"

"I'll send a card, too. How would that be?"

He took a deep breath. His chest felt constricted.

"Let's not do this," he said. "Not like this. I don't want to try to be light and gay about it. I can't do it right now."

She took his hand. She raised it to her mouth and kissed it.

"You're right," she said.

"I don't want to be gloomy, but we can't be frivolous about it."

"Yes, you're right."

"How is Thomas anyway?"

"Unchanged, really."

"My brother has been a little bumpy lately. Mom's trying to track it down. It's hard."

"I'm sorry to hear that."

"My buddy Pete goes over to see him sometimes. I didn't even know that, but a nurse mentioned it to my dad. They were friends, too, my brother and Pete, but we were closer. Anyway, it touched me to find that out."

"I like Pete already."

"How are the fries?"

"I don't think they're great, but I could eat a horse."

He stood and moved to the bed and grabbed something out of his suit jacket. He kissed her and handed it to her.

"What is this?" she asked, obviously pleased.

"Open it and see."

She opened it quickly. It was a charm bracelet. It had two charms, Charlie knew. One of Humpback Rock to mark the northern end of the Blue Ridge Parkway, and one of the Biltmore.

"Oh, Charlie," she said, taking it out and draping it over her wrist. "I've always wanted one. And these . . . they're so dear. I'm squinting to see. I recognize the Biltmore . . . yes, it's the Biltmore. And this other one? It sounds familiar. . . ."

"It's Humpback Rock. It marks the northern end of the Blue Ridge Parkway."

"Yes, yes, I remember now."

She finished with the buckle and raised her wrist and jiggled it in the light. Then she carefully studied it once more.

"I meant to say you're my north and south, but that's too corny even for me."

"It works, Charlie."

She stood and came and sat on his lap. She kissed him and she held the bracelet out where she could see it, where the light coming from above could find it.

Margaret woke softly. For a moment she thought she was in the farmhouse, the old oak casting its shadows through the bedroom window. But then she felt Charlie beside her. They had fallen asleep. They had slept in each other's arms. They had not had sex. They had kissed forever, over and over, and when the moment had come to go further, she had clung to him. She could not do that; she could not give herself again that way, although she burned to do so. It was too dangerous, and he understood, he always understood, and so they had stayed on top of the bedspread, necking like teenagers, saying the things they wanted to say.

Margaret lifted her head and saw light beginning at the edge of the window.

"I have to go," she whispered.

He pulled her closer.

"You have to go, too," she said.

She slid out of the bed and used the bathroom and washed

her face, used her finger to smear toothpaste on her gums. When she returned, Charlie had the bedside light on and he had started to dress.

"I'll walk you down," he said.

"No, Charlie. I don't want you to. I don't want to prolong this anymore. I'll be okay. I'll get to Blake's just as Gordon is waking."

He nodded. She went into his arms.

"Everything, everything, everything," he whispered.

"Yes," she said.

She kissed him and turned and went out the door. At the end of the hallway she saw dawn pushing through the windows. Cloudy day, she thought. Rain coming.

Asters

(Seven years later)

Chapter
Twenty-eight

The boy's hands felt cold and raw as he dribbled the basketball, but the rest of his body was well heated and moved with the easy athleticism of a thirteen-year-old. He was tall and thin, nearly six feet, and dribbled and shot without the awkwardness that sometimes accompanied early adolescence. He wore ankle-high Converse sneakers, a University of Maine hoodie, and a pair of gray corduroys so worn in the knees that the abraded ribs glistened in the afternoon light. The *poing* of the ball and the squeak of his sneakers made the only sounds on the Margaret Chase Smith Elementary School blacktop, except when the ball hit against the metal backboard or *ching-g-ged* through the metal chain beneath the basket.

He had warmed up already, shooting from five feet, then ten feet, then the three-point line in a circle around the goal. Although he liked all aspects of the game, he prized jump shooting above all other skills. His grandfather had shown him early shots of Jerry West, the great Los Angeles Laker from the

1970s, and Gordon had accepted West as a jump-shot model. West had been a pure shooter, better than Bird, Gordon believed, better than Havlicek, and as he moved around the clamshell backboard, his shots arcing nicely, he practiced coming quickly off a pass and shooting all in one fluid motion. He hit more than he missed, but when he missed, that was good, too, because he followed the rebound, trapped the ball, then turned and spun and launched a fadeaway, à la Jerry West, and then quickly followed his own shot. The rule was: if the shot went in, he returned to his place in his around-the-world journey on the court. If the shot missed, he trapped it again, spun, and shot until the net finally calmed the ball properly.

It was October and cold in Maine and the wind hit the side of the brick elementary school building and raised an occasional dust devil. Gordon hardly noticed. He did not notice the geese that passed overhead to his east, their wings silently paddling southward. He did not notice the light passing and breaking through the clouds except when it affected his shot. He failed to notice that several of the puddles left by the day's earlier rain had turned to ice. They looked thin and brittle and not convinced of their own desire to remain.

But something—something cold and quiet and deep—made him look up and see his grandfather's pickup coming down Tallytown Road. He knew at a glance it was his grandfather: no one else drove an old GMC truck, powder blue faded to gray, with one headlight half as bright as the other. No one drove as slow, either. Gordon grabbed the ball and held it for a second against his hip. A wind came up and made one of the grammar school swings twist and buckle and ting a little on its chain. The same wind chased the dust devil into the corner of the building beside the art room, and Gordon turned to watch a gum wrapper dance for a moment before flicking down and sideways, then joining more leaves in the swirl.

His grandfather turned into the elementary school parking lot and Gordon knew.

His dad was dead. It was as simple as that. His grandfather wouldn't leave the cows at milking time for anything short of an emergency. How long, he wondered, had this moment been coming? He turned back to the basket and launched a shot that swished so perfectly onto the bottom of the net that it caused the ball to shrug back up for an instant. Then gravity plunged the ball through and Gordon grabbed it nearly out of the net, leaping high and landing in time to see his grandfather slip out of the truck, one foot in, one foot out, and make a small "come here" wave. And for the rest of his life, although he didn't know it at the time, Gordon would remember this single moment: dusk, October, the chill of late afternoon, the gassy thrum of his granddad's pickup, the orange weight of the ball against his hip, the dust devil rising and falling on each wind like breath stolen from somewhere else and spent to no good end.

Blake heard the news from Carrie, a casual friend, a fellow library board member, in the Shop 'n Save, several feet away from the mustard-ketchup-pickle-barbecue-sauce section. It had just happened, Carrie said. She had just heard. She, Carrie this was, had heard from her cousin Ginny, who worked at the veterans' center and had been calling about pizza, who wanted what on what—it was Tuesday and pinochle night at Carrie's— and in passing Ginny mentioned that they had lost one of the long-termers, a guy named Kennedy, and asked if it wasn't the case that Carrie knew the family. Of course she did, Carrie said, and she repeated the line to Blake—*Of course she did*—who could merely receive the information and continue to stare at the brittle end of Carrie's hair where it flipped in a curl like a ram's horn near her jawline.

"That's Tom Kennedy," Blake said softly. "Margaret's husband."

"I thought so," Carrie said, her eyes satisfied as if she had solved a puzzle. "That's so sad. It's ironic that it even came up. I mean, Ginny didn't know there was any connection."

"When did it happen?" Blake asked.

"Just a little bit ago. Not even an hour, probably."

Blake placed her hands carefully on the grocery cart handle and closed her eyes. Poor Tom Kennedy, she thought, gone after all these years. Poor Margaret. She opened her eyes and saw Carrie still regarding her carefully.

"A little prayer?" Carrie asked.

"No, not really. Just remembering Tom before all the sickness. I knew him as a kid. He was as good a man as I ever knew."

"He won the medal, didn't he?" Carrie asked, although she knew it well enough without asking, Blake knew.

"Yes, the Congressional Medal of Honor. The highest award our country can give."

"I suppose . . ."

"Yes, it's probably a blessing," Blake interrupted, not quite wanting Carrie to speak the words. "It's probably time."

"Are you two still close?" Carrie asked. "You and Margaret?"

"Best friends for years. I have to go to her."

"I'm sorry to drop it on you like this. I didn't know all the connections exactly. My husband always says I talk before I think."

"I'm going to get going, Carrie," Blake said, beginning to push the cart slowly, her body moving automatically. "Hearing it like this, it kind of hit me hard."

"Sorry, I didn't mean to just drop it on you . . . ," Carrie repeated.

"No, it's okay. It had to happen someday. The poor man."

"If I hear anything, I'll call you."

"Thank you," Blake said.

Outside in the car, Blake sat for a moment after loading the groceries. How strange she felt. Tom Kennedy. Margaret Kennedy. And poor Grandpa Ben, that good man, and little Gordon. She sat for a while and watched people moving back and forth.

She tried to remember what she had in the way of groceries and whether she could go directly to Margaret's or would have to stop on the way home to unload. She picked up her cell and dialed Sean, her husband, and told his message center what

had happened when he didn't answer. *Tom Kennedy,* she said.
You never met him.

—☙

Margaret made a fire in the old hearth. It was late afternoon,
evening really, and she wanted a fire. Grandpa Ben favored
the woodstove, knowing that a fireplace was an impractical
indulgence, but tonight, just this evening, Margaret wanted a
fire.

She performed the task without thinking much about it.
She lit a roll of paper, saw it threaten to go out, then catch more
merrily and begin to burn, grabbing a bouquet of pine tinder
as it caught. Margaret stayed on one knee beside it, feeding it
carefully, letting it grow. She broke off a few pieces from a
birch log, the thick paper bark on the backside of the wood,
and that made the fire's commitment final. A bright orange
flame began to fill the fireplace with light, and Margaret
watched for a moment without thinking.

The memory of the phone call intruded only a little.
Thomas was gone. Tom. Her husband. The call had been calm
and quiet, a short declaration from one of the hospital
administrators—what was her name? Margaret tried to recall
and couldn't; she had taken the place of Mrs. McCafferty—
who had asked at the outset if this was Margaret Kennedy, wife
of Thomas who was a patient in the Bangor Veterans' Center.
Margaret had known, of course. The administrator had wanted
to make sure she did not deliver such information to the wrong
party, and when Margaret agreed that in fact she was Margaret

Kennedy, the administrator had said she was sorry to inform her that her husband, Thomas Kennedy, had expired shortly before afternoon rounds.

Expired, the woman had said. Not died, not passed away, but expired. Like milk, Margaret couldn't help thinking. Like old cans of tomato sauce.

When she satisfied herself that the fire would increase, she rose and closed the evening blinds. She did not let herself think of Thomas. Not yet. She went into the kitchen and poured herself a scotch, letting it swirl and turn in one of the short highball glasses she sometimes used when she wanted a drink. She poured one for Grandpa Ben, too, and carried both glasses into the living room and sat and waited. A minute or two later she heard the truck arrive. Two doors closed, and then the back door opened and they entered the kitchen.

"In here," Margaret called. "I've started a fire."

She stood. When Gordon came into the room she gathered him in her arms. His skin felt cold and wet. She marveled, not for the first time, that he was taller than she. When she let him go, he stood awkwardly, apparently not sure what to say. She put both hands on his cheeks and smiled.

"It's okay, sweetheart. It's fine," she said.

"What was it . . . ," he began to ask.

"Just time," she said and kissed his cheek. "Just time."

She hugged Grandpa Ben and then handed him his glass of scotch.

"I thought you might like a drink," she said to Ben.

He nodded.

"Now, sit with us for a second, sweetheart," she said to Gordon. "You can run upstairs in a minute. I just wanted to go through things."

She sat down in one of the two easy chairs. Ben went and put a few more sticks of wood on the fire, then he took a seat, too, the ice in his scotch glass making a winter sound.

"What happens now?" Gordon asked.

He still hadn't taken a seat. Margaret decided to let him do whatever he needed to do. He moved closer to the fireplace and put his back toward it.

"Well," Margaret began, "we haven't discussed much about it. I suppose we avoided it. A simple ceremony? Is that what you had in mind, Ben?"

"Yes."

"Time has passed by a little," Margaret said, trying to frame things so Gordon would understand. "It's been a long time since Tom was part of the everyday world."

"I know," Gordon said.

"I mean, his contacts, his friends . . . it's been a long time. We've always thought cremation, if that's okay with everyone still. Then we could have a small service and inter the ashes. Is everyone okay with that?"

Both Ben and Gordon nodded.

"Maybe a week, four or five days from now?"

"Is that what people usually do?" Gordon asked.

"Yes, a little time. It allows people to make a trip up. My

parents will want to be here. Maybe we can arrange to have Father Kamili say a few words. Ben, would you like that?"

He nodded.

"All right then. The American Legion will want to do something, I imagine. I'll let them know. We'll put a notice in the paper, too. Maybe some of Thomas's old football friends will show up. The Millinocket Minutemen."

She smiled. She took a small sip. Yes, she thought, the fire was lovely and needed. She studied Gordon's face. He was a handsome boy, slightly fair with the redness she had contributed, and with Thomas's heavy brows. Sometimes, in the right light, she reminded him of a young Elvis or Marlon Brando— a bright, glimmering handsomeness that surprised her. She knew him well enough, though, to see he didn't know how to behave exactly. His father was dead, but in reality his father had been dead for many years.

"Gordon," she said, "don't feel you have to do one thing or another. Don't feel any pressure . . . maybe that's the wrong word . . . any expectation, maybe. I'm not sure what I'm trying to say. Your dad has been sick all of your life, and you'll feel some sort of expectation to mourn in a certain way, and maybe you can't match that with your feelings right now. That's what I'm trying to say. Your dad was a fine man, but I realize, we both realize, your granddad and I, that you didn't have a chance to know him. I'm sorry for that. I'm trying to say just let things come to you. It's all okay. Do you know what I'm saying?"

Gordon nodded.

Then Gordon saw what Margaret had not. She watched

him cross the room and bend down to Ben and take his grandfather in his arms. This loving boy. He held his grandfather
while the old man cried. And Thomas was in the room if only
for an instant.

—☙

Blake knocked softly on the Kennedys' kitchen door, then
pushed slowly through it. She glanced at Margaret's muck
boots sitting patiently on the porch. If the boots had not
been present, she would have looked for her old friend in the
barn. She knocked again out of courtesy just as a wind rose
and tucked hard against the house. Leaves shook free of the
oak beside the front porch and scattered across the barnyard.

Gordon opened the door as she went through it.

"Hello, Gordon," Blake said and gently looped one arm
around the boy's neck and kissed him quickly on the cheek.
"I'm sorry about your dad. Very sorry. He was a good man."

"Thank you."

"Is your mom home?"

He nodded and she followed him into the kitchen. It felt
good to be out of the wind. She glanced around the kitchen.
Nothing much had changed. It remained an old farm kitchen,
functional and solid, with a fifties-style linoleum-topped table
settled against one corner. She had seen a table not unlike it in
an antiques store in Portland the week before. She hadn't made
the connection before seeing it now.

"Mom's in the living room," Gordon said. "She has a fire
going."

"Okay. Where's Grandpa Ben?"

"The barn."

Blake slipped out of her jacket and hung it on the back of a kitchen chair, then walked down the short connecting hallway and stepped into the living room. Her footsteps brought Margaret onto her feet.

"How did you hear?" Margaret asked. "I just called you and left a message with Phillip."

"From Carrie at the Shop 'n Save. It was just one of those coincidence things. She had just heard from someone at the hospital. I ran some groceries home and then came right over."

Margaret smiled. It was a tender smile. Blake went to her friend and hugged her.

"I'm sorry, Margaret. He was such a fine man."

"Yes, he was," Margaret answered.

"I have such warm feelings about Tom right now. And about you. Tommy Kennedy."

Blake felt Margaret hug her harder. Blake closed her eyes and held her friend. She stayed in Margaret's arms for what seemed like a long time. When Margaret released her, Blake had to wipe her eyes.

"Sit, please," Margaret said, clearing the sections of a newspaper to make room. "I wanted a fire this afternoon. Isn't that odd? I like the flames."

"I love a fire," Blake said, sitting. "And it's a day for it."

"Yes, so do I. I always have. I've just been reading the death notices. Morbid, I suppose, but I wanted to see how they're done. We'll have to post one."

"There's time for that, sweetie. We could do that tomorrow."

"I know, but I feel if I can be efficient about things . . . it helps somehow."

Blake reached over and held Margaret's hand.

"And how are you feeling?" Blake asked. "Has it sunk in at all?"

"Oh, a little. I mean, it was such a long time coming that no one can say it was a surprise. Poor Tom. I miss him, Blake. I miss him as a person. But I'm glad it's over. Glad for him, for me, for Ben, and for Gordon. It's the proverbial second shoe to drop. Finally it's come and that's a relief in a way. I'm being honest. I think I mourned for him so long that I don't have much left."

"I understand," Blake said.

"Would you like some tea? A drink?"

"No, I won't stay long. Sean is leaving tomorrow on a business trip, and I want to check in on Phillip."

Margaret stared at the fire.

"I guess we need to have people back after the ceremony. I called my parents and they're going to come up. I'm having trouble knowing who else might show up. He's been gone from the world for so long."

"I'm glad your folks are coming."

"You know, I've thought about this day, about him dying, so many times that you would think it's been rehearsed and clear in my mind. But it's not. It's still a surprise. Nothing has changed, and then everything has changed. I can't quite get my mind around it."

"It's all just happening now, Margaret."

"I understand that in one part of my mind, but my heart is twisted up."

Blake squeezed Margaret's hand. Then she moved closer. She pushed back Margaret's hair a little.

"You stood by him," Blake whispered. "I've never seen anyone else stand by someone as you did. I've never said this to you, but it gave me faith. It gave me faith that humans could be true. It restored me. After Donny, I sometimes thought, well, Margaret is in the world, too. You were like a counterweight to all the craziness that went on around the divorce. You don't know, but many people saw it, sweetheart. Your son saw it and that's everything."

Margaret hung her head. She pressed a wad of tissues to her eyes and cried softly. Blake hugged her again. Something in the fire popped and a small ash flew out and landed on the hearth. Margaret took a deep breath, then looked up and tried to smile.

"The fire feels good," Blake said, rising. "How's Ben taking it?"

"He's Ben. It hurts, I know it hurts, but I keep thinking that this is the tail of the comet. We had the comet a long time ago. That's the phrase that keeps going around in my head."

Blake bent down and hugged Margaret one last time. A thick wind hit the house again and the fireplace puffed out a small ball of smoke. Blake shook her friend's hand lightly and then went out. Gordon sat at the kitchen table eating a bowl of cereal.

"Do you know what a great mom you have?" Blake asked as she slipped into her coat.

But Gordon didn't hear. He had earbuds in and Blake realized he had music jamming his hearing.

Chapter
Twenty-nine

How strange it was, Margaret thought, that on the day of her husband's funeral she must also be a hostess. She wondered about it as a custom, how it had become expected. Were the details of food and housecleaning supposed to take one's mind off the tragedy at hand? If so, it didn't work particularly well, because as Margaret moved around the kitchen, trying to keep her black dress clean and not spotted with sink water, she merely felt put-upon.

But at least her mother was there. Whatever differences they had had in the past, she could count on her mom. Her parents had arrived the night before and parked their Jay Feather camper back behind the barn, plugging into a receptacle that Ben had placed there for them years ago. Her father was dressing in the camper; her mother was upstairs, slipping into her own mourning dress. Ben and Gordon had already driven over to the cemetery. Everything was running a little late.

"Mom, we have to get a move on," Margaret called up the stairs, her hands still wet from the sink.

"Right there, honey."

"The caterers are pulling in now."

"Okay."

Margaret returned to the kitchen and watched the catering van pull close to the house. Two young girls jumped out of the front. Margaret was relieved to see an older woman climb out from the middle of the vehicle. Almost immediately the woman began giving the girls orders. The girls began sliding doors open and ducking inside while the woman came up the stairs and knocked. Margaret let her inside. She was a short, wiry woman who smelled faintly of cigarette smoke, but she gave off an air of competency as well. She wore black trousers and a black smock. She held out her hand; one of the knuckles, Margaret noticed, had been jammed and flattened into something resembling a tree burl.

"Dorothy Gibson, Mrs. Kennedy. I'm sorry about your loss," the woman said.

"Thank you, Dorothy. Please call me Margaret."

"We're a whisker late, I know, but don't you worry about anything. We have everything in hand. Just point me to the kitchen and we'll take care of things from there."

Margaret gave Dorothy Gibson a brief introduction to the kitchen. Margaret was pleased to see Dorothy did not stand on ceremony; she opened cabinets, poked around in the refrigerator, and otherwise made herself familiar with her tools.

"This will all do nicely," Dorothy said when they finished. "You'll be back around two?"

"I think so."

"No worries. We'll have some appetizers ready to go, then we'll wait about a half hour after most of the people arrive to serve. People like a drink first. Does that sound about right?"

"Perfect. Thank you."

Finally Margaret's mom stepped into the kitchen. She wore a black dress that was slightly baggy on her but suitable. She looked good, actually, Margaret noted. She had lost weight and had been doing yoga with a women's group and her posture and bearing seemed better. The softer winters agreed with her. Her skin held a better tone than when she had lived in Maine.

"This is my mom, Renee," Margaret said, introducing the two women.

"Daddy should have the car ready," Renee said after shaking Dorothy's hand. "I saw him from the upstairs window."

The two girls arrived with dishes covered by foil. They were cute, probably high schoolers, Margaret saw, and they wore matching black skirts and sweaters. Margaret shook their hands, too, when they put down their dishes, then she corralled her mother and led her outside.

"What a day," Renee said when she stood on the stairs waiting for the car. "You couldn't ask for a prettier one."

"I'm glad it's a pretty day for Thomas."

"Me, too," Renee said.

Margaret felt her mom slip her arm through her own. They stood in the sunlight until her dad arrived with the car.

—◌

Ben Kennedy did not know what he thought about cremation. He didn't mind the concept, exactly, but it seemed a bit too tidy. He had moved enough final things in his life to know the weight of the dead, and it was somehow that weight that reassured him in its endings. The small urn full of ashes that stood on the table beside the hole—a posthole, really, Ben thought, nothing more—contained the mortal remains of his son, Thomas, and that seemed impossible. Cows, dogs, cats, they required spadework, sometimes the backhoe, and he had never considered it before, but the process of burying the creature had been its good-bye. He did not know if he could find the same finality in a jar of ashes, regardless of what the undertaker, Todd Lyle, told him about such things. But, he decided, now was not the time to raise such an issue. Walking beside his grandson in the good October light, Ben made a conscious decision to let things go. Whatever had happened to his boy was finished now. That was as clear as a bell.

Ben saw the parish priest, Father Kamili, standing and talking to some of the mourners. Hard to miss him, Ben realized, the priest being an African. From what he understood, half the Catholic churches in the country now had priests from away because the local boys didn't buy into it any longer. That was all right by him. A priest always seemed a postage stamp to Ben, not the whole letter, and when he came up he shook the man's hand and introduced him to his grandson.

"I see the resemblance," Father Kamili said, shaking Gordon's hand. "Naturally."

"And I'm John Harigan," a man standing beside the priest

said, extending his hand. "I doubt you remember me, but I played football with Tommy at Millinocket. Some of the boys are showing up."

"Well, that's fine," Ben said, trying to place him.

It didn't seem possible that a man Tom's age was bald and spread out into his suit jacket the way this man seemed to be. But then, Ben figured, his own son was dead, turned to ash, and whoever would have guessed that could have come to pass?

Then cars began arriving in numbers. Something about the position of the sun caught the chrome and anything shiny on the vehicles and flashed it back at them, the refracted light running like cats across the dull grass. Ben stood back behind the table with his son's ashes, doing his best to recognize the waves of mourners walking slowly up the hill. It was the casket that was missing, he realized, his eyes giving nothing away. The casket gave things a substantial feeling. Burying a can of ash didn't seem worth gathering people for. A casket, on the other hand, spoke to the weight of the event.

"Hello, yes, hello," Ben said. "Thanks for coming."

Old faces. New faces. A group of seven American Legion boys, old buzzards, really, walked up the hill and got ready to do something or other. Ben found it difficult to concentrate. He wasn't sure what he had expected, but this wasn't it. He felt annoyed and cranky; what were they all doing here? Thomas was gone, his son was gone, and that wasn't something all the dark clothing in the world could alter.

In the midst of his confusion, he felt his grandson put his

hand on his elbow and guide him to his seat. He was glad for that. He wanted a rest. His legs felt weak and his breathing moved solidly in his chest. Like ice melting. Like tea spreading in a cup of hot water.

"Mom's here," Gordon whispered when Ben sat down, his grandson's breathing tickling him slightly. "They just pulled up."

—◌⊃

So this was it, Margaret thought, trying to weigh the sight of so many old friends and neighbors scattered across the hillside. She looked out the window, her forehead nearly against the glass, and tried to sort out her feelings. The October sunlight felt in contradiction to their business. It called for the harvest, for the taking up, not the putting under. But maybe, too, it was weather for a final tally. At least, she thought, they did not have rain. Rain might have been too much. Thomas did not deserve rain.

"I guess they want us in here," her dad said, pointing to the open spaces marked by orange cones for the family. He pulled the car in and shut it off. How strange it felt to be in the backseat by herself; it was a return to childhood, her parents driving while she occupied herself with the passing scenery. But today was different, of course, and she waited while Mr. Lyle, the undertaker, stepped forward and opened her door.

"Good afternoon, Margaret," Mr. Lyle said. "People are gathered."

"I see," Margaret said, stepping out.

"It's a beautiful day."

"Yes, it is."

"There's been a small change to the program events," Mr. Lyle said, his voice going low, as if revealing something he was unsure about. "If it's all right with you."

"What do you mean?"

"They've sent an honor guard," Mr. Lyle said. "These are really quite remarkable young men. I didn't agree to any change until I had an opportunity to speak with you. It just occurred . . . the honor guard, I mean. They just arrived."

"Do you mean the American Legion men?" Margaret asked, confused.

"No, this is an honor guard. I gather it's an elite guard. There's a form you can fill out to have an honor guard for veterans . . . for their funerals, but this wasn't my doing. I didn't think you'd want that particular service."

"How did they get here? How did they know . . ."

"The squad leader . . . I'm sorry, I don't honestly know the vernacular here. I am not a military man myself. The squad leader said it was arranged in Washington. Because of the medal, I suppose. It's a little unclear to me, too."

"Yes, all right," Margaret said, not entirely sure she was called on to make a decision. It was possible that all Congressional Medal winners received an honor guard. And what was it Mr. Lyle said? They could fill out a form and be provided with an honor guard? She felt annoyed with Todd Lyle; he pretended formality and politeness, but his eye remained on the bottom line and she found that a particularly disagreeable trait in an undertaker.

How peculiar it all was. She watched heads turn to see her

as she began up the hillside. *As if I were a bride,* she thought, amazed. She walked alone, her parents tagging behind her. Then she saw Blake. Sweet Blake, who came close and kissed her cheek.

"If you need anything," Blake whispered, "anything at all."

"I'm all right, Blake. I'm numb, actually."

Then the ring of people grew around her and she greeted as many familiar faces as she could. Old friends. Friends of Thomas's, friends of hers. Acquaintances, a few farmers, a milk buyer probably there for Ben. As she made her way closer to the small awning, she realized she should have given the interment more thought. She had left it in Mr. Lyle's hands, and, as she had already noted, he did things on a short purse. There was nothing wrong with the arrangement, but neither did it speak to Thomas's warmth and character. It was a Chevrolet funeral, and Margaret felt a short stab to the heart when she realized her husband deserved more.

The priest, Father Kamili, led them in an Our Father when Margaret finally sat beside Ben. She felt Gordon's hand resting on her shoulder; his other hand rested on his grandfather's. She reached back and covered his hand with hers.

Then ritual. One of the sacraments, she remembered. Strangely, she recalled the responses, the meter of the ceremony, with little effort. Father Kamili handled the service well. His voice had a pleasing lilt; a Caribbean tumble that made his sentences end in unpredictable ways. Ben had been correct to want a priest, she understood now. Belief or no belief, eternal life or no eternal life, the ceremony gave structure to a moment without structure.

When Father Kamili finished, the honor guard appeared on the crest of the hill.

She felt Gordon's fingers dig slightly into her shoulder. The soldiers—there was no denying it—looked resplendent. They carried rifles and marched in perfect step, not rushed, not hasty in any detail. She felt people turn and draw in their collective breath. Margaret glanced at the American Legion fellows, the elderly men in ill-fitting uniforms, and she saw them settle back in their chairs, as if they understood they would not be needed. The guard came solemnly down the hill, their buckles shining, their steps precise. They looked beautiful and young, masculine in the finest way, and she realized they did not move their eyes to accommodate their feet, did not look down. One of them, the soldier farthest on the left, commanded them, saying words in a short, military grunt that made little sense to her. When they arrived at the awning, the commanding officer produced a flag—where had it been? she had not seen it—and the men began to fold it. She had seen such things on television, everyone had, but she had never seen it in person. She squeezed Gordon's hand and reached over and took Ben's arm. She felt him trembling.

Yes, she thought, *this is what Thomas deserved. This is a small part of what he deserved.*

Behind her, she heard Gordon begin to sob. She stood quickly and collected him in her arms. She held him fiercely. His sobs would not cease.

"Your daddy was such a good man," she whispered passionately in his ear. "You should be very, very proud of him. You're his son and you have his goodness and I am proud of you."

He nodded against her. From behind him, she watched Blake step closer and take Gordon's free arm.

Then it was time to receive the flag. She sat slowly and waited.

"On behalf of the president of the United States and the people of a grateful nation," the commanding guard said in a clear, well-modulated voice, "may I present this flag as a token of appreciation for the honorable and faithful service your loved one rendered this nation?"

"Thank you," Margaret whispered.

The flag felt heavy and dense, a perfect triangle, the stars facing upward. Margaret took it and held it on her lap. The commanding soldier stepped back and saluted her while the rest of his squad marched slowly up the hill. When they gained a hundred feet from the awning they came to attention, then pointed their rifles at the distant clouds and fired a volley. The sound shocked Margaret. Then a second volley, and a third, and Margaret, loosely conscious of their numbers, realized it was a twenty-one-gun salute. Seven times three. The smoke from the small explosions turned white in the October afternoon. She clung to Gordon's hand and squeezed mercilessly when a lone trumpeter blew taps from the peak of the hill. In those sweet, sad notes, she did her best to say good-bye to Thomas. *Dear man,* she thought. *Rest.*

—☙—

"A twenty-one-gun salute is the highest honor a soldier can receive," her dad said on the ride home. "That's what one of the Legionnaires said . . . the skinny one, Fred, I think. He said that if a Medal of Honor winner wanted to attend the State of the Union address, they would make room for him no matter what. He could get in ahead of all the big-shot politicians."

"Make sure we remember to tell Gordon," Margaret said.

"How did they know about this anyway?" her mom asked, twisting in the car seat to ask the question. "I mean, we're in Maine."

"I don't know, Mom," Margaret said. "Mr. Lyle said they came from Washington. It might have something to do with Tom's medal. Maybe all medal winners are given a guard."

"Well, it was very moving," her mom said. "I'll remember it as long as I live."

"Those rifles were loud, weren't they?" her dad said.

Margaret nodded. A headache had begun along her scalp line and she put her forehead against the car window, hoping the coolness would ease the pain. She felt relieved to have the interment behind her. Ben and Gordon had placed the urn in the ground; she had thrown a handful of dirt on top of it. It was done. It made no sense any longer to wish anything had been done differently, or with more élan, because it was final in a way she had not been able to imagine. She was a widow—she could not think the word without thinking of spiders—and Thomas was a soldier fallen in war.

It took no time to arrive home and she saw a few people had already found drinks and stood on the porch, enjoying the last of the afternoon. Her dad dropped them off at the door and a man, a friend of Thomas's, a football player on their high school team, came quickly down the stairs and helped them out. Her dad pulled the car around back to make room for other vehicles. Her mother took her arm and led her up the stairs. Margaret smelled wood smoke coming from the chimney. Gordon, she was certain, had done that for her.

"Here we are," her mother said when she gained the landing.

In many ways, Margaret realized, it felt exactly like a party. It had been years since they had had people in, but she recalled the feeling. Her mother went in to use the ladies' room and Margaret found herself alone on the porch, not exactly sure what to do next. She shook hands with two or three people who came forward and introduced themselves. Blake took the flag from her and it was not until she did so that Margaret remembered it was in her hands. She whispered to Blake that she would like a scotch, please, with plenty of ice. And two aspirins. Blake nodded and went off to fetch the drink.

"Tommy was quite a football player," someone said in her hearing. "Tough as anything. Strong, too. I remember . . ."

Slowly, Margaret made her way into the house. She smelled the fireplace immediately. Her instinct told her to go into the kitchen, to find Dorothy and check that everything was in hand, but then she realized it was not her role this day. What did it matter, anyway? The reception was not meant to impress; it was a social duty, not an unfair one, she decided, and she resolved to let others worry about its outcome. She wanted to sit beside the fire, to have the aspirin and cold scotch go to work on her headache. In an hour, maybe two, it would all be over in any case, and then the house would empty and become quiet and the rhythm of farm life would close around them.

She said hello to two more people, smiled, accepted a kiss. And when she looked for Blake and the drink, standing on her tiptoes to see, her eyes fell on a face so familiar it felt like a blow to her senses.

Charlie King stood beside the fireplace, his eyes meeting hers as they always had.

—❧—

In that moment, she understood. She understood where the honor guard had come from, how they had been sent, by special request, from a diplomat she once knew. For a moment everything except their glance disappeared, and she took a step toward Charlie, her eyes on his, and she could not be sure if he came to say hello or good-bye, to pay his respects and leave or to join her life forever. Gordon stood beside him, their backs to the fire, and she could see they had talked; they had a familiar way about them, two guys, two basketball players, hanging out by the fireplace. People stepped aside as she moved toward him, toward Charlie King, toward the man who had once escorted her to a ball. And it was October, and the sun would fall into the hills quickly, and the phoebe had left weeks ago, and the great oak covering the house stood bare in the autumn coolness. The fireplace burned brightly, and she imagined its smoke going up into the heavens, a white plume slowly catching the wind and traveling to the sea. Winter would come on a quiet evening, she knew. Soon, soon it would arrive. It would come by following the rivers from the mountains into the valleys, the snow falling like ashes of things partially remembered and consumed, and all the world would retreat inside, paused and waiting for spring, for warmth, and for the heavy heads of common lilacs.

Acknowledgments

Thanks first to Tupper Hillard, my old buddy and fellow quarterback, who read this manuscript to check the military details. He's a graduate of West Point and a man who threw a tight spiral in his day. Thanks for your many years of friendship and your readiness to do a former teammate a favor.

Much gratitude to my editor, Denise Roy, and to all the folks at Plume. Thanks for your help in making this a better book than it started out being. I'm pleased by the work we've done here and I hope you are, too. Can't wait to see what's next.

As always, thanks to everyone at the Jane Rotrosen Agency, but especially to Andrea Cirillo and Christina Hogrebe. You don't know half of what you do for people. You don't know half of what you've done for me.

I also wanted to say a special thanks to Peggy Gordijn at the Rotrosen Agency, who keeps sending my novels around the world and selling them to foreign markets now and then. It's such a kick to see something you've written appear in a foreign language, and before our paths crossed it rarely happened. So thank you. And to Mike McCormack, many thanks for all you do behind the scenes.

I also wanted to thank Plymouth State University in New Hampshire, my teaching home for more than two decades. It's a place I love. The administration granted me a sabbatical this past year, freeing me for a time to concentrate on this novel. Plymouth State University is one of the good places in the world, and I am a lucky man to work with such fine colleagues.

And finally to Wendy and Justin and our sweet dog, Laika. Always hurry home.